# Beneath Still Waters

Annie Seaton

*Daughters of the Darling: 4*

---

Annie Seaton lives near the beach on the mid-north coast of New South Wales. Her career and studies spanned the education sector, including working as an academic research librarian, a high school principal, and a university tutor until she took early retirement and fulfilled her lifelong dream of a full-time writing career.

Each winter, Annie and her husband leave the beach to roam the remote areas of Australia for story ideas and research. She is passionate about preserving the beauty of the Australian landscape and respecting the traditional ownership of the land. For those readers who cannot experience this journey personally, Annie seeks to portray the natural beauty of the Australian environment—its spiritual locations, stunning landscapes and unique wildlife.

Readers can contact Annie through her website, annieseaton.net, or find her on Facebook and Instagram. To stay up to date with her new releases, subscribe to her newsletter on the home page of her website:

http://annieseaton.net

# Also by Annie Seaton

**Daughters of the Darling**

*From Across the Sea*
*Over the River*
*By the Billabong*
*Beneath Still Waters*
*Under Darling Skies*
**A Bec Whitfield Mystery**
*Bowen River*
*Shadows on the Shore*
*Storm Season*
**Duckinwilla Days**
*Coming Home*
*Secrets and Surprises*
*Wishes and Whispers*
*Chasing Dreams*
*New Beginnings*
*All Together Now*
**Home to the Outback**
*Lucy*
*Angie*
*Jemima*
*Isabella*
**Pentecost Island Series**
*Pippa*
*Eliza*
*Nell*
*Tamsin*
*Evie*
*Cherry*
*Odessa*
*Sienna*
*Tess*
*Isla*
**Anthologies**

**The Happy Outback Hotel (2026)**
*Outback Strangers*
*Outback Secrets*
*Outback Dreams*
*Outback Hearts*
*Outback Spirit*
*Outback Promise*
*Outback Horizon*
*Outback Silence*
*Outback Whispers*
*Outback Flame*
**The House on the Hill series**
*Beach House*
*Beach Music*
*Beach Walk*
*Beach Dreams*
*The House on the Hill Boxed Set*
**Sunshine Coast Series**
*Waiting for Ana*
*The Trouble with Jack*
*Healing His Heart*
*Sunshine Coast Boxed Set*
**Porter Sisters Series**
*Kakadu Sunset*
*Daintree*
*Diamond Sky*
*Hidden Valley*
*Larapinta*
*Kakadu Dawn*
**Second Chance Bay Series**
*Her Outback Playboy*
*Her Outback Protector*
*Her Outback Haven*
*Her Outback Paradise*
*The McDougalls of Second Chance*

*Pentecost Island 1-3*
*Pentecost Island 4-6*
*Pentecost Island 7-10*
**The Richards Brothers**
*The Trouble with Paradise*
*Marry in Haste*
*Outback Sunrise*
*Richards Brothers Boxed Set*
**Love Across Time**
*Come Back to Me*
*Follow Me*
*Finding Home*
*The Threads that Bind*
*Love Across Time Boxed Set*
**Bindarra Creek**
*Worth the Wait*
*Full Circle*
*Secrets of River Cottage*
*A Clever Christmas*
*A Place to Belong*
*Hearts in Harmony*

*Bay (Boxed Set)*
**The Augathella Girls Series**
*Outback Roads*
*Outback Sky*
*Outback Escape*
*Outback Wind*
*Outback Dawn*
*Outback Moonlight*
*Outback Dust*
*Outback Hope*
**Augathella Girls Anthologies**
*Augathella Girls 1-4*
*Augathella Girls 5-8*
**Augathella Short and Sweet**
*An Augathella Surprise*
*An Augathella Baby*
*An Augathella Spring*
*An Augathella Christmas*
*An Augathella Wedding*
*An Augathella Easter*
*An Augathella Masquerade Ball*
*Augathella Short and Sweet 1-3*
*Augathella Short and Sweet 1-4*

**Standalone Books**
*Whitsunday Dawn*
*Undara*
*Osprey Reef*
*East of Alice*
*An Aussie Christmas Duo*
*Four Seasons Short- Sweet*
*Deadly Secrets*

*Adventures in Time*
*Silver Valley Witch*
*The Emerald Necklace*
*A Clever Christmas*
*Christmas with the Boss*
*Her Christmas Star*

# Dedication

*To my dear Aunty Maureen, my loyal reader and supporter, who passed this year in the ninety-fifth year of her wonderful life.*

*Endurance, foresight, strength, and skill;*
*A perfect Woman, nobly plann'd,*
*To warn, to comfort, and command;*
*And yet a Spirit still, and bright*
*With something of angelic light.*

William Wordsworth - *Perfect Woman*

# Chapter 1

*March*

Caitríona O'Byrne-Wainwright held tightly onto her husband's hand as they crossed the wide street in Broken Hill, heading towards the solicitor's office to sign the documents that would change their lives forever.

'I still can't believe we're doing this, Logan,' she said as they stepped onto the kerb. 'Are you sure it's the right thing to do?'

'How many times have we had this conversation, sweetheart?' His grin was wide, and happiness filled her as she looked at the man she'd been married to for almost a year now.

'About fifty times,' she admitted.

'I'm sure it's a great start for us. It gives us some independence—the land on this side of the river is much better than my little patch across the river from *Ceann Mara*. And it gives us the freedom to choose the stock we run. I'm looking forward to putting some of my ideas into action.'

His smile was wide as she shook her head. 'Okay, no more doubts. I'll stop asking if we're doing the right thing.'

Logan checked his watch as they walked along the street. 'Want a coffee? We've got time—still half an hour until we meet James at his office.'

'Sounds good.' Cat nodded as they crossed the road.

'Did you have any luck getting onto Shea yet?'

'No, she's still not answering her phone. I was hoping we could meet up today.'

'Have you spoken to her since she was home at

Christmas?' Logan asked.

'No. I'm going to give Mum a call. If Mum hasn't been able to talk to one of her chickadees for that long, she'll be getting Dad to get the plane out and fly down here to check on her.'

'I remember you saying that Shea didn't seem herself when she was home.'

'She was too quiet. She's always been the outgoing one of the five of us. When I asked her if she was okay, she said work was really busy. I let it go because I know how much she loves being busy at the clinic.'

The Goat and Bucket coffee shop on Sachin Street was buzzing with the mid-morning rush. Young people perched on stools along the wide counter, middle-aged women chatted over pots of tea, and a few elderly couples sat by the windows, watching the street life unfold.

Cat sniffed appreciatively. 'Best coffee in Australia, I reckon.'

'And how much of Australia have you travelled?' Logan asked with a teasing smile.

'I lived in Sydney, remember? I was in Newtown, where the coffee was excellent. But this place—they do it very well.'

'It's good to hear you talking normally about your time at uni without getting that look you used to have,' Logan said gently. 'Have you heard from the girls lately?'

'Yes, Scart's going to try and come out here for the June long weekend now that she's graduated and working. And Jill's still busy, but she said she needs a touch of outback reality. I was surprised how much Jill loved it out here, the couple of times she's visited.'

Logan cleared his throat. 'Did I tell you I've made an appointment with the builders for tomorrow?'

'No,' Cat said slowly, 'and you know full well you didn't tell me that. What builders?'

'Well, since Reg's house burned to the ground, we need somewhere to live over there. It's too hard rowing across the river in the punt every day, and it's too far to drive around. I figured we need to build a place as quickly as possible.'

'I didn't think we'd be able to afford that yet,' Cat said, frowning.

'I'm going to cash in one of my investments. I think it's something we need to prioritise.' Logan's voice grew softer. 'We won't be two for long—we're going to need somewhere to raise our children.'

Cat's hand drifted down and brushed lightly against her flat stomach. 'Don't get your hopes up. I'm only two weeks late.'

'I know, but a man can hope,' Logan said, squeezing her hand.

Cat smiled as caution mixed with hope. They'd been careful not to talk about it too much, but the hope had been there. Their own property, a new house, and now maybe a new life growing inside her—it felt like too much good fortune to trust all at once.

'One thing at a time,' she murmured, but she didn't move his hand from where it rested against her stomach.

##

The offices of Pearce & Associates sat on the corner of Argent and Oxide Streets, housed in a graceful heritage building that spoke of Broken Hill's prosperous mining past. The brass nameplate beside the heavy wooden door gleamed in the afternoon sun, and a flutter of nervous anticipation ran through

Cat as Logan held the door open for her.

The reception area was fitted out with polished wood shelves holding leather-bound law books, accompanied by a grandfather clock ticking steadily in the corner. Behind the reception desk sat a woman who appeared to be in her early thirties, her glossy auburn hair pulled back in a sleek chignon that complemented the tailored navy suit, which had probably cost more than a good breeding heifer.

'Mr and Mrs Wainwright?' the woman asked, rising gracefully from her chair. 'I'm Nina, Mr Pearce's secretary. He's expecting you.'

Nina's eyes lingered on Logan, her welcoming smile becoming warmer. Logan, to his credit, seemed oblivious, his attention focused on Cat.

'Please, take a seat,' Nina said, gesturing to the leather chairs. 'Mr Pearce will be with you in just a moment. Can I get you tea or coffee?'

'Water will be fine for me, thank you,' Cat replied, settling into one of the chairs. The leather creaked softly beneath her.

'Make that two,' Logan added, checking his watch. Nina disappeared through a door behind her desk, her heels clicking on the polished floorboards. Cat watched her go, then turned to Logan with raised eyebrows.

'She seems efficient,' Cat said.

'Nina? Matches the place.'

Before Cat could respond, a door opened and a tall, distinguished man in his fifties emerged. Terence Pearce had silver hair and kind eyes behind wire-rimmed glasses, and his handshake was firm.

'Mr and Mrs Wainwright, wonderful to see you both again. I trust you're ready to become the new owners of *Dunleavy*?'

'As ready as we'll ever be,' Cat resisted rolling her eyes as she accepted the glass of water that Nina placed before her with another brilliant smile—again directed at Logan.

'Excellent. Now, I have all the documents prepared. The vendor's representatives signed yesterday, so we just need your signatures, and we can complete the settlement.'

Once they were settled in his office, Terence spread the papers across his mahogany desk, pointing to various clauses and conditions. Cat tried to focus on his words, but her mind kept wandering to the enormity of what they were about to do. *Dunleavy*—2,000 acres of prime grazing land, with river frontage and established infrastructure. Well, what was left of the buildings after the fire.

'The insurance payout for the main house has been transferred to the vendor, as agreed,' Terence continued. 'That leaves you with a clean slate to build whatever you like.'

'And the sheds?' Logan asked. 'The report mentioned some structural damage.'

'The north shed will need repairs, but the rest are sound. There's also the matter of the original homestead cottage closer to the river—it's small, but habitable if you need temporary accommodation while you build.'

Cat felt a chill run down her spine at the mention of the house that had burned to the ground. That was the house where Erin had been held, where that man—Miles, or whatever his real name was—had searched for the money Reg's son had hidden there. It had all burned to ash in the fire last winter.

'The cottage will suit us as a temporary home,' Logan

said, squeezing Cat's hand. 'Just until we get the new house built.'

Nina appeared at Cat's elbow with a gold pen. 'If you'd like to sign here, Mrs Wainwright.'

Cat took the pen, her hand trembling slightly as she signed her name to page after page. With each signature, her excitement grew. This wasn't just a property purchase—it was their future, their own station where they would build their life and a family together.

'And here, Mr Wainwright,' Nina said, her fingers brushing Logan's as she handed him the pen.

Logan signed with a flourish, his satisfaction evident in every stroke. When he finished, Terence gathered the papers with a smile.

'Congratulations,' he said, standing to shake their hands. 'You are now the proud owners of *Dunleavy Station*.'

Cat grinned as the reality hit her. They'd done it. Despite all her doubts and fears, they'd taken the leap. Now all they had to do was pay for it.

'Thank you,' she managed.

'The keys,' the solicitor said, producing a small key ring with two brass keys. 'One for the cottage, one for the main gate. Mr McGilvray had these posted to us.'

Logan took the keys, weighing them in his palm. 'Hard to believe something so small can open up such a big future.'

'*Dunleavy* has a rich history,' Terence said, walking them to the door. 'I'm sure you'll add your own chapter to its story.'

'That's exactly what we hope to do,' Cat said, thinking of all the hours she and her father had spent researching the history of *Ceann Mara*, tracing the stories of the families who had worked the land before them. 'Dad and I have been documenting the heritage of our home station for years. It's fascinating to think we'll now be adding to the family history somewhere new.'

'But still on your river. Building on the past while making it your own.' Terence nodded approvingly. 'That's the Australian way, isn't it?'

As they walked back onto the street, the early afternoon sun warmed Cat's face.

'So,' Logan said, jangling the keys in his pocket, 'how does it feel to be a landowner, Mrs Wainwright? Celebration lunch?'

Cat stood on her tiptoes to kiss him, right there on the busy street. 'Like the beginning of everything,' she said against his lips. 'And yes, please. I'm starving.'

As they broke apart, Cat grinned mischievously. 'Though I have to say, I'm impressed by how oblivious you were to Nina making eyes at my handsome husband in there.'

Logan's eyebrows shot up in surprise, then he broke into a wide grin. 'Was she? I hadn't noticed.' He struck a mock-heroic pose. 'What can I say? Women have always found my rugged charm irresistible. It's a burden I bear with dignity.'

Cat laughed, swatting his arm. 'Your rugged charm? Is that what we're calling it now?'

'Hey, you married me for my devastating good looks and witty personality,' Logan said, waggling his eyebrows. 'Nina just has excellent taste.'

'I married you for your sheep-shearing skills and your ability to fix tractors,' Cat shot back, still laughing. 'Everything else was just a bonus.'

##

The Imperial Hotel hadn't changed much since the

mining boom days, with its wide verandas and ornate ironwork reminiscent of the time when Broken Hill was the silver capital of the world. Cat and Logan chose a table away from the noise of the public bar in the fresh air of the beer garden, where the afternoon sun filtered through the pepper trees and cast dappled shadows across the red brick pavers.

'I still can't believe we've done it,' Cat said, studying the menu without really seeing it. '*Dunleavy* is ours.'

'Having second thoughts?' Logan asked, though his tone was teasing.

'No,' Cat said firmly. 'Just... overwhelmed, I suppose. It's such a big step.'

Logan reached across the table to take her hand. 'The biggest step we've taken so far. Well, apart from getting married.'

Cat smiled, then glanced up as a shadow fell across their table. A man in his forties stood there, wearing a khaki shirt with a veterinary clinic logo embroidered on the pocket.

Cat recognised him immediately. 'Hello, you're Rod Le Cerf, aren't you? You used to work at the Wilcannia practice, didn't you? Before you moved down here? And you're at the Broken Hill clinic now.'

'That's right,' Rod nodded. 'I remember your family when I was at Wilcannia. I hope you don't mind me interrupting, but I saw you from inside and thought I'd say hello.'

'Not at all,' Cat said. 'Actually, we've been trying to reach Shea to let her know we're in town. Is she at work today?'

Rod shook his head. 'Shea? No, she's not... didn't you know? She left our practice last year. I stopped because I was going to ask you how she was.'

'She left? What do you mean, she left?'

'She handed in her notice. Said she had other opportunities to follow up.' Rod glanced between them. 'We do miss her.'

'Other opportunities?' Cat frowned as confusion filled her. First, Erin with all her secrets when Jack went overseas, and now Shea was keeping the family in the dark.

'What kind of opportunities?'

'I'm not sure, exactly.' Rod shifted his weight from foot to foot. 'Look, I don't want to speak out of turn. She settled in well when she came to us from Wilcannia, but then something changed in the last couple of months before she left. She seemed a bit distracted.'

Cat's hand trembled as she pushed a loose strand of hair behind her ear. 'Where is she working now? The other vet clinic?'

Rod shrugged helplessly. 'I heard she'd moved to Melbourne. But that's all I know, I'm afraid. She didn't ask for a reference, so I don't know where she went to work.'

'Melbourne?' Cat stared up at him. 'Shea hates Melbourne. She always said she could never live in a big city.'

'I'm sorry I can't be more help,' Rod said, clearly keen to escape the awkward conversation. 'I should probably get back to work. Nice meeting you both, and... well, I hope you track Shea down soon. Give her my best.'

He disappeared back into the pub, leaving Cat and Logan staring at each other in stunned silence.

'Last year?' Cat whispered. 'She's been gone at least four months and didn't even mention it when she was home at Christmas.'

Logan's jaw was tight. 'That's not like Shea at all. She

might be impulsive, but I didn't think she'd move without telling us.'

'Unless she's in trouble,' Cat said, her mind racing through possibilities. 'Or something's wrong that she doesn't want us to know about. Or maybe Mum and Dad know.'

The waitress interrupted with a bright smile. 'Ready to order?'

Cat looked at the menu again, her appetite completely gone. 'I'll just have a salad, thanks. And a lemonade.'

'Make that two salads,' Logan said absently, his attention still on Cat. 'And I'll have a light beer, please.'

When the waitress left, Logan leaned forward. 'Do you think we should call your parents?'

'Maybe,' Cat said, fumbling for her phone. 'But what are we going to say? Did they know Shea is somewhere in Melbourne?'

'Something's not right.' Logan looked as worried as Cat felt.

Pulling out her phone, she dialled her mother's mobile number, a myriad of thoughts running through her head as the phone rang. Maybe they did know already and hadn't mentioned it at Shea's request. But that didn't make any sense.

Laura O'Byrne answered on the second ring, her voice bright and bubbly.

'Cat, darling! How did the signing go? Are we formally neighbours now?'

'We are all done.'

'Congratulations. Are you staying in Broken Hill or coming home today?'

'Tomorrow, Mum,' Cat said, trying to keep her voice

steady.

'Right, a family celebration dinner. I'll talk to the girls and see who's going to be home.'

'First, Mum, can we talk about Shea?'

'What about Shea? Have you caught up with her today? Is she all right?'

'I'm not sure,' Cat admitted. 'We've just found out she left her job at the vet clinic here before Christmas. She's apparently moved to Melbourne, but Rod—her boss—didn't know why or where exactly. Did you and Dad know that?'

The silence on the other end of the line stretched so long that Cat wondered if the call had dropped out.

'Mum? Are you there?'

'I'm here,' Laura's voice was tight. 'You said she moved to Melbourne before Christmas? Are you sure?'

'Yes. And she never answers my calls anymore. It's always texts. We thought she was just busy at work, but—'

'But she doesn't have a job there anymore,' Laura finished. 'Oh, Cat. I had a feeling something was wrong. A mother's instinct, you know? But I told myself I was being silly. I've talked to her every week, but she's been quieter than usual. She's lost that usual Shea vivaciousness. And no, Dad and I had no idea she'd left Broken Hill. She never said a word, and we haven't been there yet this year.'

'What should we do?' Cat shook her head at Logan to let him know that Mum was as much in the dark as they were.

'I'll call Shea until she answers, and I'll ask her outright where she is and what she's doing,' Laura said decisively. 'How could she think she could get away with that?'

'Laura,' Logan said, leaning close to the phone so that Laura could hear him. 'We've got the builders' meeting tomorrow, but after that we're free. We could drive down to Melbourne from here if you like.'

'Thank you, Logan, but no. Come home,' Laura said. 'Tom and I will find out what's going on. Shea is a grown woman, but she's still our daughter. She wouldn't just move without telling us unless she had a good reason.'

Cat ended the call more worried than before. At least now Mum knew, and she would go and tell Dad straight away, but the knot in her stomach tightened with each passing minute.

'Months of lies,' Cat said quietly, staring at her phone. 'Every time we asked about her day, she must have been making up stories about work. Unless she's at a clinic in Melbourne?'

'She could be.' Logan reached across the table to squeeze her hand. 'Calm down, sweetheart. Your parents will sort it and let us know tomorrow night.'

'How could Shea do that? And why?' Cat shook her head.

Logan kept hold of her hand. 'You know what it's like to want to keep something private, Cat.'

Her eyes filled with tears. 'I do, but surely something that bad hasn't happened to Shea.'

Their salads arrived, but neither of them had much appetite, and they picked at their bowls.

'I feel like such an idiot,' Cat said suddenly. 'All those excuses about being rushed off her feet at work, and she wasn't even there.'

'You couldn't have known,' Logan said. 'None of us could.'

Cat nodded, but the hurt remained. This should have been one of the best days of their lives—signing for their own property, taking such a huge step towards their future. Instead, she felt empty; her earlier excitement had completely drained away.

'I just want to know she's okay.' Cat swallowed. 'I do know how easy it is to cover up and hide the truth.'

Logan stood and came around to her side of the table. He crouched beside her and took both her hands in his. 'Sweetheart, don't go back there. Shea is probably just being independent.'

'I'm scared. I just have a feeling.' Cat's voice hitched on a sob. 'Something has happened.'

'Whatever's going on, we'll sort it out,' Logan said firmly. 'We'll support her.'

But as they walked back to their car, her excitement about owning *Dunleavy* was overshadowed by concern for Shea. Their perfect day had been shattered by the chance meeting with Rod, and Cat couldn't shake the feeling that something was very wrong.

##

A week had passed since they had been to Broken Hill and signed the documents for their property.

Cat had managed to get a couple of texts from Shea saying, **I'll catch up with you soon. Stop worrying about me.**

Cat managed to push her worries about Shea to the back of her mind while she and Logan focused on *Dunleavy*—or what had previously been called *Dunleavy*. They both agreed to rename the station, but the problem was that they hadn't been able to come up with anything Cat was happy with yet.

'*New Horizons? Riverside Downs? River Bend*?' Logan had made dozens of suggestions, but Cat shook her head each time.

'It has to be perfect,' Cat said, 'like *Ceann Mara*. Our family home name is just right.'

'It's entirely up to you. Whatever you choose will be fine with me.' Logan stood by the fence with her as they looked at the ruins of the old homestead—the blackened timber, the piles of ash, the twisted metal. 'We'll get a bulldozer over here in the next week or so to clear that away, if that's okay with you.'

'Yes, it'll be good to have that gone.'

'So, what sort of name are you thinking?' Logan put his arm around her shoulders as they looked out over the land that was now theirs.

'Well, I don't know whether to make it modern and new, looking forward, or whether we need to do something that relates to the family history. Not that this land was ever part of our family's. When Dad heard that we were going to buy it from Reg, he went back through the records. He knew who owned it before Reg, but apparently, there were a couple of early settlers there not long after Thomas and Samuel started clearing *Ceann Mara*. Maybe something to do with the river and the paddle steamers? What do you think?'

Logan's arms went around her waist, and he laced his fingers over her stomach. 'What do I think? I think that whatever you choose will be fine.'

She turned in his arms and grinned up at him. 'You're no use.'

'I don't have a historical bone in my body, sweetie,' he said.

'I'm sure we'll come up with something.'

'You haven't been so focused. I've got things on my mind.' His hand caressed her skin. 'How long until you can do a pregnancy test?'

'I bought one before we left Broken Hill. I didn't tell you. I didn't want to get you excited.'

'Didn't want to get me excited? I can barely sleep at night.'

'The instructions say you have to be a certain number of days late, and I'm there now.' Cat turned and looked up into Logan's face, unable to stop smiling up at him.

'How about when we go back across the river?' he suggested hopefully.

She stood on her toes and brushed her lips across his. 'Let's go back now.'

# Chapter 2

*Melbourne - six months earlier*

Shea had driven through the night towards a city she'd never wanted to live in, carrying nothing but two suitcases and the desperate need to be invisible. The city sprawled before her like a concrete ocean, endless and impersonal—exactly what she needed. She'd only stopped for fuel and bitter coffee from service centre machines, her hands gripping the steering wheel so tightly that her knuckles had turned white somewhere past Hay. Now, in the grey dawn light filtering through Melbourne's perpetual haze, she felt simultaneously invisible and utterly exposed.

She'd chosen Melbourne because it was big enough to disappear in, far enough from home that no one would accidentally find her, and because she knew absolutely nothing about it. That anonymity felt like armour now as she navigated unfamiliar streets, following road signs towards the northern suburbs where her small budget might stretch a little further.

The radio played softly—some talk show host discussing the weekend weather—but she switched it off when the voices became too cheerful, too normal. Everything felt wrong: the flat suburban landscape after a lifetime of red earth and river gums, the constant traffic, and the claustrophobic grey sky. But wrong was what she needed. Wrong meant she couldn't pretend this was temporary, couldn't slip back into old patterns of thinking.

In Preston, she found a small, furnished flat above a bakery that smelled of yeast and sugar. The real estate agent, a harried woman with coffee stains on her blouse, barely looked at her references.

'Two weeks' bond, two weeks' rent in advance,' she said, handing over the keys. 'Lease is six months minimum.'

Six months. The number echoed in Shea's mind as she climbed the narrow stairs to her new home. Six months to figure out who she was now, and what remained of her life after everything had crumbled.

The flat was small but clean, with windows that looked out over rooftops towards a distant line of hills. Not the river, not home, but a view that hinted there was still sky beyond the city's edges. She set her two suitcases on the single bed and surveyed her new domain: kitchenette, bathroom, and living area with a couch that had seen better decades. It would do.

For three days, she lived on takeaways and the contents of her suitcases while scouring job advertisements. The *Melbourne Age* was spread across her small dining table each morning, circled with a red pen where veterinary nurse positions beckoned. But each time she picked up the phone to call, her nerve failed. How could she explain why she needed a job with no references? How could she tell a potential employer that she was running from her previous life without revealing why?

Online job boards were kinder, allowing her to craft careful emails that skirted around the truth. *Recently relocated to Melbourne. Seeking new opportunities. Happy to discuss experience in person.* She sent a dozen applications and received three responses.

The first two interviews went badly. The practices were small, family-run operations where everyone knew everyone, and her lack of references stood out like a neon sign. The second interviewer, a stern woman with suspicious eyes, asked pointed questions about why she'd left Broken Hill so suddenly.

'I just needed a change,' Shea said, hating how weak it sounded.

'References are standard in this industry,' the woman replied. 'I can't hire someone I can't verify.'

The third interview was at a larger clinic in South Yarra. Dr Martinez was in his fifties, with kind eyes behind wire-rimmed glasses and the slightly harried air of someone juggling too many responsibilities. He listened as Shea explained her situation in carefully neutral terms.

'I've been working as a vet nurse for several years,' she said, her voice steadier than she felt. 'But I've recently had to relocate quite urgently due to personal circumstances. I'm hoping you might consider my experience and qualifications rather than requiring references from my previous employer.'

Dr Martinez leaned back in his chair, studying her. 'What kind of personal circumstances?'

Shea's throat tightened. She'd rehearsed this moment, but sitting here under his gentle scrutiny, the words felt inadequate. 'There was a difficult situation. Someone I trusted... it became complicated. I needed to leave quickly for my own well-being.'

He nodded slowly, and she saw something shift in his expression—not suspicion, but understanding. 'I see. And you'd prefer your previous employer not know where you've gone?'

'Yes, sir.'

'This wouldn't be related to anything illegal or unethical on your part?'

'No, absolutely not.'

Dr Martinez was quiet for a long moment, drumming his fingers on the desk. 'I'll tell you what. I've been short-staffed here for months, and good vet nurses are hard to find. I'm willing to offer you a two-week trial period. If your work is satisfactory and you prove reliable, we'll make it permanent. No references are required, but I'll need you to be completely honest about your qualifications and experience.'

She exhaled shakily, her hands trembling as she accepted the contract. 'Yes, of course. Thank you. I won't let you down.'

'I hope not,' he said, though his tone was warm. 'When can you start?'

'Tomorrow, if you need me.'

That evening, she sat in her small flat with a proper employment contract in her hands and felt the first small stirring of something that might eventually become hope. She had work. She had a roof over her head. It wasn't much, but it was a beginning.

The routine of work saved her during those first weeks. The South Yarra Veterinary Clinic was busy enough to keep her mind occupied, but not so chaotic that she couldn't manage. Dr Martinez and the other staff—two vets, a receptionist named Claire, and another nurse called Janet—were professional and friendly without being intrusive. They seemed to sense she needed space and gave it to her, for which she was grateful.

She kept her interactions brief and professional. When Claire invited her to join them for drinks after work, she politely declined. When Janet asked about her weekend plans, she mentioned being tired and needing to catch up on errands. It wasn't entirely untrue, but it wasn't the whole truth either. The whole truth was that she was afraid of getting too close, of having to explain herself, and of losing that anonymity that was so essential to her.

Her phone buzzed constantly with messages from David.

At first, she had read them, hoping they might contain something resembling an apology or acceptance. Instead, they were variations on the same theme: **You can't just run away from this. What we had was real. You're being unfair. We need to talk.**

After the first week, she stopped reading them altogether.

The work itself was familiar comfort—prepping for surgeries, monitoring patients, assisting with examinations. Her hands remembered the motions even when her mind felt fragmented. Animals didn't ask complicated questions or expect emotional explanations. They simply needed care, and she could provide that even when she couldn't provide it for herself.

But the nights were harder. In her small flat above the bakery, with only the sounds of traffic and her own thoughts for company, the grief would surface like floodwater. She'd tried grocery shopping after work, but the sight of couples in the supermarket aisles, the baby food sections, even the casual intimacy of shared shopping lists, would send her fleeing back to her flat with whatever she could grab quickly.

This was how she found herself, three weeks after starting work, sitting in the Courthouse Hotel in North Melbourne on a Friday evening, staring at a chicken parmi she'd barely touched. The pub was busy but not rowdy, filled with after-work drinkers and diners who minded their own business. It felt safer than her empty flat, less lonely than cooking for one.

She'd noticed him earlier—the dark-haired barman who moved easily behind the bar, pulling beers and making cocktails while carrying on conversations with regulars. He had an open, friendly face and a laugh that carried across the room without being intrusive. Several times, she'd caught him glancing in her direction, but she assumed he was simply checking tables.

When he approached her table to clear away her barely touched meal, she kept her eyes down, hoping to avoid conversation.

'Not hungry tonight?' he asked, his voice carrying a warm, deep timbre that made her look up despite herself.

'It was fine,' she said quickly. 'I'm just not very hungry.'

'Fair enough.' He stacked her plate with the others he was carrying. 'Can I get you another wine?'

She shook her head. 'I'm okay, thanks.'

He didn't move away immediately. Instead, he seemed to study her with curious brown eyes. 'You're not from around here, are you? I can usually pick accents, but yours is interesting.'

Despite herself, Shea almost smiled. 'Country NSW.'

'Ah, that explains it. I'm Heath, by the way. I've seen you in here a couple of times now.'

'Shea.' The name slipped out before she could stop it.

'Nice to meet you properly, Shea from country NSW.' His grin was infectious, and she felt something inside her chest—a part that had been locked away for weeks—respond despite her best efforts. 'What brings you to Melbourne? Besides our world-famous chicken parmis.'

She pushed down the desire to connect, to share even the small, safe parts of her story. 'Work,' she said simply.

'Right. Well, if you ever want to try something other than the parmi, the fish and chips here are actually pretty decent. And the company's not bad either.' He gestured around the busy pub. 'Good place to meet people if you're new in town.'

'I should go,' she said, reaching for her purse.

'Of course. But, Shea from country NSW—you're

welcome here anytime. No pressure, no questions. Sometimes a friendly face is all anyone needs.'

As he walked away, she sat for another few minutes, watching him work. There was something steady about him, something genuine in his easy interaction with customers that she hadn't encountered in weeks. When she finally left, she caught him looking in her direction and raised her hand in a small wave. His answering smile followed her out into the Melbourne night.

Two weeks later, against her better judgement, she found herself back at the Courthouse Hotel. She'd told herself she was simply hungry and too tired to cook, but deep down she knew she was hoping to see Heath again. The admission made her uncomfortable—she wasn't ready for connections and wasn't sure she ever would be—but the memory of his easy warmth had surfaced during her lonely evenings more often than she cared to admit.

The pub was quieter on this Friday, perhaps because of the drizzling rain that had been falling since the afternoon. She chose the same table as before, ordering fish and chips this time, remembering his recommendation.

When Heath appeared at her table, his face lit up with genuine pleasure. 'Well, look who's back. And you took my advice about the fish and chips, I see.'

'They were highly recommended,' she said, surprised to find herself almost smiling.

'By a very reliable source, I'm sure.' He was carrying a fresh glass of wine, which he set down beside her plate. 'This one's on the house. Welcome back.'

Before she could protest, he'd moved on to another table,

but the gesture warmed her more than the wine did. When he returned later to clear her plate—empty this time—he lingered for a moment.

'Better than the parmi?'

'Much better. Thank you for the wine.'

'My pleasure. You look like you've had a long week.'

The observation was gentle, not intrusive, but it caught her off guard. 'How can you tell?'

'Barman's intuition. Plus, you've got that thousand-yard stare that comes from thinking too hard about things you can't change.' He tilted his head, studying her. 'Want to talk about it, or would you prefer I mind my own business?'

For a moment, she considered it—actually considered opening up to this stranger with kind eyes and a warm voice. The loneliness of the past weeks pressed against her chest like a physical weight.

'Mind your own business,' she said finally, but she softened it with a small smile. 'But thank you for asking.'

'Fair enough. The offer stands, though. Sometimes strangers make the best listeners—no judgement, no history, no expectations.'

After he walked away, she sat nursing her wine and thinking about his words. No history, no expectations. When was the last time she'd talked to someone who didn't know her, who wasn't waiting for her to be the person she used to be?

The thought both terrified and intrigued her.

The following Monday at work, Dr Martinez called her into his office during lunch break.

'How are you settling in, Shea? It's been a month now.'

'Very well, thank you. I hope my work has been satisfactory.'

'More than satisfactory. You're thorough, reliable, and the animals respond well to you. I'd like to offer you a permanent position.'

Relief flooded through her. 'Thank you. I'd like that very much.'

'There is one thing, though.' His expression grew more serious. 'Whatever situation you were dealing with—I hope you're getting the support you need. This job can be stressful, and if you're dealing with personal issues...'

'I'm managing,' she said quickly.

'I'm sure you are. But if you ever need resources—counselling, legal advice, even just someone to talk to—I want you to know you're not alone. We take care of our staff here.'

The kindness in his voice nearly undid her. For weeks, she'd been functioning on autopilot, compartmentalising her grief and fear, focusing only on the immediate necessities of survival. But sitting in his office, faced with genuine concern from someone who barely knew her, she felt the careful walls she'd built begin to crack.

'Thank you,' she managed. 'That means more than you know.'

That evening, she sat in her flat with the employment contract and felt something shift inside her chest. She had a job, a place to live, and slowly—very slowly—she was beginning to remember what it felt like to be a person in the world rather than simply a collection of reflexes and survival instincts.

Her phone buzzed with another message from David, but for the first time in weeks, she deleted it without a tremor of anxiety. Whatever power he'd held over her was beginning to loosen, replaced by the small but growing certainty that she could build something new from the wreckage of her old life.

The staff room bulletin board at the clinic was covered with the usual notices—roster changes, continuing education opportunities, and a reminder about the Christmas party she probably wouldn't attend. She was still planning to go home for Christmas, though the thought of facing her family's questions filled her with dread.

But one small flyer caught her eye: *Holistic Healing and Wellness Counselling Course. Learn to support others through life's challenges while healing yourself.*

The tagline felt as though it had been written specifically for her. Without really thinking, she pulled out her phone and found the website. *Offered by the Melbourne Institute of Alternative Healing. Next intake: January 8.*

Shea's finger hovered over the application button. This wasn't her at all. She was practical, scientific, grounded in veterinary medicine and rural common sense. Alternative healing was something she'd always been quietly sceptical about. But sitting in the sterile break room, feeling disconnected from everything else that had once made sense, maybe she needed to be more open-minded. She filled out the application form and sent it before she could talk herself out of it.

It wasn't healing, not yet. But it was a beginning.

# Chapter 3

*Murray River - 1874*

The Murray River stretched before them, gleaming in the late afternoon light, and Catherine O'Byrne felt her breath catch as she watched Daniel McKenzie secure the moorings of their borrowed dinghy. They'd travelled upriver from Wentworth to deliver supplies to *Riverside Station*, and now, with the day's work done, Daniel had suggested they take a walk along the bank while her father, Samuel, concluded his business with the station manager. They had been friends for two years, since she had started travelling the river with Papa.

'It's beautiful here,' Catherine said, her voice barely above a whisper as she smoothed her dusty travelling skirt. Even in her late twenties, she was painfully aware of her own inexperience, especially around men like Daniel—stockmen who moved with easy confidence and spoke with voices husky from red dust and hard work.

'Not as beautiful as you,' Daniel replied, his blue eyes crinkling with the kind of smile that made her stomach flutter like a bird in a cage. He was around her age, or perhaps younger; his face weathered by the harsh sun, framed by dark hair that curled at his collar. His hands were gentle when he helped her from the boat, but strong enough to handle the most difficult horse.

Catherine felt heat rise in her cheeks. 'Mr McKenzie, you shouldn't say such things.'

'Why not, if they're true?' He stepped closer, and she caught the scent of river water and leather that seemed to cling to his clothes. 'And call me Daniel. We've known each other these past two years as the steamers have come through. Surely we're beyond formalities.'

They walked along the red bank, past the river red gums that cast long shadows across the water. Catherine had been travelling with her father on the paddle steamers for two years, partly to help with the bookkeeping, partly because Samuel enjoyed their intelligent conversations.

'I must confess,' Catherine said, stepping carefully over a fallen branch, 'I much prefer this to Melbourne society.'

'Really? I'd have thought a young lady would enjoy the excitement of the city.'

Catherine laughed, a sound that carried across the water like birdsong. 'Papa built us a beautiful house in Toorak back in sixty-six—all the latest fashions, you understand. After he made his fortune in wool, he thought we should live like proper toffs.' She paused, her fingers trailing along the bark of a river red gum. 'But Mama is never comfortable with all that formality. She comes from simple Irish folk, more so than Papa did. The grand parties and calling cards feel like playacting to her.'

'And to you?'

'Oh, completely. Give me the river and the open sky over stuffy drawing rooms any day.' Catherine's eyes sparkled as she spoke. 'I love being on the paddle steamers with Papa. There's something magical about the rhythm of the wheels in the water, the way each bend in the river brings something new. We collect wool from stations all along the Murray and Darling—Uncle Thomas at *Ceann Mara*, dozens of others. Each place has its own character, its own stories.'

Daniel was watching her intently now, surprise in his expression. 'Most young ladies of your station would find such travel beneath them. I feel as though I don't know you.'

'Oh, you do know the real me, Daniel. Those young ladies are missing the best of life,' Catherine said firmly. 'Papa started with nothing but determination and an eye for good wool. He built his fortune through hard work and fair dealing, not by putting on airs. I'm prouder of him for that than for any fancy house in Melbourne.'

'You speak of him with such affection.' His voice held yearning, and Catherine glanced at him from beneath her eyelashes.

'He's given me everything—education, opportunity, adventure. But more than that, he's shown me that there's honour in honest work, in treating people fairly regardless of their station.' Catherine's voice grew softer. 'Mama used to say that kindness costs nothing but is worth everything. Papa never forgets that, even as a wealthy man.'

They had reached the fallen log now, and Daniel helped her seat herself on its smooth surface. The river murmured past them, carrying leaves and small branches towards the distant sea.

'How did your father build such a fortune?' Daniel asked, settling beside her.

'Wool, mainly. He has an extraordinary eye for sheep; he can judge the quality of a fleece just by looking at the animal. He and Uncle Thomas started with a small run near Bourke, and then expanded. Now Papa owns stations from here to Queensland, and has paddle steamers to transport the wool to market.' Catherine smiled proudly. 'He's one of the wealthiest men in the colony, but you'd never know it to speak with him. He treats everyone the same, from bank managers to boundary riders.'

'And yet his daughter prefers dusty riverbanks to Melbourne ballrooms.'

'Every time.' Catherine turned to face him fully. 'This feels real to me—the river, the work, the connection to the land. In Melbourne, everything feels like a performance. I am supposed to act like a lady. Here, with you...' She trailed off, suddenly aware of how forward she sounded.

'Here with me, what?' Daniel's voice had grown quiet, intense.

'Here with you, I can be myself.'

The silence stretched between them, broken only by the gentle sound of water lapping against the bank and the occasional plop of a fish jumping. Catherine studied his face—the brown skin from years in the sun, the laugh lines around his eyes, the way he looked at her as though she was dear to him.

'I've been thinking about you often, Catherine,' he said finally. 'When we're not on the river, when we're back at the station. I find myself watching for your father's steamer.'

'You do?' The words came out breathless, and she felt foolish for her eagerness.

'I do.' He reached for her hand, his fingers warm and rough against hers. 'You're different from other girls I've known. There's something genuine about you, something unaffected by all that wealth and position.'

Catherine's heart hammered against her ribs. No one had ever spoken to her this way—with such attention, such gentle admiration. In Melbourne, young men either pursued her for Papa's money or were intimidated by it. She had not been receptive to any of them; Daniel seemed to see her for herself alone.

'I think about you too,' she admitted, then immediately

wondered if her words were too bold.

'Do you?' His thumb traced across her knuckles. 'What do you think about?'

'I wonder what you do when we're not here. Whether you think the river is as beautiful as I do. Whether you...' She trailed off, unable to voice the deeper questions that kept her awake at night in her narrow bunk on the steamer.

'Whether I what, Catherine?'

'Whether you might care for me the way I've come to care for you.'

Daniel's expression grew serious, intense, and for a moment, Catherine thought she'd made a terrible mistake. Then he lifted her hand to his lips, pressing a gentle kiss to her knuckles.

'Sweet Catherine,' he murmured. 'Of course I care for you. I think of you constantly.'

When his lips touched hers, her whole body trembled. They were warm and gentle at first, then more urgent as she responded with an innocence that made him kiss her harder. She'd never been kissed before, had barely been alone with a man who wasn't family, and the sensation of his arms around her filled her with confidence.

'I love you, Daniel,' she whispered against his mouth, the words spilling out before she could stop them.

Daniel pulled back slightly, his eyes searching her face. 'Catherine...'

'I do,' she said, mistaking his hesitation for surprise. 'I know it's sudden, but I've never felt anything like this before. Have you?'

'You're young and very innocent,' he said carefully.

'I'm twenty-seven. That's not so young. And I may be innocent, but I know my own heart.'

He was quiet for a long moment, his hands still resting at her waist. Catherine could hear the distant sound of her father's voice carrying across the water, probably discussing freight schedules with the station manager.

'Your father will be looking for us soon,' Daniel said.

'I don't care.' The boldness of her own words surprised her, but she meant them. 'Daniel, I love you. I think you might love me too, if you'd let yourself.'

His expression changed. 'Catherine, if we... if I...' He stopped, and then started again. 'Do you understand what you're saying? What you are asking?'

She thought she did. Catherine had grown up around working stations; she understood the basics of what passed between men and women, even if her knowledge was more theoretical than practical. More importantly, she understood the yearning that had been building in her chest these past months, the way her whole being seemed to lean towards Daniel whenever he was near.

'I understand,' she said quietly.

What followed was gentle, awkward, and overwhelming all at once. Daniel spread his coat on the soft grass beneath the river red gums, and Catherine gave him her innocence with complete trust. She whispered his name like a prayer and told him again that she loved him, and if she noticed that he never said the words back, she was too caught up in the wonder of it all to mind.

Afterwards, as they straightened their clothes and Catherine tried to smooth her hair back into some semblance of respectability, the magnitude of what they'd done began to sink in. She felt different, a tender soreness that reminded her with each movement of what had passed between them. Everything around her seemed different now. There was no going back.

'Catherine,' Daniel said, his voice oddly formal as he helped her to her feet. 'What we just... this can't happen again.'

The words hit her like cold water. 'What do you mean?'

'I mean, this was a mistake. You're Samuel O'Byrne's daughter. You're from one of the wealthiest families in the colony. I'm just a stockman with nothing to offer you.'

'You've offered yourself,' Catherine said, confusion threading through her voice. 'That's everything to me.'

Daniel's jaw tightened. 'You don't understand how the world works. Your father could buy and sell this entire station without thinking twice. He'd horsewhip me if he knew what just happened, and he'd be right to.'

'My father would understand if we explained—'

'Explained what? That I took advantage of his daughter?' Daniel shook his head. 'This can't go anywhere, Catherine. I should never have let it happen.'

Something cold and heavy settled in her chest. 'But you said you cared for me.'

'I do care for you. That's why this has to stop here.' He reached out as if to touch her face, then let his hand fall. 'You'll marry someone of your own class someday. Someone who can match what your father can give you.'

'I don't want someone of my own class,' Catherine said, her voice breaking slightly. 'I want you.'

'Then you want something that can't be.'

They walked back to the river in silence, Catherine's mind reeling with hurt and confusion. She'd given him everything—her innocence, her heart, her trust—and Daniel was already pulling away, seeming desperate to pretend it had never happened.

Samuel was waiting by the dinghy; his expression held concern. 'There you are. I was starting to worry.'

'We just took a walk,' Daniel said easily, as if nothing had changed. 'Catherine wanted to take a walk along the Darling River.'

Catherine managed a smile, though it felt like her face might crack from the effort. 'It was lovely, Papa.'

The trip back to the landing place where the two rivers merged passed in a blur of churning water and polite conversation. Daniel helped her along the makeshift wooden plank onto the steamer as if she were made of glass, his eyes avoiding hers. Samuel chatted about freight schedules and river conditions, oblivious to the storm raging in his daughter's heart.

Six weeks later, Catherine sat alone on the deck of her father's steamer as it made its way upriver towards *Ceann Mara*. She'd made this journey dozens of times, but today the familiar rhythm of the paddle wheels failed to soothe her.

She pressed her hand against her stomach, still flat beneath her travelling dress, and tried to steady her breathing. Her monthly courses were now a month overdue, and the morning sickness that had plagued her for the past week left no room for doubt.

She was carrying Daniel McKenzie's child.

The irony wasn't lost on her. She'd told Daniel she preferred the river to Melbourne society, and now the river had been her downfall. Every bend brought them closer to Uncle Thomas and Aunt Caitríona and her cousins at *Ceann Mara*, closer to the family gathering where she'd have to smile and pretend nothing had changed while this secret grew inside her.

'You're quiet today, dear,' Samuel said, settling beside her on the wooden bench. His wrinkled hands rested on his knees, and Catherine noticed how the years of sun and hard work had aged her father. 'Something troubling you?'

'Just thinking, Papa.' Catherine managed what she hoped was a convincing smile. 'About Melbourne, about the future.'

'Ah.' Samuel nodded knowingly. 'You're thinking about that young Harrington fellow, aren't you? The one who's been calling on you.'

Catherine's stomach clenched. Edward Harrington was the son of one of Melbourne's most prominent banking families, and he had been paying increasingly serious attention to her at social gatherings. He was everything a father could want for his daughter: wealthy, well-educated, from an established family with impeccable connections.

'Perhaps,' she said carefully.

'He seems like a fine young man,' Samuel continued. 'His father and I have had some business dealings—all very proper, very above board. The family has an excellent reputation.'

'Yes, Papa.'

'Of course, I won't pressure you. You've seen so little of the world beyond our business travels.' Samuel's voice grew gentle. 'But a woman in your position needs to think about security, about making a good match. The world can be cruel to women who don't have the protection of a respectable marriage.'

If only he knew how cruel it had already been. If only he knew that his warnings came too late.

'I understand, Papa.'

They travelled in comfortable silence for a while, watching the red banks slide past. Catherine had always loved this stretch of river—the way the gums leaned over the water, the flash of kingfishers diving for fish, the endless sky that stretched from horizon to horizon. But today, even the beauty of the landscape couldn't lift the worry from her heart.

She thought of Daniel, still at Wentworth, working at *Riverside Station*, probably already forgetting what had passed between them. Had he given her even a moment's thought since that afternoon, or had she been nothing more than a pleasant diversion from the monotony of station life? She had been so gullible, and shame burned through her.

The worst part was that she knew she loved him. Despite his rejection, despite his dismissal of what she had offered him, her heart still quickened at the memory of his voice, his touch, his tenderness. She had built dreams around those few stolen hours, imagined a future where love conquered the practical realities of class and wealth.

Now she was facing a different kind of future entirely— one where her choices had narrowed to shame or deception, ruin or a marriage built on lies.

'Catherine,' Samuel said suddenly, breaking into her thoughts. 'Whatever you choose to do, you know I love you, don't you? You and your sister are the most precious things in my life.'

The unexpected tenderness in her father's voice almost broke her heart. 'I know, Papa.'

'Good. Because sometimes the world demands difficult choices from us, and I want you to know that nothing— nothing—could ever change my love for you.'

Her eyes stung with unshed tears. If only she could tell Papa the truth, throw herself on his mercy, and trust in that unconditional love. But she knew the realities as well as Daniel did. Samuel had worked too hard and built too much to see it all threatened by his daughter's disgrace.

As the steamer rounded the familiar bend that brought *Ceann Mara* into view, Catherine made her decision. She would carry this secret as long as she could. She would play her part in the family gathering, accept Uncle Thomas's warm embrace, and respond to Aunt Caitríona's gentle questions about her future.

And when she could hide it no longer, she would find another solution—one that wouldn't destroy the life her father had built or the reputation that meant everything to their family's future.

Perhaps, if she were very careful and very lucky, no one would ever have to know what had really happened on that autumn afternoon when she'd mistaken a man's desire for love.

# Chapter 4

As Christmas approached, Shea reluctantly made the long drive home to *Ceann Mara*. Her small car felt fragile on the highway, buffeted by road trains and weighed down with carefully selected gifts that wouldn't reveal too much about her changed circumstances. She'd practised her story—keeping it vague—during the six-hour journey: still working as a vet nurse, enjoying the variety of cases, looking forward to some professional development opportunities in the new year.

The lies sat heavy in her chest, but the alternative—explaining what had really happened, seeing the worry and questions in her family's eyes—felt impossible.

Christmas Eve dinner was a grand affair. Laura had outdone herself with a pre-Christmas feast—golden roast chicken, vegetables from her garden, and fresh-baked bread that filled the homestead with an enticing aroma. The long dining table at *Ceann Mara* gleamed with good silverware and festive red and green placemats Laura brought out each December.

Shea sat quietly, pushing food around her plate while the familiar sounds of family conversation washed over her. Cat and Logan sat close together, whispering and laughing with newlywed contentment. Róisín and Seth exchanged private glances across the table. Jack's hand found Erin's under the table, and Shea felt a sharp pang of loss watching their easy intimacy.

'You've been very quiet tonight, Shea.' Erin turned her attention to Shea. 'Everything alright at work?'

She forced a smile. 'Just tired. It's been a busy year.'

'You mentioned some new training opportunities,' Tom

said, refilling wine glasses. 'What sort of courses are you looking at?'

'Oh, just some continuing education,' Shea said vaguely. 'Professional development, that sort of thing.'

She felt Erin's gaze lingering on her and quickly turned to Bridget, asking about her university plans. Bridget launched enthusiastically into her computer science program, and Shea let her youngest sister's excitement wash over her, grateful for the distraction.

'Before we finish dinner,' Cat said suddenly, placing her fork down carefully, 'there's something we should share.' She glanced at Tom, who nodded and reached for an official-looking document.

'A letter arrived this week from the War Graves Commission,' Cat continued.

The conversation around the table halted. Tom unfolded the letter, his fingers slightly unsteady.

'They found him,' he announced, his voice thick with emotion. 'The DNA tests were positive. Gilbert's remains were among those recovered from the mass grave at Pheasant Wood. He now has a proper grave at Pheasant Wood Military Cemetery in Fromelles.'

Silence fell over the table as Laura reached for Tom's hand, her eyes shining with tears.

'After all these years,' Laura whispered. 'He has a proper resting place.'

Shea's throat ached, overwhelmed as much by the sad family history as by the secrets she was keeping. Here was her great-great-uncle Gilbert, finally found after more than a century, while she sat at the same table, hiding her loss from the people who loved her most.

The irony wasn't lost on her—as her family celebrated finding their missing ancestor, she was working harder than ever to stay lost herself.

Later that evening, after dinner, Cat caught her arm gently.

'Are you sure you're okay?' Cat asked, her voice soft with concern. 'You seem... preoccupied.'

Shea managed what she hoped was a convincing smile. 'Just work stress. You know how I get involved with things.'

But she could see in Cat's eyes that her sister wasn't entirely convinced. She had always been good at reading between the lines.

'Don't forget our traditional Christmas Eve drinks at the billabong.'

'Oh, I'd forgotten. I'm a bit tired.' That was the last thing Shea wanted to do.

'Don't even think about not coming.' Cat stared at her.

The sisters gathered around the billabong as they always had, but Shea felt like she was watching through glass. The familiar warmth, the easy chatter, the shared intimacy—she didn't feel a part of it.

Erin talked about Jack's photographs, Cat was full of excitement about the house they planned to build when they bought their land, Róisín was animated about work, and Bridget bubbled with university plans. Their voices washed over her like background noise. How could she tell them that while they spoke of normal things—careers, relationships, futures—she was living in a rented flat in Melbourne under a different name? That she jumped every time her phone buzzed? That she'd lost a baby and couldn't even grieve properly because she was too busy looking over her shoulder?

She nodded when it seemed appropriate, managed small responses when directly asked, but inside, she felt empty. Each of her sisters had found their place in the world. And here she sat, with secrets she held close, and couldn't share even with the sisters who had once been close confidants.

The conversation flowed around her, and she let it, grateful that her quietness could pass for normal tiredness rather than the bone-deep exhaustion of someone running from her own life.

On Boxing Day, Shea left early, claiming she needed to get back to work commitments. As she drove away from *Ceann Mara*, she caught sight of her childhood home in the rearview mirror, and relief filled her as she drove away.

# Chapter 5

Two weeks later, on a rainy Saturday afternoon, Shea sat in a converted warehouse in Fitzroy, sitting in a circle with twelve other people. The instructor, Eliza Westfield, was nothing like what Shea had expected. She was probably in her early forties, with prematurely silver hair pulled back in a loose bun, her intelligent eyes set in an unlined face that seemed to look right into you.

'Welcome to your first component of the course—Steps Towards Healing,' Eliza said, her soft voice carrying a gentle warmth. 'This course isn't about quick fixes or miracle cures. It's about learning to sit with pain—yours and other people's—without trying to fix it or run from it.'

Shea shifted uncomfortably in her chair. Running was exactly what she had been good at.

'Hi folks, let's start with introductions,' Eliza continued. 'Share your name and what brought you here. There's no pressure to reveal more than you're comfortable with.'

When it was Shea's turn, she kept it simple. 'I'm Shea. I'm a vet nurse, originally from western NSW. I moved to Melbourne recently, and I'm looking for... something different.'

Eliza's eyes lingered on her for a moment, as if she could sense the careful editing in those few sentences. 'Welcome, Shea. What part of western NSW?'

'The Darling River. My family runs a sheep station near Bourke. I have four sisters.'

'Beautiful country. I imagine it's quite a change living in the city.'

'Yes,' Shea said quietly. 'It is.'

After the session, as people filtered out of the warehouse, Eliza approached her. 'Would you like to grab a coffee? There's a place around the corner that does excellent coffee.'

Shea hesitated. She'd been avoiding social situations, keeping to herself in her small rental apartment and speaking to no one except when work required it. But something about Eliza's manner—direct but not pushy, interested but not intrusive—made her nod.

The café was one of those Melbourne coffee places with mismatched furniture. Worn leather armchairs sat beside bright orange plastic stools, while faded velvet sofas in deep burgundy faced off against sleek modern benches. Bookshelves lined the walls, crammed with everything from dog-eared paperback novels to pristine art books. Colourful wall hangings—macramé plant holders and vintage concert posters—covered nearly every inch of exposed brick. A collection of succulents in mismatched pots crowded the windowsills, and fairy lights strung haphazardly across the ceiling cast a warm, honey-coloured glow over everything.

Shea inhaled deeply as they found a table by the window, breathing in the rich aroma of freshly ground coffee beans mingled with the earthy scent of old books and a faint hint of sandalwood incense. It was a chaotic kind of place where every corner held something different. Eliza ordered for both of them without asking.

'So,' Eliza said, wrapping her hands around her mug, 'a vet nurse interested in wellness counselling. That's not a combination I see often.'

'I suppose I'm looking for a different way to help,' Shea said carefully. 'Veterinary work is very clinical, very focused on fixing things. Sometimes people need something else.'

'And sometimes we need something else for ourselves,' Eliza observed gently.

Shea nodded, not trusting herself to speak.

'You mentioned your family has a station on the Darling. That must be a strong connection to the land, and to family history.'

'It is. My dad's actually been researching our family tree recently. We've been on the same land for generations—since the 1800s. My great-great-uncle, Samuel O'Byrne, ran paddle steamers up and down the Darling back then.'

'Paddle steamers,' Eliza repeated, her interest clearly genuine. 'What a romantic image. Though I imagine the reality was quite harsh.'

'Dad's cleared up some family mysteries. Samuel had two daughters, but Dad hasn't been able to trace them. He's trying to piece together the gaps in the family tree.'

'Family mysteries,' Eliza mused. 'They have a way of echoing through generations, don't they? Sometimes the stories we don't tell are as powerful as the ones we do.'

Something in her tone made Shea look up sharply. 'What do you mean?'

'Just that families often have patterns. Ways of dealing with difficult situations, of protecting each other—or themselves. Sometimes what looks like disappearing is actually surviving.'

A chill ran down Shea's spine. 'I never thought of it that way.'

'Tell me about your sisters,' Eliza said, smoothly changing the subject. 'You mentioned your family—are you close?'

'Very close. There are five of us girls. I'm the fourth.' Shea found herself relaxing as she talked about Cat, Róisín, Erin, and Bridget. 'They'd be horrified if they knew I was sitting in a Melbourne café studying alternative healing. Well, maybe not horrified. But definitely surprised.'

'You haven't told them you're here?'

Shea's coffee suddenly tasted bitter. 'Not exactly. They think I'm still working in Broken Hill.'

Eliza didn't ask why, for which Shea was grateful. Instead, she said, 'Sometimes we need space to figure out who we are outside of our family roles. There's nothing wrong with taking time for yourself.'

'Is that what you think I'm doing?'

'I think you're here for a reason, and that reason will become clear when you're ready for it to be clear.' Eliza smiled. 'In the meantime, you're learning skills that will help you support other people through difficult times. That's never a waste.'

As they walked back towards the tram stop, Eliza handed Shea a business card. 'This is my brother's practice. He's a GP, but he works with people experiencing grief and trauma. If you ever need someone to talk to—professionally, I mean—he's very good at what he does.'

Shea glanced at the card: Dr H McGregor, General Practice & Counselling Services.

'Thank you,' she said, slipping the card into her wallet.

'See you next week, Shea,' Eliza said as the tram approached. 'And remember—healing isn't about forgetting what happened. It's about learning to carry it differently.'

As the tram carried her back towards South Yarra, Shea

stared out at the city lights beginning to twinkle in the gathering dusk.

## 

Shea thought a lot about what Eliza had taught them in that first session, and had the opportunity to put what she'd learned into practice that same week, when she sat with an elderly lady after Dr Martinez had put her cat to sleep.

Mrs Patterson's sobs had finally quietened to soft hiccups, but her hands still trembled as she clutched the empty cat carrier. Shea sat beside her in the clinic's quiet room, maintaining the gentle presence she'd learned in her counselling course.

'Fifteen years,' Mrs Patterson whispered. 'Whiskers was with me for fifteen years. Since before my Harold died.'

Shea resisted the urge to offer platitudes about Whiskers being "in a better place" or "no longer suffering". Instead, she stayed silent, letting the woman's grief fill the space between them.

'Tell me about a favourite memory with Whiskers,' Shea said finally, her voice soft.

The woman's tear-stained face brightened slightly. 'She used to sit on Harold's chair every evening at six o'clock, waiting for him to come home from work. Even after he passed, she'd still go to that chair at six. Like she was keeping watch for him.'

'That sounds like love,' Shea said simply. 'Both for Harold and for you.'

'Do you think... do you think pets know when we love them?'

'I think Whiskers knew she was cherished every single

day of her life,' Shea replied, meaning every word. 'That's not something death can take away.'

Mrs Patterson nodded, dabbing at her eyes. 'The house is going to feel so empty.'

'It will, for a while. But the love doesn't go away, even when the presence does. That's something you get to keep.'

After Mrs Patterson left, Shea sat in the empty room for several minutes, processing the session. She'd drawn on everything Eliza had taught her about holding space for grief, about not rushing to comfort, but simply being present with pain. It had felt natural, right—like using muscles she'd forgotten she had.

For the first time since arriving in Melbourne, she felt her old self stirring.

# Chapter 6

Despite her progress in the counselling course, the nights were still difficult. One night, Shea jolted awake from a nightmare, her heart racing and sweat dampening her nightshirt. In the dream, she'd been back in Broken Hill, walking to her car after a late shift, when a figure had stepped out from behind the building. David's voice, cold and angry: 'You can't just disappear, Shea. I'll always find you.'

She lay still in the darkness of her Preston flat, listening to her own rapid breathing and the distant hum of Melbourne traffic. The dream had felt so real she could almost smell the red dust of the clinic car park, could almost feel David's hand gripping her arm.

A shadow moved past her bedroom window.

Shea's breath caught. There it was again—a dark shape blocking the streetlight for just a moment. Someone was outside, looking up at her window. The certainty hit her like ice water: David had found her. Somehow, he'd tracked her down, and now he was out there, watching, waiting.

Her pulse spiked as she crept to the window. The street below was empty except for parked cars and the occasional cat picking its way between garbage bins. No figure lurking in doorways, no one craning their neck to peer up at first-floor windows.

First floor. The tension she'd been carrying for weeks finally broke. Her flat was on the first floor—at least four metres off the ground. No one could look in her windows from street level, not unless they were carrying a ladder.

Shea sank onto her bed, running shaking hands through

her hair. She was being ridiculous. David didn't even know she was in Melbourne, let alone her address. The shadow had been a bird, or a tree branch moving in the wind, or nothing at all—just her traumatised mind creating threats where none existed.

But as she lay back down, pulling the covers up to her chin, she couldn't shake the feeling that somewhere out there, David was still looking for her. The rational part of her mind insisted it was impossible, but her body remained tense, alert, listening for footsteps that would never come.

She didn't sleep again that night.

##

By Easter, Shea had completed her first semester of the wellness counselling course, and to her surprise, she'd not only excelled but found herself genuinely passionate about the work. The theories that had once seemed abstract now made perfect sense, and her practical nature had adapted to the more intuitive aspects of the training. She understood grief counselling in a way that went beyond textbook knowledge—an understanding born from her own raw experience.

'You have a natural gift for this,' Eliza had told her after a particularly challenging role-playing exercise where Shea had helped a fellow student work through simulated pregnancy loss. 'The way you hold space for people's pain without trying to fix it—that's not something that can be taught.'

Shea's friendship with Eliza had deepened over the months. They often grabbed coffee after sessions, and Eliza had become something of a mentor, guiding Shea through the more difficult emotional territory the course occasionally stirred up. There was also Heath, whose Friday night presence at the

Courthouse Hotel had become a welcome constant in her Melbourne routine.

Tonight was one of those Fridays, and Shea found herself looking forward to their easy conversation. She'd arrived early and claimed her usual table, ordering the fish and chips that had become her standard Friday meal.

'Well, if it isn't my favourite country girl,' Heath said, appearing at her table with his characteristic warm smile. He set down a glass of wine without being asked—he'd learned her preferences months ago.

'How did you know I was from the country the first time we met?' Shea asked, settling back in her chair. 'You picked it before I even told you where I was from.'

'The way you hold yourself,' Heath said, perching on the edge of the chair across from her. 'City people are always in a hurry, always looking over their shoulders. You move like someone who's used to having space around them.'

'Interesting observation for a barman.'

'Well, I'm not really a barman,' Heath grinned. 'I'm only here Friday nights, helping out my brother-in-law. He owns this place, and Friday's his busiest night. I figure I owe him a few favours.'

'What do you do the rest of the week?'

'I'm a doctor, actually. GP in a practice at Carlton. Fridays are my mental health night—pulling beers is surprisingly therapeutic after a week of consultations.'

Shea looked at him with new interest. 'A doctor who moonlights as a barman. That's definitely not something you see every day.'

'And a vet nurse studying alternative healing,' Heath countered. 'We're both a bit unconventional, aren't we?'

They talked easily about their childhoods—Heath's suburban Melbourne upbringing with weekend trips to the beach, Shea's life growing up on the family sheep station. She found herself sharing more than she usually did, telling him about mustering sheep with her sisters, swimming in the billabongs during scorching summer afternoons, and the way the Southern Cross looked so bright above the Darling River that you could read by starlight.

'Four sisters,' Heath said, shaking his head in amazement. 'That must have been chaos.'

'Organised chaos,' Shea laughed. 'Mum had us all on roster systems—who helped with cooking, who fed the chooks, who got to ride in the front of the ute. Though being fourth in line meant I rarely got the front seat.'

'Only one quiet sister for me, a lot older than me, too.' Heath admitted. 'Always wondered what it would be like to have more siblings. The noise alone must have been incredible.'

'Oh, it was. Especially when we were teenagers. Three bathrooms for seven people—you learned to be strategic about shower times.' Shea paused, remembering. 'But it was wonderful too. Someone always had your back, even when you were fighting with them. What was it like just with one sister?'

'Quiet,' Heath grinned. 'Very, very quiet. And my parents' undivided attention she left home, which was both a blessing and a curse. Every scraped knee was a medical emergency, every school report analysed like a thesis. Growing up out there must have been very different. I love getting out to remote country.'

'It's different,' Shea said. 'I can imagine silence would take some getting used to if you're a city person. But once you understand it...'

'Sounds like you miss it.'

'I do.' The admission surprised her with its honesty. 'I love the work I'm doing here, but Melbourne is a temporary stop. Serving a purpose.'

Heath studied her for a moment, then seemed to make a decision. 'Would you like to have dinner with me sometime? Somewhere that's not the pub?'

A flutter of interest stirred in Shea's chest, followed immediately by the familiar wall of anxiety. 'Heath, I...' She paused, choosing her words carefully. 'I'm not really in the right headspace at the moment. It's not you—you're a great guy. It's kind of you, but—'

'Fair enough,' Heath said, his smile understanding rather than disappointed. 'But if you ever change your mind, the offer stands. And in the meantime, I enjoy our Friday night conversations too much to let them go. Forget I asked.'

'No need. I enjoy talking to you too,' Shea assured him, grateful for his laidback presence.

# Chapter 7

*Early June*

Sunday afternoon was bleak and cold, with a Melbourne drizzle that seemed to seep into everything—the old weatherboard walls of her flat, her bones, her spirit. Shea pulled herself out of the threatening doldrums and curled up on her sofa with a cup of tea and one of the psychology books Eliza had recommended, but she found herself staring out of the rain-streaked windows more than reading.

Days like this made her ache for *Ceann Mara* with a physical pain. At home, even the worst weather had a purpose—rain meant the paddocks would green up, the river would rise, the stock would have good feed. Here, the grey sky just depressed her, offering nothing but cold and the smell of wet concrete.

She missed the way Sunday afternoons stretched endlessly at the homestead, with Mum cooking something that filled the whole house with warmth and her sisters sprawled across the verandas reading or arguing or planning their week. She missed the red earth that stained your boots and the way the Darling River caught the late afternoon light like hammered gold. Most of all, she missed the silence—not this city quiet punctuated by traffic and sirens, but the deep, breathing silence of the outback that let you hear your own thoughts.

When her phone rang, she glanced down at the screen, almost letting it go to voicemail—weekends were her sanctuary from the world. But when she saw Eliza's name on the screen, she picked up.

'Shea, I hope I'm not interrupting your weekend.' Eliza's voice was always a pleasant combination of husky and brisk that sounded like she'd just finished laughing at something. Warmth ran through Shea at the sound, and she couldn't help smiling. Over the months, she and Eliza had formed a solid friendship that she valued more than Eliza would ever know.

'Not at all. Just doing some reading. Meet at the café?'

'Twenty minutes?'

'Perfect.'

'And Shea? Bring an open mind.'

Shea closed her book and stretched. Whatever Eliza had in mind, it would be better than sitting here dwelling on homesickness and grey skies. She pulled on her leather boots and her long wool coat, something she'd never needed at *Ceann Mara*.

The rain had eased to a fine mist by the time she stepped outside, but the wind still carried that sharp Melbourne bite that seemed to cut right through you. She pulled her coat tighter and headed for the tram stop, wondering why Eliza had said to keep an open mind.

Twenty minutes later, she stepped into the warmth of their favourite coffee shop, grateful for the fire crackling in the old stone grate. The familiar mix of coffee aromas and book-scented air enveloped her as she looked around. Eliza was already settled at their usual corner table, two steaming mugs waiting.

'What's up?' Shea asked, unwinding her scarf as she slid into the mismatched chair across from her friend at their usual corner table.

'I have something I want to talk to you about,' Eliza said

as they settled into their familiar corner table at the eclectic café near the warehouse.

'That sounds ominous.'

'Not ominous,' Eliza laughed. 'Opportunistic, maybe. I know how much you don't like living in the city, and I've got a suggestion for you.'

Shea raised an eyebrow. 'I'm listening.'

'My cousin Ruth is a vet in Wentworth—you know, the little town at the confluence of the Murray and Darling rivers. She's been looking for a qualified vet nurse to help the other vet when she retires, someone reliable and experienced. When I mentioned you, she was very interested.'

'Wentworth,' Shea repeated slowly. The name stirred something in her memory—Dad's research, the paddle steamers, the river junction.

'I know what you're thinking,' Eliza continued. 'Medical family, right? My brother's a doctor, Ruth's a vet. I should probably confess now that, as well as practising in the alternative arena, I'm also a lecturer in psychology at Melbourne Uni.'

This was news to Shea. 'You are? What made you change?'

Eliza's expression grew more serious, her fingers tracing the rim of her coffee cup. 'Personal tragedy. I lost my husband in a car accident five years ago. Conventional therapy wasn't helping me process the grief—all the clinical approaches I'd been trained in felt inadequate when I was the one in pain. A friend suggested I try some alternative healing approaches, and they saved my life.'

'I'm sorry,' Shea said quietly. 'That must have been devastating.'

'It was. But it also led me to this work, and now I get to help people like you find their own path through darkness.' Eliza leaned forward. 'That's actually my ulterior motive in suggesting Wentworth. I have a friend there, Ritchie, who runs an alternative healing practice. She works out of this beautiful cottage by the river, and I think you're ready to do some work there—not just as a student, but as a practitioner.'

Her interest was piqued. 'Tell me more about Wentworth.'

'It's small, peaceful, right on the river junction where your family's paddle steamers used to run. Ritchie's cottage is this gorgeous old stone building with gardens that go right down to the water. You'd love it, Shea. I know you well enough now to be sure of that.'

'And the vet work?'

'Ruth and her business partner, Ronald, run a mixed practice—small animals in town, farm calls out to the stations. It's exactly the kind of variety you're used to, but without the isolation you're feeling here.'

Shea stared out the café window at the busy Melbourne street, weighing the idea. Wentworth. The river. A chance to continue her counselling work while returning to something closer to home.

'When would she need someone?'

'As soon as possible. Ruth's been looking for a nurse for three months.' Eliza pulled out her phone. 'I can call her right now if you're interested.'

'Yes,' Shea said, surprising herself with the certainty in her voice. 'Yes, please call her.'

By the end of the week, everything was arranged. Ruth McLean had interviewed Shea over the phone and offered her the position immediately. Ritchie had welcomed the idea of having another counsellor to refer clients to. Shea had given her two weeks' notice at the South Yarra vet clinic and started planning her move.

Friday night came around again, and Shea made her way to the Courthouse Hotel one last time. She'd been looking forward to telling Heath about her decision, to saying goodbye properly to the friendship that had been such a lifeline during her Melbourne months.

But when she arrived, a different barman was working behind the bar—a younger man she didn't recognise.

'Is Heath working tonight?' she asked when she ordered her wine.

'Nah, he's not on tonight,' the barman said. 'Family thing, I think. Can I get you anything to eat?'

Disappointment hollowed out her chest. She'd wanted to thank him, to explain why she was leaving, to make sure he understood it wasn't about his dinner invitation.

'No, thanks, but I'll leave him a message.'

The Wednesday evening shift at the South Yarra clinic had been particularly challenging—two emergency surgeries and a difficult euthanasia that had left Shea emotionally drained. She was looking forward to the quiet of her Preston flat, perhaps a cup of tea and an early night before her final day at work tomorrow.

She was surprised to find Heath waiting outside the clinic when she emerged at half past seven, leaning against the brick wall with his hands in his jacket pockets.

'I hope you don't mind,' he said, straightening when he

saw her. 'I thought I'd walk you to the tram stop. It's getting dark.'

'That's kind of you, but you didn't need to—'

'I wanted to.' His expression was serious but gentle. 'I got your message. Shea.'

'I didn't know if you'd get it. I wanted to say goodbye, but you weren't there last Friday night.'

'Family emergency. My aunt had a fall and needed someone to sit with her at the hospital. She's fine now, but I felt terrible about missing you.'

'You don't need to explain—'

'Actually, I do. Because your note got me thinking.' His voice was warm, that same gentle confidence appreciated in all their conversations. 'You said you were moving to the country, and I know I said I'd forget about asking you to dinner, but I keep thinking... well, how about a dinner to say goodbye?'

Shea found herself smiling despite the emotional hangover from the day at the clinic. 'Heath—'

'I know what you said before, and I respect that. But you're leaving anyway, so there's no pressure about where it might lead. Just... one nice evening to talk before you go. What do you think?'

Standing outside the clinic in the fading light, Shea pressed her hand to her chest. The finality of leaving, or maybe just hearing from him when she'd thought that door was closed. Maybe she was simply tired of always saying no to kindness.

'Just dinner?' she asked.

'Just dinner. I promise. Saturday night?'

Shea nodded.

Heath's hand held her elbow as they walked towards the tram stop, their footsteps echoing on the quiet street.

##

Saturday arrived grey and drizzling, the kind of Melbourne weather that always dampened spirits. Shea spent longer than usual choosing what to wear, finally settling on a royal blue winter dress she'd bought during her first week in the city but never worn—it had seemed too hopeful then, too much like the sort of thing the old Shea would have chosen.

Looking at herself in the mirror now, determination overrode the touch of nervousness. This wasn't a date, she reminded herself. It was goodbye to a new friend and practice. Practice for the person she was going to be in Wentworth, someone who could have normal conversations with kind men without feeling the need to flee.

Despite her best intentions, her thoughts went back to the night she made the biggest mistake of her life.

# Chapter 8

*Nine months earlier - Broken Hill*

Shea should have trusted her instincts about the staff drinks that Friday night. She had planned to make an appearance, have one beer, and slip away early, like she usually did. But Dr Richards had announced his retirement, and somehow one drink became three, and David Mason, the new vet taking over the practice, had been persistent in keeping her glass full and her conversation focused on him.

'You're different from the other vet nurses,' he'd said, leaning closer than necessary in the crowded pub. 'More serious. More intelligent.'

It should have been a compliment, but something about the way he said it made her uncomfortable. David had a way of talking that made everything sound like a judgement of her, of other people, of situations he deemed worthy or unworthy of his attention.

'I should head home,' she said around ten o'clock, but David had been insistent.

'Come on, Shea. The night's still young. Besides, I've got that bottle of wine I've been saving. The good stuff from the Barossa.'

She'd hesitated, knowing she had already had more to drink than she was comfortable with. But David was her superior at the practice, and he had been increasingly attentive over the past few weeks in ways that felt both flattering and pressuring.

'Just for a nightcap,' he said, his hand finding the small of her back as he guided her towards the door. 'I promise I'll be a perfect gentleman.'

Shea woke the next morning in David's bed with a sick feeling that had nothing to do with the wine. She remembered fragments of the night—David's hands more insistent than gentle, her own protestations dismissed as coyness, the moment when saying no became more complicated than saying yes.

David was already awake, propped on one elbow, watching her with an intensity that made her skin crawl.

'Morning, beautiful,' he said, his voice carrying a possessive note that hadn't been there before. 'I've been thinking about us.'

'Us?' Shea pulled the sheet higher, looking for her clothes scattered around the room.

'Last night changed things, don't you think? We can't pretend there's nothing between us now.' David's hand moved towards her face, and she flinched away. 'I was thinking we should make this official. Let people at work know we're together.'

'David, I need to go home. I need to think—'

'Think about what?' His voice sharpened. 'About whether you want to be with someone who actually appreciates you? Someone who can advance your career instead of holding you back?'

The implication was clear, and it made Shea's stomach turn. She gathered her clothes and dressed quickly while David continued talking about their "relationship" as if it were a foregone conclusion.

'I'll pick you up for dinner tomorrow night,' he said as she headed for the door. 'There's a new place in Broken Hill I want to try.'

'I didn't agree to dinner,' Shea said, pausing with her hand on the doorknob.

David's expression darkened. 'I think you're forgetting how this works, Shea. We're colleagues. We need to maintain a professional relationship.'

The threat was subtle but unmistakable. Shea left without another word, but had no intention of submitting to a threat.

***

For the next two weeks, she managed to avoid being alone with David. She took her lunch breaks at different times, found excuses to be in the field when he was in the office, and kept their interactions strictly professional. But he was persistent in ways that felt increasingly invasive.

He left flowers on her desk. He "coincidentally" appeared at the grocery store when she was shopping. He sent text messages that started friendly and became progressively more demanding when she didn't respond immediately.

'You can't avoid me forever,' he said one afternoon, cornering her in the supply room. 'People are starting to talk about why you're being so cold to me.'

'I'm not being cold. I'm being professional.'

'Is that what you call it?' David moved closer, blocking her path to the door. 'Because from where I'm standing, it looks like you're playing games—leading me on and then pulling away.'

'I never led you on, David. That night was a mistake.'

His eyes glittered, and his face flushed with anger. 'A mistake? Is that what you tell yourself? Because I remember you being very willing.'

The way he said "willing" made her feel sick. 'I need to get back to work.'

'We need to talk about this properly. Tonight. Dinner.'

'I said no.'

'And I'm saying yes. Seven o'clock. The Italian place on Argent Street.' He stepped aside finally, but his voice followed her out of the room. 'Don't make this harder than it needs to be, Shea.'

She went to dinner because refusing felt more dangerous than agreeing. David was charming at first, ordering expensive wine and discussing his plans for expanding the practice. But as the evening wore on, his tone became more possessive, more controlling.

'I've been thinking about moving you to a more senior position,' he said over dessert. 'Someone with your skills deserves more responsibility. More independence.'

'I'm happy with my current role.'

'Are you? Because from what I've observed, you're capable of much more than basic vet nursing. With the right guidance, the right support, you could really advance your career.'

The subtext was clear: cooperate with his romantic expectations, and her career would flourish. Resist, and things would become difficult.

When he walked her to her car, David's hands were more aggressive than they'd been in the restaurant. His kiss was demanding, possessive in a way that made her push him away.

'David, stop. I don't want this.'

'Yes, you do. You're just scared of what people will think.'

'No, I don't. I don't want to see you outside of work anymore.'

David's expression shifted from confidence to anger so quickly that it made her step backwards.

'That's not your decision to make, Shea. We're involved now. You can't just decide you want out because you're having second thoughts.'

'I can, and I am. Please respect that.'

'Respect?' David laughed, but there was nothing humorous about it. 'You sleep with me and then want to pretend it never happened? That's not how the world works. It's time we moved in together.'

Shea got into her car and locked the doors immediately. Through the window, she could see David standing under the streetlight, his face twisted with something that looked like fury mixed with entitlement.

The harassment started the following week. David found reasons to criticise her work in front of colleagues. He scheduled her for the most unpleasant tasks and the longest hours. He made comments about her "reliability" and "professional judgement" that were technically workplace appropriate but clearly personal.

Three weeks after that dinner, Shea realised her period was late. The pregnancy test she bought confirmed her worst fears.

She sat in her car in the pharmacy parking lot, staring at the two pink lines, feeling her world collapse around her. They'd used protection, but clearly it hadn't been enough. The thought of being tied to David forever through a child made her physically ill.

She couldn't tell him. The man who'd already made her life miserable over a single night would see a pregnancy as permanent ownership. Termination was not an option—she simply couldn't do that, no matter how complicated the circumstances.

Her only option was to leave. She started quietly looking for positions in Melbourne, crafting applications late at night when she was sure David wouldn't call or text.

***

The miscarriage happened on a Thursday morning during a routine vaccination clinic. Shea felt the cramping start around ten o'clock, but she pushed through until the pain became impossible to ignore. By noon, she was bleeding heavily enough that Janet, the practice secretary, insisted on driving her to the medical centre.

'Probably just stress,' Shea had lied, but Dr Williams confirmed what she already knew. She'd lost the baby she'd been too terrified to want, but somehow had started to mourn anyway.

'These things happen,' Dr Williams said gently. 'Especially early in pregnancy. There's nothing you could have done differently.'

Shea spent the rest of the day at home, grieving something she hadn't even had time to process. The relief was overwhelming and guilt-inducing in equal measure.

She didn't know that Janet had called the practice to explain her absence. Or that Janet, meaning well, had breached patient confidentiality and mentioned the miscarriage to David.

He appeared at her door that evening without warning, his face a mask of fury that made her step backwards into her hallway.

'How dare you,' he said, pushing past her into the house. 'How dare you kill my child?'

'David, it wasn't—I didn't—'

'Don't lie to me. Janet told me everything. You were pregnant, and now you're not, and you never said a word.' His voice was rising, becoming more aggressive with each word. 'That was my baby, Shea. Mine. You had no right to make that decision without me.'

'I didn't make any decision. I had a miscarriage. They happen—'

'Bullshit. You went and got it taken care of because you couldn't stand the thought of being tied to me. Well, congratulations. You're still tied to me. You work for me, you live in my town, and now I know exactly what kind of person you really are.'

David was pacing her living room like a caged animal, his hands clenched into fists. Shea had never been physically afraid of him before, but something in his stance had shifted into territory that felt genuinely dangerous.

'You need to leave,' she said, trying to keep her voice steady.

'I'll leave when I'm ready to leave. We're not done talking about this.'

'Yes, we are. Get out of my house, David.'

He turned to look at her then, and the expression on his face made her blood run cold. 'You think you can just dismiss me? You think you can use me and then throw me away like garbage?'

'I never used you. I never wanted any of this.'

'You wanted it enough that night. You wanted it enough to spread your legs for me.'

The crude language was meant to hurt, to reduce what had happened to something ugly and shameful. Shea felt tears of anger and humiliation burning behind her eyes, but she refused to let them fall while he was watching.

'Get out. Now. Or I'm calling the police.'

David laughed, but it was a sound full of malice. 'Call them. Tell them how you murdered your own baby and then tried to hide it from the father. See how sympathetic they are.'

He moved towards the door finally, but paused with his hand on the knob. 'This isn't over, Shea. You can't hide from what you've done. And you can't hide from me.'

Shea waited until she was sure David's car was gone before she started packing. She threw clothes into suitcases without folding them, grabbed her important papers from the filing cabinet, and loaded everything into her car with shaking hands. Everything else she left behind, including a month's rent and her notice to vacate the apartment in an envelope on the table.

She didn't call anyone. She didn't leave forwarding information or explain her sudden departure. She simply wrote a brief resignation letter, left it on the kitchen counter with her rent and house keys, and drove towards Melbourne through the night.

The physical pain of the miscarriage was nothing compared to the emotional devastation of realising how completely she had misjudged David's character. She'd known he was intense and had sensed something controlling in his personality, but she'd never imagined the depths of cruelty he was capable of when he didn't get what he wanted.

As the lights of Broken Hill disappeared in her rear-view mirror, Shea felt as though she was in limbo, running away from everything and towards nothing. She had no job waiting in Melbourne, no friends to take her in, no clear plan beyond putting distance between herself and the man who had made it clear he considered her property to be disposed of at his discretion. There was no way she was going to tell her family how foolish she'd been.

The miscarriage had saved her from one kind of lifelong connection to David, but his final words echoed in her mind as she drove through the darkness. She might be leaving Broken Hill, but she had a terrible feeling that David's influence on her life was far from over.

She was twenty-five years old, heartbroken, physically fragile, and completely alone. But for the first time in weeks, she could breathe without fear. It would have to be enough to start over.

# Chapter 9

*Mid-June*

Heath had suggested they meet at the restaurant rather than him picking her up—a consideration that showed he understood her need for control over the situation. When Shea arrived at the little Greek taverna in Fitzroy, her emotions barely under control, he was already there, studying the wine list with interest.

'Perfect timing,' he said, standing as she approached. 'I was just trying to decide between the *Assyrtiko* and the *Vermentino*. What do you think?'

'I think you're showing off your wine knowledge to impress a country girl,' Shea replied briskly, settling into her chair.

'Is it working?'

'Depends on whether you can pronounce them correctly.'

Heath laughed, and just like that, the tension she'd been carrying began to ease. The conversation flowed as naturally as it did at the pub—easier, perhaps, without the background noise and Heath's obligation to serve other customers.

They talked about books, about travel, about the peculiarities of Melbourne coffee culture versus country hospitality. Heath told her about his medical training, about choosing general practice because he liked the variety and the ongoing relationships with patients. Shea found herself talking about veterinary nursing, about the satisfaction of helping animals who couldn't advocate for themselves, about the way farming families often loved their working dogs more than most people loved their relatives.

'You miss it,' Heath observed over the shared baklava. 'Country life.'

'I do. Melbourne's been good to me—I needed to be here for a while. But it was always temporary.'

'What's calling you back? Besides family.'

Shea considered how much to reveal. 'I suppose I want to feel useful again. Like I'm connected to something that matters beyond just myself.'

'And you don't feel that in Melbourne?'

'I feel... safe in Melbourne. But safety isn't the same as living.'

Heath was quiet for a moment, twirling the stem of his wine glass between his fingers. 'That sounds like something someone says when they've had to choose safety over living for a while.'

The observation was gentle but perceptive, and her breath caught. 'Perhaps.'

'I hope your new town gives you both,' Heath said simply.

They walked to the coffee shop Shea had chosen—a tiny place tucked down a laneway that served coffee so strong it could wake the dead. Heath took one sip and raised his eyebrows.

'Christ, that's got some bite to it.'

'City coffee's too weak,' Shea said with mock disdain. 'This is more like what we drink at home.'

'Are you trying to put hair on my chest?'

'I'm trying to see if you're tough enough to handle country standards.'

'I think I'm failing your test.'

'Spectacularly,' Shea agreed, but she was smiling now, genuinely relaxed.

They talked until the café began closing around them, the conversation ranging from serious to silly and back again. Heath told her about his childhood ambition to be a marine biologist, derailed by a fear of sharks. Shea confided her teenage dream of being a wildlife photographer, abandoned when she realised she preferred helping animals to observing them from a distance.

'I should get you home,' Heath said as they emerged onto the still-busy Saturday night streets. 'I promised ten o'clock.'

'It's barely nine-thirty. Are you trying to get rid of me?'

'I'm trying to be a man of my word. But if you want to walk around the block a few times to kill time, I'm not opposed to that.'

They did walk, taking the long way back to Shea's tram stop, the conversation gradually growing more personal. Heath spoke about the loneliness of being an only son with one much older sister, the pressure of having parents who expected him to cure the world. Shea found herself talking about her sisters, about the comfort and complexity of being part of such a large, close family.

'They must be worried about you being so far from home,' Heath said.

Shea's step faltered slightly. 'They don't know I'm unhappy. I've gotten rather good at... managing their expectations.'

'That sounds exhausting.'

'Sometimes it is.'

At the tram stop, Heath turned to face her properly. 'Shea, I don't know what brought you to Melbourne or what's taking you away, and I respect that you don't want to share those details. But I want you to know—tonight has been one of the nicest evenings I've had in a long time. Not because of the food or the coffee, but because of the company.'

Warmth rose in her chest. 'It has been nice, hasn't it?'

'If you ever find yourself back in Melbourne, or if you ever want someone to talk to who doesn't have any expectations or agenda, I hope you'll remember that I'm here.'

'Thank you. For tonight, for... for reminding me that I can still do this. Have normal conversations, enjoy someone's company without...'

'Without what?'

'Without feeling like I need to run away.'

Heath's expression grew serious. 'Shea, I hope you know that whatever happened to make you feel that way, it wasn't your fault. And whoever made you feel like that, they were wrong. Can I text you so you have my number?'

She agreed and quickly gave him her number; he put it into his phone, and a few minutes later, her phone pinged.

The tram was approaching now, its headlights cutting through the evening mist. Shea stepped closer to Heath and, acting on impulse, stood on her tiptoes to kiss his cheek.

'Thank you,' she said simply. 'For being kind. For being patient. For giving me a lovely evening when I really needed one.'

'Take care of yourself, Shea from the Darling River,' Heath said as she boarded the tram. 'I hope your new town appreciates what they're getting.'

As the tram pulled away, Shea pressed her face to the window and watched Heath standing under the streetlight until he disappeared from view.

She probably wouldn't call him—by the time she was ready for someone like Heath, too much time would have passed, too much distance would have grown between them. But keeping his number was like a reminder that there were good men in the world who understood that kindness was important.

As Preston flashed past the windows, Shea allowed herself to imagine, just for a moment, what it might have been like to meet Heath under different circumstances. In another life, where she hadn't been broken and put back together with all the pieces slightly out of place. In another life, where she could have said yes to dinner dates and coffee walks and lazy Sunday mornings without hesitation.

But this wasn't another life—this was the life she had. And in this life, she was moving to Wentworth in five days to start over, to build something new from the careful foundation of her healing.

Still, as she climbed the stairs to her flat, Shea smiled. Tonight had been proof that she was stronger than she'd realised, more ready for the future than she'd dared to hope. If she could manage an entire evening with Heath—laughing, talking, enjoying herself—then perhaps she was ready for whatever Wentworth might bring.

Tomorrow, she would pack up her life in Melbourne. On Monday, she would drive north towards the rivers and a new beginning.

But tonight, she would go to sleep thinking about Greek food and terrible coffee and the way Heath's eyes crinkled when he laughed at her jokes. Tonight, she would fall asleep smiling.

# Chapter 10

*Melbourne 1874*

After being on the rivers, the Toorak mansion confined Catherine like a prison. She stood at her bedroom window, watching the manicured gardens where no leaf dared to fall out of place, and pressed her hand against her stomach. Three months now, and still her secret remained hidden beneath her dress. But not for much longer.

'Catherine?' Her mother's gentle voice came from the doorway. 'May I come in?'

Catherine turned from the window, managing a smile for her mother. Breda O'Byrne was still beautiful, with the kind of quiet elegance that had first caught Samuel's eye all those years ago in Ireland. She had been barely thirty-two when Samuel had brought them both to Australia to start a new life.

'Of course, Mama.'

Breda closed the door softly behind her and crossed to where Catherine stood. 'You've been so quiet since you returned from *Ceann Mara* with your father. And you barely touched your breakfast again this morning.'

Catherine's throat tightened. The morning sickness had eased somewhat, but her secret pressed down on her more heavily each day. 'I'm just tired from all the travelling.'

'Catherine.' Breda's voice was gentle but firm. 'I carried you in my womb and have known and loved you from then to the woman you are now. I know when something is troubling you deeply.' She paused, her eyes searching Catherine's face. 'How long since your last monthly courses?'

The direct question caught Catherine off guard, and her carefully constructed composure crumbled. 'Mama, I—'

'Three months? Four?'

Catherine's eyes filled with tears. 'Three months and two weeks.'

Breda's expression didn't change, but she reached out and drew Catherine into her arms. 'Oh, my dear girl.'

'I'm so ashamed,' Catherine whispered against Breda's shoulder. 'I never meant for this to happen. I thought he loved me, I thought—' She pulled back slightly, her voice becoming bitter. 'Perhaps I was foolish to believe any man would truly want to marry an old maid of twenty-seven. Maybe Daniel saw me as convenient rather than marriageable.'

'Hush.' Breda stroked Catherine's hair with gentle hands. 'Don't speak of yourself that way. You are a beautiful, accomplished woman. The right man would consider himself fortunate to have you, regardless of your age.'

Catherine told her mother everything—about Daniel McKenzie, about their meetings over the past two years as the steamers travelled the river routes, about that afternoon when she'd given him her heart and her innocence only to have him reject both.

'He said I was too good for him,' Catherine finished miserably. 'That Papa would horsewhip him if he knew. And then he simply... dismissed me. As if what happened between us meant nothing at all.'

Breda was quiet for a long moment, still holding Catherine close. When she finally spoke, her voice was very soft. 'Catherine, I need to tell you something about our past—about why we came to Australia.'

Catherine pulled back to look at her mother's face. 'What do you mean?'

'When your father left Ireland, I was keeping house for my brother John at the vicarage in Kilgarvan. You were fourteen years old when he finally returned for us.' Breda's hands trembled slightly as she smoothed Catherine's hair. 'Those were hard years, Catherine. Samuel had gone to Australia to seek his fortune, and I was left to raise you, living in the vicarage with your uncle.'

Catherine nodded, remembering those difficult years before Papa had come back for them. 'I remember how excited you were when his letters started coming more frequently, saying he was established and ready for us to join him.'

Breda's voice grew thick with old memories. 'Samuel never forgot us, never stopped working towards the day he could bring us to Australia.'

'And when he came back, he married you properly before we sailed,' Catherine said softly, remembering that hasty but joyful ceremony.

'He wanted to make everything right, wanted us to arrive in Australia as a proper family.' Breda cupped Catherine's face in her hands. 'You were old enough at fourteen to understand what that meant for our respectability, our future. Samuel gave us everything—security, status, love. But the world... the world is not always forgiving to families whose circumstances were once... irregular. Samuel is a good man, Catherine. The best of men. But the world... the world is not forgiving to women like us.'

Catherine felt a glimmer of hope. 'Then perhaps Papa would understand—'

'He would, I do not doubt that. But understanding and

accepting are different things. Samuel has worked so hard to build his reputation, his standing in society. A scandal like this...' Breda shook her head. 'It would destroy everything he's built, not just for himself but for you and young Róisín as well.'

The hope died as quickly as it had been born. 'Then what am I to do?'

Before Breda could answer, there was a soft knock at the door.

'Mama?' Ten-year-old Róisín's voice called through the wooden panels. 'Are you in there with Catherine? Cook says luncheon will be ready soon, and Papa is asking for you both.'

Breda and Catherine exchanged glances. Róisín had their father's keen observational skills and was already beginning to notice when something was amiss in the household.

'Just a moment, darling,' Breda called back, then lowered her voice to Catherine. 'We'll continue this later.'

'Mama, is Catherine ill?' Róisín's voice carried genuine concern. 'She's been so quiet lately, and she didn't eat much at breakfast again.'

Catherine wiped her eyes quickly and moved towards the door. When she opened it, Róisín stood in the hallway, her dark hair neatly braided and her blue dress pressed to perfection. At ten, she was already showing signs of the beauty she would become, with Samuel's intelligent eyes and Breda's delicate features.

'I'm fine, Rosie,' Catherine managed a smile for her younger sister. 'Just tired from all the travelling.'

Róisín studied Catherine's face. 'You've been tired a lot lately. And sad. Did something happen at *Ceann Mara*?'

'Nothing for you to worry about,' Catherine said gently,

reaching out to smooth Róisín's already perfect hair. 'Now, shall we go down to Papa before he sends out a search party?'

'All right,' Róisín agreed, but her expression suggested she wasn't entirely convinced.

As Róisín made her way towards the stairs, Breda caught Catherine's arm gently. 'We'll support you,' she said firmly, her voice low enough that Róisín couldn't hear. 'Whatever you decide, your father and I will stand by you. If you want to go away somewhere until the baby comes, we can arrange that. If you want to raise the child, we'll find a way. You're not alone in this, Catherine.'

'But Papa doesn't know yet.'

'No. And if you prefer to keep it that way, at least for now, I'll respect that decision.'

Catherine walked to her dressing table and picked up a silver-framed photograph of Samuel standing proudly beside his first paddle steamer. This man had worked hard to give them a wonderful life, and she found the thought of destroying Papa's hard-won respectability with her disgrace unbearable.

'I want to see Daniel first,' she said quietly. 'I need to tell him about the baby. Perhaps... perhaps when he knows, he'll reconsider. Perhaps he'll do the right thing.'

Breda's expression was carefully neutral. 'And if he doesn't?'

'Then I'll decide what to do next.' Catherine set down the photograph and turned back to her mother. 'But I need to try. I need to give him the chance to be honourable.'

'Very well. But Catherine—don't pin all your hopes on his response. Men like that, men who can walk away from what they've done... they rarely change their minds when faced with consequences.'

Two days later, Catherine told Samuel she wanted to accompany him on his next business trip upriver. Her father was delighted—he'd been worried about her listless behaviour and thought the river journey might restore her spirits.

'We'll go as far as Swan Hill,' he said, spreading maps across his study desk. 'I need to inspect the new wool stores there, and we can visit several stations on the way.'

'Will we stop at *Riverside Station*?' Catherine asked, trying to keep her voice casual.

'I expect so. Why?'

'I just remember it as being particularly beautiful. All those river red gums.'

Samuel smiled. 'My daughter, the nature lover. Yes, we'll likely stop there for supplies.'

The paddle steamer churned steadily upriver, carrying Catherine towards what she hoped would be a resolution to her dilemma. She stood at the rail, watching the familiar landscape slide past, and tried to rehearse what she would say to Daniel.

*I'm carrying your child. We must marry. Too blunt.*

*Daniel, I need to speak with you about our afternoon together. Too vague.*

*I love you, and I'm having your baby. Too pathetic.*

Nothing sounded right. How does one tell a man who had rejected her that she now carries his child and needs his protection?

When they reached *Riverside Station*, Catherine's heartbeat thundered in her ears as Samuel conducted his business with the station manager. She waited for her opportunity, then asked if she might take a walk along the riverbank while the men finished their discussions.

'Take care not to wander too far,' Samuel called. 'We'll be departing within the hour.'

Catherine made her way towards the workers' quarters, her stomach churning with nerves and morning sickness. She found one of the stockmen mending harness outside the bunkhouse.

'Excuse me,' she said, her voice barely above a whisper. 'I'm looking for Daniel McKenzie. Is he about?'

The stockman looked up, squinting against the afternoon sun. 'McKenzie? He's not here anymore, miss. Left about six weeks back with his missus.'

Catherine's head spun. *His missus.* 'Where did he go?'

'Goldfields, I reckon. There's been talk of new strikes up Beechworth way. Half the young fellows hereabouts have headed up there to try their luck.' The stockman returned to his work. 'Can't say as I blame them. Station work don't pay much compared to what they're promising in the diggings.'

Catherine stood frozen, her carefully rehearsed words crumbling to dust. Daniel was gone, vanished into the goldfields like so many young men chasing dreams of instant wealth. And with a *wife*. Even if she could find him, he had a wife.

'Miss? You all right?' The stockman was looking at her with concern. 'You look a bit pale.'

'I'm fine,' Catherine managed. 'Thank you.'

She walked back towards the river on unsteady legs, her last hope dissipating like morning mist. When they docked at Swan Hill a few days later, Catherine made her decision.

'Papa,' she said as the steamer prepared to dock. 'I won't be continuing with you.'

Samuel looked surprised. 'Why not? Are you feeling unwell?'

'A little. I think I'd like to rest here for a day or two, then make my own way back to Melbourne.' Catherine had been planning this conversation, and the lie came easier than she'd expected. 'Mrs. Henderson at the boarding house is an old friend of Mama's from her seamstress days. I'm sure she'd be happy to have me stay.'

'I don't like leaving you—'

'Papa, I'm a grown woman. Surely, I can manage a few days in Swan Hill without coming to harm.' Catherine managed a smile. 'Besides, you've always said the river towns are safer than Melbourne. Too small for serious trouble.'

Samuel still looked uncertain, but Catherine pressed her advantage. 'I promise I'll send word as soon as I leave to come home. And Mrs Henderson will take excellent care of me.'

'Very well. But I want you on the first available steamer back to civilisation, do you understand?'

'Of course, Papa.'

That evening, after Samuel's steamer had disappeared around the bend, Catherine stood in her small room at Henderson's Boarding House counting the money Breda had pressed into her hands before she left Melbourne—enough to keep her for several months if she was careful. Three days later, she bought a ticket to take a Cobb and Co coach from Swan Hill to Wentworth, where she had decided to settle. She couldn't explain to herself why she chose Wentworth, but wondered if she held on to the hope that one day she would see Daniel again.

A week later, she stood at the confluence where the Darling River met the Murray, two waterways joining to become more powerful together. The irony wasn't lost on her. She had come here hoping to join her life with Daniel's, only to find herself more alone than ever.

But perhaps alone was what she needed to be. Perhaps this remote river junction, far from Melbourne society and its expectations, was exactly where she belonged. Here, she could disappear from her old life without destroying her father's reputation. Here, she could face whatever came next on her own terms.

Catherine pressed her hand to her stomach, where her child grew beneath the respectable façade of her travelling dress. 'It's just you and me now,' she whispered. 'But we'll manage. We O'Byrne women are stronger than we look.'

# Chapter 11

*Mid-June*

Two days later, after her dinner with Heath, Shea loaded her car with her few possessions and pointed it northwest towards Wentworth. As Melbourne's suburbs gave way to the countryside, then to the vast plains of northwestern Victoria, calm filled her.

She crossed the Murray into New South Wales at Curlwaa and followed the Silver City Highway to Wentworth. When she saw the sign at the outskirts of town, her heart gave an unexpected flutter. The town was smaller than she'd imagined, a handful of streets clustered around both rivers, but there was something immediately welcoming about it.

Ruth McLean met her at the veterinary clinic, a modern building on the main street with large windows and a cheerful blue and white sign. Ruth was in her sixties, with greying brown hair and the kind of practical briskness that reminded Shea immediately of her mother.

'Welcome to Wentworth,' Ruth said, showing her around the clinic. 'I can't tell you how relieved I am to have you here. It's been a long three months waiting to retire. Ronald is away for a couple of days, but you'll meet him later in the week. He's a cranky curmudgeon on the surface, but he has a heart of gold.'

When she left the clinic, she called into the graceful cottage on the river where Ritchie ran the wellness centre in her front room. She asked Shea to work casually every second Saturday when she wasn't required at the vet clinic, and she agreed readily.

That afternoon, Shea moved into a small cottage she'd rented on the eastern side of the river, just five minutes from the clinic, and across the river from Ritchie. The house was nothing fancy—two bedrooms, a small kitchen, and a living room with French doors that opened onto a deck overlooking the Darling River.

Standing on that deck as the sun set over the water, watching the gentle current carry the day towards the sea, Shea felt something she hadn't experienced in months: peace.

Not healing, not yet. But peace, and she thought that might be enough to build on.

##

Six weeks into her new life in Wentworth, Shea had found her rhythm. The winter wind puffed gently from the south, raising goosebumps on her skin. She sat motionless on the wooden park bench, staring at the trees at the point where her beloved Darling River merged with the mighty Murray. If she focused on the water as it flowed together—two currents becoming one—she was able to breathe evenly and deeply, keeping her mind anchored to the present moment. It was a grounding technique she'd learned in the first weeks of her counselling course in Melbourne, though back then she'd never imagined she'd need it so desperately.

The familiar ritual had become her lifeline: arriving at dawn, claiming the same bench, watching the gently flowing waters of the rivers merge. Some mornings, she'd think about Dad's family research, how he'd become fascinated with the paddle steamers that had churned these waters in the nineteenth century. The historical information board near the viewing tower spoke of cargo loads and passenger manifests, of a time when these rivers were highways to prosperity. Other mornings, she'd simply let the water's movement wash over her, a meditation that kept the darkness at bay.

This morning, she was seeking calm as she prepared for the long drive home to visit *Ceann Mara*. It was time.

Her phone buzzed in her pocket—a text notification. Without looking, she knew it wouldn't be anyone from her family. She'd been careful about that, screening calls and sending brief responses that revealed nothing. The last thing she needed was Mum's worried voice asking why she sounded different or Cat's intuitive questions that always cut too close to the truth. Shea had become an expert at deflection over the past months, crafting careful lies about being busy at work—work that was now different.

The phone buzzed again. This time, she pulled it out, her stomach clenching when she saw David's name on the screen. Two missed calls and now a text:

**I know you're ignoring me. We need to talk. Please Shea.**

Her thumb hovered over the block button—she'd considered it so many times, but something always stopped her. Her free hand had unconsciously curled into a fist against her thigh, knuckles white with tension. The phone felt heavy in her palm, loaded with the confrontation she feared. Then again, blocking him would only make him more determined to find her. Or perhaps it was the residual guilt he'd planted in her mind that October morning when everything had fallen apart.

But she had run. From Broken Hill, from the vet clinic, from the suffocating intensity of David's expectations and the terrible emptiness where the baby should have been, to Melbourne. Then here to Wentworth, building a new life one careful day at a time, using her new skills. Yet even now, sitting by the river that had become her sanctuary, David's words still echoed: the accusations, his obsessions, the fantasy of not being ready to "try again" immediately.

She deleted the text without reading the rest and slipped the phone back into her pocket. The water continued its eternal flow, two rivers becoming one, carrying away whatever was thrown into their current.

Dad would love this. If her family were here, he and Cat would be chattering excitedly about family paddle steamers and their determination to solve the mystery of Samuel O'Byrne and his family.

A persistent rumbling broke through her introspection. She turned slowly, her eyes sweeping across the lush green grass and majestic river red gums towards the viewing tower where tourists often climbed the steps to photograph the confluence. A procession of vintage tractors was making its way along the main road, each maintaining a respectful distance from the one in front. Shea frowned as the lead tractor turned left into the loop road that led to the park where she sat. One by one, five other tractors followed, their engines puttering in a solemn rhythm as they parked in a neat line at the far end of the car park.

She watched, puzzled, until a glance at her watch reminded her that she needed to head off. This daily routine—coming here, sitting here for an hour, watching the river—had become as essential as breathing. Her thoughts always wandered to Dad's research, to the stories of steamboat captains and river traders that had captured her imagination. The water, the history, even now these unexpected visitors with their restored machines—all of it helped her ignore the ever-present darkness that had shadowed her since that October morning last year.

Standing, she smoothed her hands down her jeans, picking off the eucalyptus leaves that had drifted down from the trees above. As she turned towards her car, a long black station wagon with a discreet white logo on its side pulled into the car park and positioned itself behind the line of tractors.

Understanding hit her like a physical blow.

The tractors weren't just vintage machinery out for a morning drive. They were a guard of honour. A farewell escort. And that black station wagon...

A burst of grief struck her chest so suddenly she gasped, drawing in a shaky breath. The darkness she'd been holding at bay for months rushed back with devastating force as she stared at the hearse, knowing that somewhere in this small river town, someone was beginning their own journey through loss.

# Chapter 12

*Friday - late July.*

Shea sat by the river as the tractor drivers formed a group and chatted, calming herself with the exercises she had learned from Eliza. She stood and took one long last look at the river, picked up her coffee cup and walked back to her car, noticing a small group of men who had been driving the tractors, standing beside them. She must have looked curious because a tall man standing behind the hearse walked over to her.

'Morning, love. Lovely day, isn't it?'

'Yes, it is. What's happening here?' she asked.

'It's a vintage tractor run. One of their members passed away last week, and this is the funeral procession just heading into town.' He gestured towards the hearse with his head. 'Bobby's coffin is in the back of the hearse. They're putting it on the slide on the back of the tractor and escorting him to his service.'

'What a lovely thing to do.' She gave him a brief smile. 'I hope it goes well.'

Shea clicked the remote and opened her car, put her empty coffee cup in the mug holder in the centre console, and took a deep breath. She had a long drive ahead. Now that she'd decided to go to *Ceann Mara* for a weekend, she wanted to be on her way. Telling her parents that she had moved to Melbourne, and then Wentworth, and hadn't told them was going to be tough. Dad, particularly, would be unimpressed; she knew she had lied by omission, and he had no time for dishonesty. She'd managed to avoid family calls and knew she'd left it too long to tell her family that she'd moved twice in the past months.

How she'd pulled off normal conversations with Mum during their phone calls was beyond her. Every time one of her sisters had rung, she'd somehow avoided the call and sent back a quick text message saying she was busy at work and would get back to them later. Cat had harped at her at Christmas, and Erin had tried to talk to her, but she'd managed to fob them both off and left quickly, saying she had to be back at work. The months since then had passed quickly, but her time in Melbourne had been healing.

She was soon on the road, leaving her small cottage on the river. The drive along the dirt road on the western side of the Darling River unfolded in familiarity. Red dust kicked up behind her vehicle, settling on the sparse saltbush and bluebush that dotted the endless plains stretching towards the horizon.

She passed through tiny settlements—Pooncarie, then Menindee—where the lakes sparkled like mirrors in the morning sun, full after recent rains. The road stretched endlessly ahead, ribboning through country that seemed to breathe with ancient stories. Kangaroos bounded away from the road's edge, their powerful legs carrying them effortlessly across the red earth, while smaller creatures—echidnas and bearded dragons— scurried for cover.

Shea knew this stretch of road by heart—the old windmill that hadn't turned in years, the gate hanging crooked where someone had clipped it with a truck, the mob of goats that always clustered under the same tree. Her hands relaxed on the steering wheel.

The river, when glimpsed through the trees, moved

slowly and deliberately, its muddy waters carrying the stories of the land towards the sea.

About an hour away from *Ceann Mara*, around three, she pulled up at a small free camping area beside the river. The sounds of the afternoon were gentle—the soft lapping of water against the bank, the melodic warbling of magpies, and the distant call of a kookaburra. She made herself a coffee and sat on the tailgate of her ute, watching the water flow past, carrying with it leaves and small branches from upstream.

The service on her phone was at zero bars, and she knew Mum would be trying to ring her today because she'd ignored a call from her yesterday afternoon as she'd locked up the clinic in Wentworth. She'd taken a photo of the historical information boards in the park there at the confluence of the rivers, unsure when Dad had ever actually been to Wentworth to look at the historical displays.

In the last conversation she'd had with Dad, he'd still been trying to trace Samuel's family history. She'd listened to Dad ramble on about what Cat had discovered, knowing that her sister was as passionate about the family history as their father was. Shea was happy to listen to him and provide suggestions. All she had to do now was tell Mum and Dad about her move and new job and manage to stay calm for the two days she planned on staying at home.

As she turned at the main gate to *Ceann Mara*, she pulled over by the mailbox—a habit ingrained from years of driving through that front gate. There were two parcels and three letters in the box, and she put them on the passenger seat before heading off towards the homestead. Her throat was tight, and she swallowed. Even the routine of getting mail from the box made her emotional. God knew how she was going to hold it together when she hugged Mum and Dad.

She pulled up a kilometre before the road split to the campground and the house, and reached for the thermos of coffee she'd made that morning. She filled her cup and took a sip, wincing at the sweetness from the extra sugar she'd put in.

'I *can* do this,' she said. 'I *will* do it. I am strong, I am capable, I am worthy of love and happiness. Today I choose courage over fear.' Shea murmured the affirmation she recited to herself each morning.

A few minutes later, she drove past the shed and smiled at the cacophony of barking dogs. That meant Dad was probably in the house. He hadn't taken the dogs out on the four-wheeler with him since the accident eighteen months ago—he hadn't been on his motorbike since then either.

They were very lucky to have him. It had been a serious accident, and the injury and his heart attack had really thrown the family. The months since then had been difficult for the whole family. Róisín and Erin had both been involved in difficult encounters since Cat's move home too.

Shea shook her head. What were the chances of three of her four sisters being involved in such horrible situations? She guessed it came down to their personalities. Mum and Dad had brought the five of them up to be caring and kind, and she guessed that made women more vulnerable to men who were going to take advantage. She certainly knew that now. Her experience with David had left her vulnerable, but in a way, it had strengthened her—she was very cautious about trusting anyone these days. Heath came into her mind; she really missed him but had avoided calling. He was a part of her Melbourne past.

Slowly, she brought the car to a halt at the front gate of the family home.

The old house sat in the late afternoon sun among the river red gums, its wide verandas wrapping around three sides. The iron roof, painted green years ago, had faded to a soft sage that seemed to blend with the eucalyptus leaves overhead. Morning glory climbed the posts, its purple flowers a splash of colour against the cream bricks, while the established garden beds burst with hardy natives—bottlebrush, grevilleas, and old-fashioned roses that Mum had somehow coaxed to thrive in the harsh inland climate.

The feeling of home washed over her, even as her chest tightened with what she had to tell her parents. Despite everything that had happened, despite the months of hiding and healing, home still called to her heart. The wide front steps, worn smooth by five generations of footsteps, led to the deep veranda where she'd spent countless hours reading, studying, and dreaming of a world beyond the river.

The screen door flew open, and Mum raced out, looking as bright as ever. Her eyes were wide, and she called over her shoulder, 'Tom! Oh my God, Shea's here!'

Mum flew down the front path, pushed open the gate, and rushed to the car. Shea took a deep breath and dug deep for emotional strength. A tear or two wouldn't go astray—it *had* been over six months since she'd been home at Christmas.

Mum's eyes glittered with tears. 'Oh, sweetheart, what a wonderful surprise! Why didn't you tell us you were coming home? You've lost weight, Shea. Are you well?'

Her voice changed from delighted welcome to motherly worry in one sentence.

Shea managed to laugh. 'Oh gosh, Mum, of course I'm

well. I'm good. And it's so good to be home.' She spread her arms and took a deep breath. 'I can't believe I haven't been here since Christmas.'

'No, and I believe you've got a few things to tell us, young lady.'

Shea's eyes widened. 'Yes, I've come home to give you some news. Where's Dad?'

'I thought he was in the kitchen, but he must have gone back to the shed. Where have you driven from today?' Her tone was cautious.

'Wentworth. It was a long drive. I haven't told you yet, I've moved.'

'So, I believe.' Mum's eyes held her steadily as they walked up the front steps. 'I believe you've got quite a lot to tell us.'

'Yes, life's been a bit of a mix over the past few months, but let's make a cuppa and sit, and then I'll tell you and Dad what I'm up to.'

'Will I ring Cat and get her to come over?'

'No, just you and Dad to start with. I'll catch up with Cat later. What about the others? Has anyone else been home?'

'Well, you've just missed Erin and Jack. They left yesterday for Menindee—Jack wants to photograph the birds while the lakes are full.'

'I drove through there at noon.' Shea pulled a face. 'What about Bridget?'

'She's in Sydney doing a course before uni starts. Very excited about it all.'

'And Róisín?'

'She and Seth are off gallivanting in Canada. Some water

management conference.' Laura shook her head with a smile. 'You girls and your adventures. I can barely keep track of who's where these days.'

'Wow, I really am out of the loop.'

'Yes, and that surprises me, sweetheart. Usually, you girls know exactly what everyone's up to.'

'It's okay, Mum. I'll explain it all in a while. Look, I'm home here now, and it's just wonderful to see you.'

Her mother held her arms open, and Shea fought to retain control as she stepped in for a gentle hug. It was time to talk about Broken Hill when everything had fallen apart.

# Chapter 13

Shea had barely settled into the kitchen chair with her cup of tea when she heard the familiar sound of her father's boots on the back steps. The dogs' barking had quieted to excited whimpering, which meant Dad was making his way inside. Warm winter sunlight streamed through the kitchen window, casting golden rectangles across the scrubbed pine table where a bright jug of bottlebrush and wattle sat on a gingham doily. The comforting smell of Mum's scones baking in the Aga filled the air, mixing with the ever-present scent of the furniture polish that Mum used to polish the banisters.

'Tom!' Laura called through the screen door. 'Look who's here!'

Her father appeared in the doorway, his rugged face breaking into a wide grin when he spotted Shea. Despite his recent heart attack, he still moved with the easy stride of a man who'd spent his life working the land, though Shea noticed he favoured his left leg slightly—a reminder of the accident that had nearly taken him from them.

'Well, well. Look what the cat dragged in. I thought I recognised that car,' he said, crossing to give her a bone-crushing hug that smelled of wool and dust and home. 'What brings you home, love? Not that we're complaining.'

'Just needed to see my family,' Shea said, accepting the hug gratefully. 'And I have some news to share.'

'Good news, I hope?'

'I think so. I've made some changes recently.' Shea glanced at her mother, who was bustling around the kitchen pretending not to be hanging on to every word. 'New job, new opportunities.'

Tom raised an eyebrow but didn't push. 'Well, we'll want to hear all about it. Though I have to say, you look a bit thin, love. Your mother's been worrying.'

'I haven't been worrying,' Laura protested, though the quick look she shot Shea suggested otherwise. 'I've just been... wondering how you've been getting on.'

'I'm fine, Dad. Really. Just been busy.' Shea took a sip of her tea, grateful for the familiar ritual of it. 'How are things here? The stock looking good?'

They fell into easy conversation about rainfall and wool prices, and the new rams Logan had bought. Safe topics, comfortable ground.

'We have some news too,' Tom said. 'We've put off the trip to Fromelles.'

'Oh?' Shea was just beginning to relax when she heard a car pulling up outside.

'That'll be Cat and Logan,' Laura said, moving towards the window. 'They said they might drop by this afternoon.'

Shea's stomach clenched. She wasn't ready for Cat's sharp eyes. Not yet.

'Shea! I knew it was your car!' The back door opened, and Cat burst through, Logan close behind her.

Shea was struck immediately by how radiant her older sister looked—there was a glow about her that hadn't been there at Christmas.

'Surprise,' Shea managed, standing to accept Cat's enthusiastic hug. Her eyes widened when she became aware of the bump in front of Cat. 'You're pregnant!'

'I am. And if you'd spoken to any of us, you'd already know that.' Cat stepped back and held her at arm's length, studying her sister's face with the intensity of a detective. 'You look different.'

'Different how?'

'Thinner. And...' Cat's eyes narrowed. 'When did you get here? How long are you staying?'

'I've just arrived. I'll probably head back tomorrow or the day after.'

'Back where, exactly?' Cat's tone had closed, becoming cooler, more pointed.

'Back to work.'

'Which would be where, precisely?' Cat wasn't letting this go. 'Because Logan and I were in Broken Hill quite a while back, and we had an interesting conversation with Rod Le Cerf.'

The blood drained from Shea's face. 'You spoke to Rod?'

'We did. Imagine our surprise when he told us you left the practice.' Cat's words were deceptively calm, but Shea could see the hurt and anger simmering beneath the surface. 'Imagine our surprise when he said you'd gone to Melbourne.'

'I—' Shea looked wildly between her parents and her sister, feeling trapped. 'I can explain.'

'Can you?' Cat's composure was cracking now. 'Because I'd love to hear your explanation for lying to all of us for months. For letting us worry about you while you've been God knows where, doing God knows what.'

'Cat,' Logan said quietly, his hand touching her arm. 'Maybe we should—'

'No.' Cat shook him off, her eyes never leaving Shea's face. 'I want to know why my sister has been lying to her family. I want to know why she's been making up stories about work while she was actually living in Melbourne. I want to know what the hell is going on.'

'I'm twenty-five years old!' Shea exploded, her own anger finally matching her sister's. 'And I'm a grown, independent woman, and I don't have to live in everyone's pocket! Maybe I wanted to make some decisions for myself without there being a family conference about it!'

'Family conference?' Cat's laugh was harsh. 'We're not talking about choosing your career, Shea. We're talking about basic honesty. About letting people who love you know where you are and that you're safe.'

'I never asked you to worry about me.'

'You didn't have to ask! That's what families do!' Cat's control was gone. 'We worry because we love you. But apparently, that doesn't mean anything to you.'

'That's not fair—'

'Fair? What's not fair is lying to Mum and Dad for months. What's not fair is making them believe you were working in Broken Hill when you were actually—'

'When I was actually what?' Shea shot back. 'Living my own life? Making my own choices? Sorry if that inconveniences you, but I don't need permission from my big sister to change jobs or move cities.'

'This isn't about permission!' Cat was almost shouting now. 'This is about basic consideration for people who love you!'

'Girls,' Laura said weakly, her face pale with shock. 'Please, don't—'

But neither sister was listening. They faced each other across the kitchen like combatants, months of hurt colliding spectacularly.

'You want consideration?' Shea's voice was cold now,

deadly quiet. 'How about considering that maybe I had reasons for wanting some privacy? Maybe I didn't want to share every detail of my life because it's none of your business.'

'None of my business? You're my sister—'

'Exactly! Your sister, not your child. Not your responsibility. You're not Mum, Cat, even though you act like you are sometimes.'

Cat flinched as if she'd been slapped. 'I'm not acting like Mum. I'm acting like someone who cares about you.'

'By interrogating me? By demanding explanations like I owe them to you?' Shea was shaking now, months of grief and guilt and rage pouring out in a toxic stream. 'I don't owe you anything. Not explanations, not details about my personal life, not a daily check-in to make sure Cat O'Byrne-Wainwright approves of my choices.'

'That's enough, both of you,' Tom said sharply, but they ignored him.

'You know what?' Cat's eyes were bright with tears and fury. 'You're right. You don't owe me anything. But don't expect me to worry about you anymore. Don't expect me to care when you disappear again for months without a word.'

'Fine by me,' Shea shot back. 'Maybe now I can live my life without your commentary on every decision I make.'

'Girls!' Laura's voice cracked like a whip across the kitchen. 'Stop this right now!'

But the damage was done. Cat and Shea stared at each other across the kitchen, both breathing hard, hurt and furious. Logan stood behind Cat, his face grim with the knowledge that this fight had gone far beyond anything that could be easily repaired.

Tom looked between his daughters with an expression Shea had never seen before—not just surprise, but genuine shock. Over their lifetimes, he'd seen his girls bicker over clothes and chores and teenage drama, but nothing like this. Nothing so raw and destructive.

'Let's all just... take a breath,' Logan said carefully. 'Maybe we should talk about something else. Something happy.' He looked at Cat, his eyes full of quiet warning. 'I'm pleased that you know about the baby now, Shea.'

'And now you know the reason why we're not going to Fromelles,' Tom said quietly.

Cat wiped her eyes, still glaring at Shea.

Shea's world tilted sideways as they stopped arguing and she finally focused on the fact that Cat was pregnant. Her water glass slipped from her nerveless fingers and crashed to the floor with a sound like breaking bones.

'I need to use the bathroom,' she managed, her voice barely a whisper.

'Shea—' Laura started.

But Shea was already moving, pushing past her family and up the stairs to her childhood bedroom. She closed the door and leaned against it, her whole body shaking with the effort of not screaming.

A baby. Cat was having a baby.

The grief that hit her was so sharp, so unexpected in its intensity, that she actually doubled over from the pain. All the careful emotional walls she'd built in Melbourne, all the progress she'd made in her counselling course, all the healing she thought she'd accomplished—it all crumbled in the face of this simple, joyous fact.

She pressed her hands to her mouth to muffle the sob that

tore from her throat. This was what she'd lost. This was the future that had died with her baby on that October morning.

Cat would have morning sickness and cravings, and the joy of feeling her child move. She would have Logan's hand on her growing belly, his excitement and protection and love. She would have baby showers and nursery preparations and all the beautiful anticipation of new life.

And Shea would have none of it. Would never have any of it, because the thought of trusting another man, of being vulnerable again, felt impossible. David had broken something in her that she wasn't sure could ever be repaired.

A soft knock at the door interrupted her chaotic thoughts.

'Shea?' Laura's voice was gentle through the wood. 'Can I come in?'

Shea wiped her face and opened the door. Her mother took one look at her tear-stained cheeks and red eyes and stepped inside, closing the door behind her.

# **Chapter 14**

'Oh, sweetheart,' Laura said softly. 'What's really going on?'

Something in her mother's voice—the tenderness, the unconditional love, the complete absence of judgement—broke the last of Shea's resistance.

'Just some trouble with a guy,' she whispered, the words scraping her throat raw. 'In Broken Hill. Last October. It... it didn't end well.'

Laura sat on the bed and held out her arms, and Shea collapsed into them like the broken child she still was inside. 'Tell me,' Laura murmured into her hair. 'Tell me what happened.'

Shea put her fist to her mouth. 'It... it didn't end well,' she whispered, the words scraping her throat raw. 'That's why I moved. I needed to get away. That's all.'

She told her mother nothing of the baby—she talked about how difficult David was. 'We worked at the same surgery—he was my new boss—and he wouldn't accept that I wanted to break it off. So, I moved to Melbourne.'

'Why Melbourne, love?' Laura asked as she smoothed Shea's hair back from her forehead. Despite the cool air in her bedroom, Shea was perspiring.

She wasn't going to tell Mum that she went to Melbourne because she could hide there, that there was much less chance of David finding her in a city of five million people. She finally admitted to herself that she was scared of him, but there was no way she was going to tell her family that. She played down the difficulties and said that she didn't want to work with him anymore. 'It just seemed like the right place for a fresh start,' Shea said carefully. 'Big enough to disappear in, you know? And I thought there might be more opportunities there.'

Laura seemed to accept this, her fingers still gentle in Shea's hair. When Shea had finally calmed, Laura said, 'Come on, let's go back down for dinner. Are you okay to come down? You and Cat can be civil, can't you?'

'Yes, Mum. I'll just wash my face and come down.'

'Good girl.'

Shea walked slowly to the ensuite and splashed cold water on her face, avoiding her reflection in the mirror. She still felt shaky, still raw from the confrontation downstairs, but also strangely relieved. She'd told Mum something, at least. Not everything, but something. It was a start.

She made her way down the familiar staircase, her hand trailing along the polished banister worn smooth by decades of O'Byrne hands. The homestead felt quieter now, the tension from earlier easing.

She wasn't surprised to see that Cat and Logan had gone. Mum and Dad were sitting at the kitchen table, and Laura was speaking quietly to Tom.

'Where are Cat and Logan?' she asked.

'Cat was a little upset,' Laura said gently. 'They've gone home.'

'I'm sorry, Mum. We shouldn't have fought like that.'

Tom nodded, his eyes holding hers. 'Your mother tells me you've had some man trouble.'

Shea forced a laugh. 'I guess that's one way to put it, Dad.'

'These things happen, love,' Tom said, reaching across to

squeeze her hand. 'The important thing is that you're safe and you're here now.'

Shea felt tears prick her eyes again at her father's simple acceptance. 'Thanks, Dad.'

'So, tell us about Melbourne,' Laura said, settling back into her chair. 'What did you do there? How did you manage?'

Shea took a deep breath, grateful to be on safer ground. 'I got a job at a vet clinic in South Yarra. Nice people, good work. And I met this woman, Eliza, who has become a close friend. She was teaching an alternative wellness course, and she talked me into enrolling to fill in my evenings.'

'Alternative?' Tom raised an eyebrow. 'That's a bit different from veterinary nursing.'

'It is, but I found I really enjoyed it. Learning about how to help people through difficult times, how to just... be present with them when they're struggling.' Shea's voice grew stronger as she talked about something that genuinely mattered to her. 'I discovered I had a natural ability for it.'

'That doesn't surprise me,' Laura said warmly. 'You've always been the one to notice when people are hurting, even when you were a little girl.'

'Well, that's how I ended up in Wentworth. Eliza had a cousin there—a retiring vet who needed a nurse—and there's also a wellness practitioner there who was looking for someone with counselling skills. So, it seemed perfect. I get to use both sides of my training, and...' Shea spread her arms with a forced but brilliant smile, 'I'm so much closer to home. I can drive up here for weekends now instead of it being such a major expedition.'

Tom's face brightened considerably. 'That's wonderful news, love. Wentworth's not far at all. What, six hours?'

'About that. It's beautiful there, Dad. Right at the confluence of the Murray and the Darling. You'd love it—all that river history you're always researching.'

'The paddle steamer route,' Tom said, his eyes lighting up with interest. 'Samuel would have known that area well. That's where a lot of the wool trade went through.'

'Exactly. There are still some of the old buildings from that era. It feels like... like I'm connecting with family history in a way.'

Laura reached over and squeezed Shea's hand. 'I'm so glad you found somewhere that feels right for you, sweetheart. And that you've made a friend like this, Eliza. She sounds like a good influence.'

'She is. She's taught me a lot about... well, about healing. About moving forward from difficult experiences.' Shea met her mother's eyes meaningfully. 'I'm doing much better now, Mum. Really.'

'I can see that,' Laura said softly. 'You look stronger than you did at Christmas. More like yourself again.'

Tom stood up and moved to the Aga. 'Right then, how about some dinner? Your mother's made enough to feed a small army, and I'm not letting you leave here until you've put some weight back on those bones.'

As her father busied himself with plates and her mother fussed over the stove, something eased in Shea's chest. She wasn't telling them everything—might never tell them everything—but she'd told them enough. Enough to explain her absence, her secrecy, her need to start over somewhere new.

And for now, in the familiar kitchen filled with the aroma of Mum's cooking and the unconditional love of her parents, it was enough.

'So,' she said, accepting a plate laden with roast lamb and vegetables, 'tell me about the property Cat and Logan have bought. Is it Reg's *Dunleavy*? They mentioned that at Christmas.'

And as her parents launched into the story of the land purchase and the building plans, Shea let the conversation wash over her, simply grateful to be home and determined to make the most of whatever time she had before she had to return to the careful new life she was building by the rivers.

'I should go and apologise to Cat,' Shea said when her plate was clear. 'I was horrible to her, and she was only worried about me.'

'That would be a good idea,' Laura said gently. 'She loves you very much, you know. You all do—love each other fiercely. That's why these fights hurt so much when they happen.'

'I know.' Shea looked between her parents. 'But please, don't tell her or the other girls about my relationship problems. Let's just say I wanted a career change, moved to Melbourne for study, and now I've found this perfect opportunity in Wentworth. Can we keep it that simple?'

Tom nodded immediately. 'Of course, love. Your private business is your private business.'

Laura reached over and squeezed Shea's hand. 'Whatever you're comfortable with, sweetheart. We'll follow your lead.'

'Thank you.' Shea felt another wave of relief. Her parents' unquestioning support, their willingness to protect her privacy even from her sisters, meant more to her than she could express.

Laura glanced at Tom, a small smile playing at the corners of her mouth. 'Well, since we're sharing news, let us tell you a bit about what's been happening here. Your father and Cat have found Samuel.'

'Found Samuel?' Shea looked confused. 'What do you mean?'

'Samuel O'Byrne,' Tom said, his eyes lighting up with excitement. 'Your great-great-uncle. We've been trying to trace what happened to him after he left the river trade, and we finally tracked him down. In Toorak of all places!'

'Toorak?' Shea nearly choked as she sipped her water. 'As in Melbourne Toorak?'

'The very same,' Laura laughed. 'Your father's been like a detective, following paper trails and land records. Turns out Samuel made quite a fortune in the wool trade and built himself a grand mansion in Melbourne's most fashionable suburb.'

Tom leaned forward eagerly. 'Built in 1866, it was. Forty rooms, extensive gardens, the works. He was living like a proper gentleman by the end of his life. Quite a change from his humble beginnings on the river.'

'That's incredible,' Shea said, genuinely amazed. 'So, while I was hiding out in Melbourne feeling sorry for myself, I was actually walking in Samuel's footsteps?'

'In a way, yes,' Tom grinned. 'Though I suspect his circumstances were rather more comfortable than yours.'

'What happened to the house? Is it still there?'

'Oh yes, it's still there. Been converted into apartments now, very expensive ones. But the original structure is intact.' Laura's eyes sparkled with mischief. 'Your father's planning a trip down to see it.'

'We should all go,' Shea said impulsively. 'Next time I'm down in Melbourne for my counselling course, you could come with me. We could see Samuel's house, maybe do some more research.'

Tom's face lit up like Christmas morning. 'Would you? That would be wonderful, love. There's so much more I want to find out about what he did after he left the rivers.'

'Of course, Dad. I'd love to help with the family history research. It feels... fitting, somehow. Like I'm meant to be part of uncovering Samuel's story.'

Laura and Tom exchanged a meaningful look, and Shea warmed with the knowledge that offering to be a part of the family history research had pleased her parents.

# Chapter 15

*1874 – Wentworth*

The morning sun cast long shadows across the dusty main street as Catherine made her way to Egge's General Store. Two months in Wentworth had taught her the habits of the small river town—the early bustle as paddle steamers prepared for their journeys, the afternoon quiet when the heat drove everyone indoors, the evening revival when the temperature dropped and families emerged onto their verandas.

Wentworth, in 1874, was a town built on water and wool. The confluence of the Murray and Darling rivers made it a natural stopping point for the paddle steamers that carried cargo and passengers between the inland stations and the ports of South Australia. Catherine had grown accustomed to the sound of steam whistles echoing across the water, the chug of engines, and the shouts of wharf workers loading bales of wool onto the great vessels. She avoided the riverfront when the larger paddle steamers that her father owned called in at Wentworth.

'Morning, Miss Catherine,' called Mary Egge as she entered the store. The smell of flour and tea leaves mingled with tobacco and leather, creating the distinctive scent she'd come to associate with civilisation in this frontier town.

'Good morning, Mary.' In a town where questions were rarely asked and answers rarely volunteered, she answered to Miss Catherine.

'Expecting another steamer today,' Mary remarked, measuring out sugar into a brown paper bag. 'The *River Queen*'s due from Swan Hill. Might have mail for you.'

Catherine's heart quickened. She'd written to her mother twice since arriving in Wentworth, carefully worded letters that she hoped she could show Papa. She desperately waited for a reply, some connection to the life she'd left behind.

'Thank you. I'll check at the wharf.'

As she paid for her provisions, the store door opened to admit Mrs Kate Delaney, a plump woman in her fifties who ran the boarding house down near the river. Catherine had grown fond of Kate since her arrival—she was one of the few people who seemed genuinely interested in making her feel welcome.

'Catherine, love,' Kate bustled over with her arms full of packages. 'I was hoping to catch you. My daughter-in-law's having a difficult time with her birthing, and I wondered if you might come have a look at her?'

Catherine hesitated. Word had somehow got around that she had medical knowledge—probably because she'd helped old Mr Fletcher with his infected leg wound, drawing on what she'd learned watching her mother treat similar injuries as she'd grown up. But helping with a birth felt like stepping into deeper waters.

'I'm not trained as a midwife, Mrs Delaney.'

'No, but you've got gentle hands and a calm way about you. And you know more than most of us about healing. Young Annie's been labouring since yesterday evening, and Mrs Patterson's at her wits' end.' Kate's eyes were worried. 'There's no proper doctor for fifty miles, and the closest midwife is up at Balranald.'

Catherine thought of her own condition—she was nearly six months along now, though her loose dresses and careful posture kept her secret safe. Soon, she would be the one needing help bringing a child into the world. Perhaps learning what she could now would serve her well when her time came.

'I'll come,' she said quietly. 'But I make no promises about what I can do.'

'That's all anyone can ask, dear.'

An hour later, Catherine was in the small cottage behind Delaney's boarding house, where Annie lay exhausted on a narrow bed. The girl—she couldn't be more than seventeen—looked up at Catherine with desperate, frightened eyes.

'Please,' Annie whispered. 'Something's not right. The baby should have come by now.'

Catherine washed her hands carefully and knelt beside the bed. Drawing on memories of helping her mother with difficult lambings at farms in Kilgarvan, she examined Annie gently. The baby was positioned awkwardly, she realised—turned the wrong way, making the birth nearly impossible.

'Annie, I think I can help,' Catherine said, her voice more confident than she felt. 'But I need you to trust me and do exactly as I say.'

What followed was the longest hour of Catherine's life. With careful manipulation and constant encouragement, she managed to turn the baby, and finally—finally—a healthy boy slipped into the world, crying lustily as Annie wept with relief and exhaustion.

'How did you know what to do?' Kate Delaney asked later as they cleaned up. 'That was as skilled as any midwife I've seen.'

'My mother,' Catherine said simply. 'She taught me to watch, to listen, to trust what my hands told me.'

Word of Annie Delaney's successful birth spread quickly through Wentworth's small community. Within a week, Catherine had been called to help with a child's broken arm and an elderly man's fever. She found herself settling into an unexpected role—not quite a doctor, not quite a midwife, but someone the community could turn to when medical help was needed.

'You've found your calling, I hear, Miss Catherine,' remarked Captain Thomas Morrison when she called at the *River Queen* to see if there was mail. The paddle steamer captain had become something of a friend, stopping to chat whenever the steamer called in at Wentworth. He was perhaps forty, aged by years on the river, with kind eyes and a gentle manner that reminded Catherine painfully of her father.

'I'm not sure I chose it,' Catherine replied, settling beside him on the wharf. 'It seems to have chosen me.'

'Best callings often do.' Morrison studied her thoughtfully. 'You know, there's talk in town about building you a proper place of your own. Mrs Delaney's boarding house is all very well, but if you're going to stay on permanent-like, you should have somewhere that's truly yours.'

Catherine's hand drifted unconsciously to her stomach. 'I'm not sure I can afford—'

'Actually,' Morrison interrupted, 'that's what I wanted to talk to you about. I had a passenger on my last run from Adelaide. A gentleman by the name of Samuel O'Byrne said he was looking for his daughter, Catherine. Would that be you, by any chance?'

Catherine's blood turned to ice. 'You didn't tell him I was here?'

'Course not. Man's business is his own, and a lady's business is hers. But he left instructions with the bank in Wentworth. If a Miss Catherine O'Byrne should ever need funds, they're to provide whatever she requires.' Morrison's eyes were gentle. 'Seemed like he cares about you a great deal.'

Tears stung Catherine's eyes. Even now, even after she'd disappeared without explanation, Papa was trying to take care of her. 'Did he say anything else?'

'Just that he hoped you were safe and happy, wherever you were. And that if you ever wanted to come home, there'd always be a place for you.'

That evening, Catherine walked down to the river confluence and sat on a fallen log, watching the waters merge in the gathering dusk. The Darling's muddy brown joined the Murray's clearer flow, two currents becoming something stronger together. She pressed her hands to her growing belly and spoke aloud to the child within.

'Your grandfather loves you already, even though he doesn't know you exist,' she whispered. 'He's giving us a chance to build something here, something good.'

Three days later, Catherine visited the Wentworth Bank and spoke quietly with the manager. Within a week, she'd purchased a small block of land near the confluence, with enough money left over to hire local men to build a modest cottage. Nothing grand—just two bedrooms, a kitchen, and a sitting room—but it would be hers.

'You're staying then?' Kate Delaney asked as Catherine packed her few belongings to leave the boarding house.

'I'm staying,' Catherine confirmed. 'This feels like home now.'

'Good. The town needs someone like you. And...' Kate lowered her voice, 'when your time comes, I'll be there to help. We take care of our own here.'

Catherine looked at her in surprise. 'You know?'

'Love, I've birthed six children of my own and helped with dozens more. I'd have to be blind not to notice.' Kate's smile was warm and understanding. 'No judgement here. Just friendship and support when you need it.'

As winter turned to spring, Catherine settled into her new cottage. She planted a vegetable garden, learned to bake bread in her small oven, and gradually transformed the simple structure into a home. Her medical practice grew by word of mouth—people travelled from stations fifty miles away to seek her help with difficult births and stubborn injuries.

One evening in late August, as rain drummed on her iron roof and a fire crackled in her grate, Catherine sat at her small wooden table and wrote to her mother:

*My dearest Mama,*

*I pray this letter finds you and Papa in good health. I know you must both be worried about my long absence, but I hope you can forgive me when you understand my reasons.*

*I am well and safe in a small town on the Murray River. I have established myself here as a healer of sorts—nothing grand, but the community has accepted me and I can help people in ways that bring me genuine satisfaction.*

*Papa's generosity has allowed me to purchase a small cottage where I am quite comfortable. Please tell him that his kindness means more to me than I can express, and that I think of both of you every day.*

*I must tell you that my time is near. I know the circumstances were not ideal, but I am not ashamed of this baby. I find myself looking forward to motherhood with a joy I didn't expect.*

*The child will be born in mid-spring, and I have good friends here who will help me through my confinement. Mrs*

*Delaney, who runs the boarding house, has become like a mother to me, and Captain Morrison of the paddle steamer ensures I have everything I need from the outside world.*

*I am not ready to come home yet—perhaps not ever—but I wanted you to know that I am building something good here. Something that feels worthwhile. I am becoming the woman I was meant to be, and I believe that when you meet your grandchild, you will understand why I made the choices I did.*

*Please give Papa my love, and tell him that his daughter is finally, truly happy.*

*Your devoted Catherine*

She sealed the letter and set it aside to post when the next steamer arrived. Outside, the rain continued to fall, filling the rivers that had become her sanctuary. In less than two months, she would be a mother. The thought both terrified and exhilarated her.

# Chapter 16

*Late July*

The next afternoon, the four-wheeler roared to life with a familiar putter that reminded Shea of childhood adventures with her sisters, racing across the paddocks and down to the river. She guided it along past the airstrip and the back road that connected *Ceann Mara* to the neighbouring property, the track worn smooth by decades of O'Byrne vehicles making this same journey.

It had belonged to Reg McGilvray, and there'd been drama last year when Erin had been involved in a situation with a guy who'd been camping at the property. The old homestead had burnt down that night, and now Cat and Logan had bought it, and they were living temporarily in the original cottage near the riverbank.

As she drove towards the back gate, Shea looked around the property with fresh eyes. She passed the airstrip where they'd watched Dad take off and land in his Cessna hundreds of times, and then later on, Róisín, her eldest sister, had got her pilot's licence.

The Darling River curved lazily through the landscape, the banks dotted with river red gums that cast long shadows in the afternoon light. She glanced over at the campground where a couple of caravans had set up for a few weeks, with some camper trailers dotted around campsites at the edge of their billabong on the other side of the track. She shook her head, amazed at the work that Mum did to keep the campground side of their property going—the bookings, the facilities, the endless maintenance.

She climbed off the four-wheeler and unlocked the chain that divided the two properties. Logan and Cat had renamed their place, but no one had told her what they'd settled on yet. She was a little bit worried about the reception she would get from Cat. They'd always got on so well, and having that set-to had been the first time they'd ever argued like that.

She locked the gate behind her and continued along the river road towards their property.

When she'd been home at Christmas, she hadn't come over here, and she hadn't seen the burnt-down homestead. As she approached the blackened ruins, tears filled her eyes as she remembered playing with the two McGilvray boys who'd lived there. Dad said they'd both turned bad, following a life of crime, and were both in jail now. Poor things, she thought to herself, wondering what Mrs McGilvray would have thought of how her sons had ended up.

Following the track down towards the river, she spotted the old cottage tucked amongst the river red gums. Her eyes widened in surprise at the transformation—flower boxes overflowing with geraniums and petunias, a vegetable garden already showing green shoots, and most surprisingly of all, tiny baby clothes fluttering on the washing line.

She parked the four-wheeler and stared at the small garments dancing in the breeze. Cat was seven months along, so she guessed it was time to get baby clothes ready. But there they were: miniature singlets, impossibly tiny socks, and a yellow jumpsuit that looked like it would fit a doll.

'Shea!' Cat appeared on the cottage verandah, her face lighting up despite the tension between them. 'I heard the four-wheeler coming down the track. I hoped it was you.'

'Hi, Cat.' Shea approached slowly, unsure of her reception. 'I came to apologise. I was awful to you yesterday.'

'Oh, love.' Cat stepped down from the verandah and pulled Shea into a fierce hug. 'I'm sorry too. I shouldn't have come at you like that. I was just so worried, and you know me, when I'm worried, I get bossy.'

Logan emerged from the cottage, work clothes dusty and a welcoming smile on his face. 'I'll leave you to it,' he said, squeezing Shea's shoulder as he passed. 'I've got some fencing to check down by the river.'

Cat turned towards the front of the cottage. 'Do you want to sit out here and look at the water? I've got the kettle on.'

'Yes, that would be nice.'

They settled on the cottage's front steps, mugs of tea warming their hands as they watched the Darling flow past in its unhurried way. The silence between them was comfortable now, sisters again rather than adversaries.

'I went through a hard time,' Shea said finally. 'Trying to decide what I really wanted to do with my life. That's why I left Broken Hill and ended up in Melbourne. I'd been seeing someone—David—but we were completely incompatible. When I realised it wasn't going anywhere, I decided I needed a complete change of scene.'

'I can understand why you didn't tell us you were questioning your career,' Cat said carefully. 'But I can't understand why you didn't tell us you were struggling. We could have helped.'

Shea picked at the wooden step with her fingernail. 'Like I said when we argued, I'm a big girl now. I guess I didn't want to admit to having doubts when all of you seemed so sure of your paths. Look at Bridget—here she is doing her course before university, and she's been following the same dream since she was about twelve years old. And was running her own software business when she was at boarding school!'

Cat nodded thoughtfully. 'And Erin's really settled down now. She and Jack are making a proper go of it, and apparently her writing is coming along in leaps and bounds.'

'And Mum said Róisín's getting promoted in the water authority,' Shea added. 'Everyone seems to have it all figured out except me.' She swallowed and looked at Cat, forcing a bright smile to her face. 'And look at you. You're going to be a mum.'

'I know, it's exciting!' Cat's face glowed with happiness. 'We didn't plan it, but I guess that's the best way sometimes.'

'And you've got baby clothes on the line,' Shea observed, proud that her voice stayed steady.

'I noticed you looking.' Cat laughed. 'I've been buying online. I have way too much. Mum's just as bad.'

'Mum and Dad are excited about being grandparents,' Shea managed.

'They are. But enough about me,' Cat said, shifting to face her sister properly. 'Tell me more about you. Tell me about where you're living and what you're doing.'

Shea described her life working at the vet surgery in Wentworth, the part-time work at the wellness centre, and the counselling course she'd completed. She told Cat about Eliza and what an amazing person she was, and how she'd only found out before leaving Melbourne that Eliza was also a professor at the university.

'She seemed like someone I could just have coffee with

after class,' Shea said. 'Turns out she was this incredibly qualified academic who'd been through her own difficult times and found healing in alternative therapies.'

'She sounds wonderful. And no other partners on the scene since you had that break-up with David?'

Cat's question was casual, but Shea caught the slight frown that accompanied it. She knew her sister well enough to recognise suspicion when she saw it.

'No, nothing like that. I'm focusing on my work, on building something meaningful. The counselling, especially—I never expected to find something I was passionate about like that.'

'It suits you,' Cat said warmly. 'You've always been the one to notice when people are hurting. Remember how you used to look after everyone at primary school?'

'Some things don't change, I suppose.'

They talked for another hour as the sun began to sink towards the horizon, painting the river gold. The conversation flowed easily now, the earlier tension dissolved in shared laughter.

'I should head back,' Shea said eventually, standing and brushing dust from her jeans. 'I'm leaving early tomorrow morning to drive back to Wentworth.'

'Already? You only just got here.'

'I know, but I've got work on Monday, and it's a long drive.' Shea hesitated.

'Make sure you ring the others while you're here,' Cat said. 'Everyone's been worried about you.'

'I didn't mean that to happen.'

'As long as we know you're okay now,' Cat said firmly, standing to hug her sister. 'We all love you, and love means worrying. But I'm glad you're happy now, glad you've found your place.'

'I'm sorry,' Shea said simply. 'For the secrecy, and for everything.'

'Water under the bridge,' Cat replied, gesturing towards the river. 'Literally.'

As Shea climbed back onto the four-wheeler, Cat called after her. 'And Shea? Next time you're struggling with something, promise you won't shut us out. We're family. That's what we're for.'

Shea waved and started the engine, but Cat's words followed her all the way back to *Ceann Mara*.

# Chapter 17

*August*

The winter afternoon was perfect for sitting on the verandah at *Ceann Mara*, and Cat had positioned herself in the old wicker chair where the late sunlight streamed through the pepper trees. She had a folder of documents spread across her lap—photocopies from the State Library, birth certificates, marriage records, and shipping manifests that she and Tom had been collecting over the past months.

'Found anything new?' Tom asked, settling into the chair beside her with two steaming mugs of tea.

'Actually, yes.' Her excitement kicked in, and the baby immediately followed. She rubbed her stomach and grinned. 'I think we might have another one interested in the family history, Dad.'

Tom smiled at her affectionately.

'Look at this birth certificate from 1864.' She held up a faded photocopy. 'Catherine O'Byrne had a sister—Róisín O'Byrne, born two years after Samuel arrived back.'

Tom leaned forward eagerly, adjusting his reading glasses. 'Róisín? Same spelling as our Róisín.'

'Must be where the family name comes from. And here—' Cat shuffled through her papers, pulling out another document. 'I found Catherine's birth certificate.'

They sat in comfortable silence for a moment; each lost in their own thoughts about these long-dead relatives whose lives they were slowly piecing together.

'I keep thinking about Shea,' Cat said suddenly. 'About

how she's still being so secretive about what really happened with that boyfriend of hers.'

Tom glanced at his daughter. 'Your mother said she told them it was just incompatibility, that they wanted different things.'

'Dad, you and I both know that's not the whole truth.' Cat set down her mug with more force than necessary. 'Shea doesn't run away from incompatibility. She's one of the most direct people I know—if someone wasn't right for her, she'd just tell them so and move on.'

'What are you thinking then?'

Cat stared out at the river, watching a pair of pelicans glide across the water. 'I think something bad happened. Something that scared her enough to make her flee to Melbourne without telling anyone. And now she's determined to keep it private.'

'She seemed better when she was here,' Tom observed. 'More like her old self.'

'On the surface, maybe. But did you notice how she reacted when Logan and I announced the pregnancy? She went white as a sheet and had to leave the room.'

Tom's expression grew troubled. 'I thought she was just overwhelmed by your argument.'

'No, Dad. There was something else there. Something about babies or pregnancy or...' Cat trailed off, not wanting to voice her growing suspicions.

'What can we do? We can't force her to tell us.'

Cat was quiet for a long moment, her mind working. 'We could go to Broken Hill. Ask around quietly. Find out what really happened there.'

'Cat—it's Shea's business.'

'It's Shea's happiness, and her mental health. I'm not talking about confronting anyone or causing drama. But Broken Hill's not that big, and Shea worked there for months. Someone must know something about why she left so suddenly.'

Tom looked uncomfortable with the idea. 'Your mother specifically asked us to let Shea handle this in her own time.'

'And I respect that. But what if she's in danger? What if this man is a threat to her?' Cat leaned forward earnestly.

'You think it was that serious?'

Cat thought about her sister's sad eyes at Christmas, the way she'd flinched from affection, the careful distance she maintained even when she was trying to seem normal.

'I think our bright, confident, fearless sister disappeared for months and came back as someone who can barely stand to be touched. I think she's learned to lie to us so convincingly that we almost believe her casual explanations. And I think she's still scared.'

Tom was quiet, processing this assessment. 'What would you do in Broken Hill?'

'Just ask questions. Visit the vet clinic where she worked, maybe chat with some of the locals. Get a sense of what the situation was like before she left.' Cat's concern was clear. 'If I'm wrong, if it really was just a simple break-up, then I'll drop it and never mention it again. But if I'm right...'

'If you're right, then what? You can't fix whatever happened to her.'

'No, but I can make sure she knows she's not alone, and that she's safe. That she doesn't have to carry it by herself.' Cat looked at her father directly and kept her voice steady. 'Something terrible happened to me, and I held it in. Believe me, it's not healthy. Wouldn't you want to be able to help Shea, too?'

Tom sighed heavily. 'Of course I would. But there's a difference between wanting to help and needing to know details that might be too painful to share.'

'I'm not talking about forcing her to relive trauma. I'm talking about understanding enough to truly support her.' Cat gestured to the documents in her lap. 'Look at what we're doing with Catherine and Samuel—we're uncovering family secrets, piecing together stories that were hidden for generations. Why is it different when it's happening in our own time?'

'Because Catherine and Samuel are dead, and their pain can't be made worse by our interference.'

Cat considered this, then shook her head. 'But maybe understanding their story teaches us. Maybe there are lessons there about how we handle crises, how we support each other.'

Tom picked up Catherine's birth certificate, studying it again. 'Why did she disappear from the family records after the 1870s?'

'I've been wondering about that too. She vanished completely—no marriage records, no death certificate we can find, nothing. It's like she just... disappeared from history.'

'Maybe she went somewhere else, started over with a new identity.'

'Or maybe she died young, somewhere remote where records weren't kept properly.' Cat's words were slow as she thought it through. 'The 1870s were hard times. Disease, accidents, childbirth complications...'

They sat in contemplative silence, both wondering about the lost stories of their ancestors and the hidden pain their own family might be carrying.

'I'll think more about Broken Hill. I might make some calls.'

'And if you find out something serious happened?'

Cat met her father's eyes steadily. 'Then I'll know how to love my sister better. And I'll make sure whoever hurt her understands that Shea O'Byrne has a family who won't let anyone harm her twice.'

Tom nodded slowly, recognising both the wisdom and the fierce protectiveness in his daughter's words. 'Be careful, Cat. Some things are private for good reason.'

'I will be. But Dad—' Cat gathered the historical documents, holding them like evidence of family resilience. 'Shea's going to be okay, too. We just need to make sure she knows she's not facing whatever this is alone.'

# Chapter 18

*September 1874 - Wentworth*

The pains began at dawn, pulling Catherine from restless sleep like waves dragging her from the shore. She lay still for a moment in her narrow bed, one hand pressed to her swollen belly, listening to the familiar sounds of Wentworth waking up—the distant whistle of a paddle steamer, the lowing of cattle being driven to water, the creak of cart wheels on the dusty road.

Her gate creaked, and footsteps sounded on the two front steps. 'Catherine, are you home?' Kate Delaney had taken to calling in on her each morning for the past week.

'Kate,' she called, her voice carrying through the thin cottage walls. 'Kate, it's time.' Another contraction gripped her, stronger this time, and she knew with absolute certainty that today her child would be born.

Within minutes, Kate bustled through the door, her grey hair already pinned back and her sleeves rolled up for work. Behind her came Maggie O'Sullivan, the Irish woman who ran the small hotel, and surprisingly, Mrs Patterson—Annie's mother, whose own successful birth had helped establish Catherine's reputation in the community.

'I knew it would be today,' Maggie said. 'The way you were walking yesterday.'

'Right then, love,' Kate said briskly, taking charge. 'Let's get you comfortable. Maggie, put the kettle on. Mrs Patterson, those clean rags we prepared are in the chest by the window.'

Catherine marvelled at how quickly her small cottage filled with purpose. These women, who had started as strangers and gradually become close friends, moved around her cottage quietly.

'How far apart are the pains?' Kate asked, helping Catherine from her bed to the wooden chair they'd positioned near the window for the best light.

'Every few minutes now,' Catherine gasped as another contraction seized her. 'Oh, Kate, I'm frightened.'

'Course you are, dear. That's natural for a first baby.' Kate's hands were gentle as she examined Catherine. 'But you're a strong girl, and we're all here with you. This baby's going to come whether you're frightened or not, so we might as well get on with it.'

Maggie appeared with steaming tea, the cup rattling slightly in her hands. 'Drink this, Catherine. It's got raspberry leaf in it—helps with the birthing.'

'How do you know so much about this?' Catherine asked between pains, grateful for something to focus on besides the growing intensity of her labour.

'Had seven of my own back in County Cork,' Maggie replied with a tired smile. 'Lost three to fever, but the others are grown now. My eldest daughter's probably birthing babies of her own by now.'

'Why did you leave Ireland?' Mrs Patterson asked, settling herself in the corner with her mending basket. Catherine had soon learned that conversation helped pass the long hours of labour, keeping both the mother and her helpers distracted from the work at hand.

'The hunger took our farm,' Maggie said simply. 'My husband heard there was work on the riverboats here in the colonies, so we took what little we had and came. He died of a fever two winters past, but I've made a life here. This place accepts people as they are, not as they were.'

Catherine nodded, understanding the sentiment completely. She knew her parents' history, and Wentworth was a place where questions weren't asked and pasts could be left behind. She'd found acceptance here that would have been impossible in Melbourne's more rigid society.

The morning wore on, punctuated by Catherine's increasing discomfort and the steady stream of women who appeared at her door. Word had somehow spread through the small community that their healer was having her own time of trial. Mrs Henderson brought fresh bread, still warm from the oven. Young Annie Patterson arrived with wildflowers gathered from the riverbank, her baby strapped to her chest.

'I wanted to be here,' Annie said shyly. 'After what you did for me and little Tom. I wanted to help if I could.'

'You helped by having such a beautiful boy,' Catherine managed between contractions. 'He's thriving, isn't he?'

'Growing like a weed. And talking already—well, baby talk, but he's trying.' Annie's face glowed with maternal pride. 'You gave me that gift, Catherine. You and your gentle hands.'

By afternoon, Catherine's cottage buzzed with quiet conversation and shared concern. The women took turns holding her hands through the worst pains, offering sips of water, adjusting the pillows behind her back. They shared stories of their own births, their losses, their hopes for their children.

'My first labour was thirty-six hours,' Kate confided during a brief lull. 'I thought I was going to die. My own mother wasn't speaking to me—disapproved of my husband, she did—so I had only Mrs O'Malley from down the lane. But she stayed with me through it all, just like we're staying with you.'

'What happened to your mother?' Catherine asked, curious despite her discomfort.

'Oh, she came around once she saw her grandson. Couldn't resist a baby, no matter how she felt about his father.' Kate's eyes crinkled with remembered fondness. 'That's the way with grandparents, you know. They forget their grievances when there's a little one to spoil.'

Catherine thought of her own father, of the money he'd provided through the bank, of his message that there would always be a place for her at home. Would he feel the same about an illegitimate grandchild?

As the sun began to sink towards the horizon, Catherine's pains intensified dramatically. Kate examined her again and nodded with satisfaction.

'Nearly there now, love. I can see the baby's head. With the next pain, you need to push with everything you've got.'

What followed was the hardest work Catherine had ever done. Harder than helping with difficult births, harder than nursing fever patients back to health, harder than leaving her family to start over in a strange place. With each contraction, Catherine gripped the rough wooden bedframe until her knuckles went white. The pain came in waves now, building and cresting before giving her brief moments to catch her breath. Sweat beaded on her forehead despite the cool river breeze through the window. She pressed her back against the wall, finding leverage as her body took over, pushing instinctively. Her breathing came in short gasps between the surges of pain that demanded everything she had.

'Here she comes!' Kate cried suddenly. 'One more push, Catherine!'

And then, in a rush of fluid and relief and overwhelming

sensation, her daughter slipped into Kate's waiting hands. The baby's cry filled the cottage—strong, healthy, indignant at being thrust from her warm, dark world.

'A girl,' Kate announced, tears streaming down her cheeks. 'A beautiful, perfect girl, dear Catherine.'

Catherine reached out with shaking hands as Kate placed the baby on her chest. The child was tiny but beautifully formed, with dark hair plastered to her small head and eyes that looked directly into Catherine's.

'Elizabeth,' Catherine whispered, the name coming to her as naturally as breathing. 'Her name is Elizabeth.'

'Elizabeth Morrison,' Maggie repeated softly. 'A good, strong name for a river baby.'

The women bustled around, cleaning Catherine and the baby, tidying the cottage, and preparing a meal for the new mother. But Catherine barely noticed their activity. She was entirely absorbed in studying her daughter's face, counting her tiny fingers and toes, marvelling at the perfect shell of her ears.

'She's going to be a beauty,' Mrs Patterson observed, peering at the baby with the expertise of a grandmother. 'Look at those long eyelashes.'

'And strong too,' Annie added. 'Listen to those lungs.'

As if responding to the praise, Elizabeth quieted and gazed up at her mother with unfocused but alert eyes. A fierce, protective love unlike anything Catherine had ever experienced filled her. 'I won't let anyone hurt you,' she murmured to her daughter. 'I'll make sure you have everything you need to grow strong and happy.'

'She's lucky to have you for a mother,' Kate said, settling beside Catherine's bed. 'You've got healing hands and a good heart. That's more important than a marriage certificate.'

Catherine looked around at the women who had surrounded her through her ordeal—Kate with her practical wisdom, Maggie with her gentle strength, Mrs Patterson with her grandmother's experience, and young Annie with her grateful friendship. None of them had asked about Elizabeth's father. None of them had suggested she should be ashamed or seek forgiveness for her choices.

'Thank you,' she said simply. 'All of you. I couldn't have done this alone.'

'You wouldn't have had to,' Kate replied firmly. 'That's what we do here—we take care of each other. Elizabeth is going to grow up surrounded by women who love her, who'll teach her to be strong and independent.'

As evening fell and the other women gradually departed to their own homes and families, Kate stayed to help Catherine through the first night. She showed her how to position Elizabeth for feeding, how to support the baby's head, and how to recognise the different cries that meant hunger, discomfort, or simple need for comfort.

'You're a natural,' she observed as Catherine successfully soothed Elizabeth's fussing. 'She knows you're her mama.'

Catherine gazed down at her sleeping daughter. Yes, she was Elizabeth's mother; she had chosen this child, fought for her, created a home and a life where she could thrive.

'I want to write to my family,' Catherine said suddenly. 'I want them to know about Elizabeth.'

Kate nodded approvingly. 'That's as it should be. Babies need all the love they can get, and from what you've told me, your parents sound like those who'd welcome a grandchild.'

'I hope so,' Catherine murmured, already composing the letter in her mind. She would tell them about Elizabeth's birth, about the community of women who had helped her, about the life she was building by the rivers. She would invite them to be part of this new chapter if they chose to be.

Outside, the Murray and Darling flowed together in the darkness towards the distant sea. Inside the cottage, Catherine held her daughter close and felt something she hadn't experienced since that afternoon with Daniel McKenzie: she felt complete.

She had created life, brought it safely into the world, and surrounded it with love. Whatever challenges lay ahead—and she knew there would be many—she would face them with the same strength that had seen her through today.

And Catherine knew, holding her sleeping daughter in the gentle lamplight, that they were going to be just fine.

# Chapter 19

*August*

The morning started like any other at the Wentworth Veterinary Clinic. Shea was preparing for a fully booked day when Ronald appeared in the doorway of the treatment room, his expression as cranky as usual.

'Shea, there's someone here to see you. Says he knows you from Melbourne.'

Shea's hands stilled on the equipment she was packing. Her first thought was David—somehow, he'd tracked her down, despite her careful precautions. Her heart began to race, and she had to force herself to breathe steadily.

'Did he give a name?' she managed, pleased that her voice sounded relatively calm.

'Heath McGregor. Says he's a doctor.' Ronald's expression softened slightly.

*Heath.* Shea's relief was so profound that she had to lean against the examination table for support. 'Heath's here?'

'You do know him then? He's in the waiting room.'

Shea made her way to the front of the clinic, her mind racing. What was Heath doing in Wentworth? And how had he found her? She pushed through the door to the waiting area and stopped short.

There he was, standing by the window overlooking the river, wearing neat chinos and a button-down shirt instead of his usual pub polo shirt and shorts. He looked different, and his face lit up with that familiar warm smile when he saw her.

'Shea.' He stepped towards her and then paused. 'I hope

you don't mind me turning up like this unannounced.'

'Heath, what on earth are you doing here?' She could hear the bewilderment in her own voice. 'How did you even find me?'

'It's a long story.' Heath glanced around the clinic, taking in the professional surroundings. 'Could we perhaps talk somewhere private? I have some explaining to do.'

'Come back at ten. I'll have my break then.' Shea still couldn't believe he was here.

An hour and a half later, they sat at a picnic table in the riverside park where Shea came for her morning reflection. The winter was crisp, and the confluence of the rivers moved beside them. Heath seemed to be gathering his thoughts, and Shea waited, studying his profile against the water.

'First, I should apologise,' he said finally. 'I haven't been completely honest with you.'

Shea felt a familiar chill of anxiety. 'What do you mean?'

'As well as being a GP, I've also done a lot of counselling. I didn't feel comfortable sharing that as I didn't want to frighten you away.'

'Frighten me?'

'Shea, when someone's recovering from trauma, the last thing they need is to feel like they're being professionally assessed. I wanted you to feel comfortable talking to me as just... Heath. As you did the first few nights we spoke, when you saw me as Heath, the barman. By the time you left Melbourne, I wanted you to know I was a GP too.'

'But how did you know I was recovering from trauma?'

Heath was quiet for a long moment; his gaze fixed on the flowing water. 'Because I recognised the signs. The way you held yourself, the careful distance you maintained, the way you flinched sometimes when people got too close. Eliza also told me about you. She gave you my card.'

'That was you? The doctor on the card?' Shea wasn't sure how she felt about that.

'Yes, but it was all coincidental. You meeting Eliza, then coming into the pub. If I were that way inclined, I'd say it was meant to be. But I'd rather call it a happy coincidence. Eliza is my older sister.'

Shea widened her eyes. This was getting a bit overwhelming. She was quiet for a moment, but she still knew deep down that she could trust Heath.

'A happy coincidence indeed,' she finally said.

'I knew you were holding back. I've seen it before, in patients. In myself.'

'In yourself?'

'I lost my wife four years ago,' Heath said quietly. 'Sarah. We were living on a remote station in the Northern Territory—I was the only doctor for three hundred kilometres. She was pregnant with our first child.' He paused, swallowing hard. 'There were complications during the birth. Things went wrong very quickly, and despite everything I tried... I lost them both.'

Shea's breath caught. 'Heath, I'm so sorry.'

'I blamed myself for a long time. I was supposed to be able to save people, especially the person I loved most in the world. After the funeral, I couldn't bear to stay in the Territory. I came back to Melbourne, threw myself into further study, tried to understand trauma and recovery because I needed to understand my own grief.'

The pieces were falling into place now—his understanding, his gentle way of listening in the pub.

'And that's how you recognised I was going through my

own issues?' Shea asked softly.

'Partly. But also, because I've made it my specialty since then—helping people who've experienced trauma. I'm now moving to rural areas, where patients don't have access to traditional mental health services.' Heath looked at her directly. 'When I met you at the pub, I also saw your strength, your determination to heal yourself.'

'So our friendship was... what? A professional interest?'

'No.' Heath's response was immediate and firm. 'Our friendship was real, Shea. Those conversations meant as much to me as they seemed to mean to you.'

Shea studied his face, but all she saw was the same honest warmth she'd come to associate with their Friday evenings.

'You still haven't explained how you found me here,' she said. 'Or what you're doing in Wentworth.'

Heath shifted uncomfortably on the bench. 'I'm here for a six-week rural placement. The Wentworth area has been without adequate medical coverage for months, and the health service asked me to do an assessment and provide temporary support.'

'That's another coincidence.'

'Yes,' Heath said. 'It is.'

Something in his tone made Shea look at him more sharply. 'Heath, is there something else you're not telling me?'

He was quiet for a long moment, clearly wrestling with something. 'I may have... influenced the placement decision slightly. When I learned you'd moved to a country town in this area, I suggested to my supervisor that Wentworth would be an ideal location for my rural medicine placement.'

'You followed me here?' Shea wasn't sure whether to be

flattered or alarmed.

'Not followed, exactly. More like... hoped our paths might cross again.' Heath looked genuinely uncomfortable now. 'I know how that sounds, and I know I should have been upfront about my qualifications from the beginning. But Shea, when you left Melbourne so suddenly, I realised I'd developed feelings for you that went beyond friendship.'

'Feelings?'

'I care about you. More than I expected to, more than I probably should have given the circumstances of how we met.' Heath's voice grew softer. 'I wanted to see you again, to be honest about who I am, to find out if what I felt might be mutual.'

Shea stood up abruptly, pacing to the water's edge. Her stomach lurched as the implications hit her—everything she'd believed about their meeting, about his motivations, suddenly called into question. Heath was a doctor—a qualified, experienced doctor who specialised in exactly the kind of work she'd been training for. He'd recognised her trauma from professional and personal, experience, and had been careful not to reveal his medical background because he understood how that knowledge might have undermined their developing friendship. That made her question whether his interest was clinical rather than personal, whether she was a case study rather than a woman worth knowing.

And now he'd said he'd arranged to come to Wentworth because he had feelings for her.

'This is an awful lot to process,' she said, without turning around.

'I know. And I'm sorry for not being completely honest from the start.' Heath followed her to the water's edge. 'But I want you to know—everything about our conversations, our connection, the way I feel about you—that's all the truth. The only thing I held back was my specialisation.'

Shea watched the two rivers flow, their currents merging into one mighty river. Like the recent changes in her life—two different streams of experience coming together to create something new.

'What exactly are your feelings for me, Heath?' she asked without turning around. She sensed him standing close to her, and it didn't make her uncomfortable.

'Honestly? I think I'm falling in love with you,' he said simply. 'I have been since our first proper conversation at the pub. You're intelligent, compassionate, stronger than you realise, and when you laugh... when you really laugh, it lights up everything around you.'

'I don't know if I'm ready for this,' Shea said honestly. 'I'm still learning how to trust my own judgement about people. How to believe in my own worth.'

'I understand. And I'm not asking for anything you're not ready to give.' Heath's voice was gentle but clear. 'I just wanted you to know the truth about who I am and to see if there might be a chance for us to explore whatever this is between us. Let these next few weeks of honesty see where our friendship leads. You might think I'm a total pain, spending more time in my company.'

Shea turned to face him, taking in his hopeful expression, the vulnerability in his posture. This was Heath—the man she'd grown to trust and care about over their Friday conversations. But it was also Dr McGregor, whose presence in Wentworth was no accident.

'Where are you staying?' she asked finally.

'The pub in town has rooms upstairs. I've booked in until I find a short-term rental.'

'And your work here?'

'I'll be covering the local medical practice, plus doing house calls to the isolated stations.' Heath paused. 'I'd also like to explore setting up some mental health support services for the region, if there's community interest.'

Despite her confusion and uncertainty, professional excitement rose in her. 'That would be incredible for this town. The nearest clinical psychologist is in Mildura.'

'Which is exactly why small towns need innovative approaches to trauma recovery and mental health support.' Heath's enthusiasm was evident. 'The work you're doing at the wellness centre—that's exactly the kind of approach that could make a real difference out here.'

They stood looking at each other across the space between them, both aware that this conversation had changed everything. Shea was grateful for his honesty and overwhelmed by his being here.

'I need some time to think about all this,' she said finally.

'Of course. I'll be around for six weeks, so there's no pressure.' Heath managed a small smile. 'But Shea? I'm glad you're here. I'm glad you found your place by the rivers. And I hope... I hope you might be a little bit glad to see me too.'

Looking at his familiar face, remembering their easy conversations and the way he'd listened without judgement during her most difficult months, Shea realised that despite the shock of his revelations, she was glad to see him.

'I am,' she admitted. 'Confused, overwhelmed, but... glad.'

Heath's smile broadened into something closer to his old

pub grin. 'That's a start.'

His presence changed everything—her quiet routine, her carefully planned new life. But perhaps change wasn't something to fear anymore.

# Chapter 20

Shea settled into bed with her book and a cup of chamomile tea, feeling more content than she had in months. Heath's arrival in Wentworth had changed her perspective—not just the growing attraction between them, but a sense that she wasn't facing her healing journey alone anymore. For the first time since leaving Melbourne, she felt genuinely hopeful about the future.

Even better, it had been ten days since David's last text message. Ten blissful days of silence from her phone, no threatening words appearing on her screen, no sudden jolts of anxiety when notifications chimed. Perhaps he'd finally given up, found someone else to focus his obsessive attention on, or simply grown bored with a game that wasn't yielding results.

The novel in her hands—a gentle historical romance she'd borrowed from the Wentworth library—felt like the perfect accompaniment to her peaceful mood. Outside her cottage windows, the Murray and Darling rivers murmured their eternal conversation, and a gentle breeze rustled the river red gums that sheltered her small sanctuary.

She was three chapters into the story when she heard it— a soft thud from somewhere outside, like something heavy being dropped or knocked over. Shea paused in her reading, listening carefully, but the sound didn't repeat. Probably just a possum investigating her rubbish bins, or a branch falling from one of the ancient trees that surrounded the cottage.

Twenty minutes later, another sound made her look up from her book. Footsteps, definitely footsteps, moving slowly around the side of the house. Her heart quickened, but she told herself it was probably Heath. He'd mentioned maybe stopping by this evening if he finished his clinic notes early, and he was considerate enough to approach quietly in case she'd already gone to sleep.

The thought of seeing him made her smile as she set her book aside and reached for her dressing gown. She'd barely tied the belt when a soft knock came at the back door—three gentle raps that somehow didn't sound at all like Heath's confident knock.

Shea hesitated at her bedroom door, suddenly uncertain. Why would Heath use the back door when he'd always come to the front? And something about the knock felt wrong, too tentative compared to Heath's normal confident taps.

She padded through the small cottage, bypassing the back door and moving instead towards the front windows where she could peer out without being seen. The moon was only a silver crescent, casting minimal light across the garden, but she could make out the shapes of the trees and the glint of the river beyond.

No sign of Heath's car in her driveway.

The front door handle rattled.

Shea's blood turned to ice water. Someone was trying to get in, testing the handle with slow, deliberate movements. The handle turned fully one way, then the other, accompanied by the soft scrape of metal against metal as whoever was outside explored the mechanism.

She backed away from the door, her breathing coming in short, sharp gasps. It wasn't Heath. Heath would call out, announce himself, and would never try to enter her home uninvited.

*David.*

The certainty hit her like a physical blow. Somehow, despite the week and a half of silence, despite her growing sense of safety, he'd found her. He was here, circling her cottage, looking for a way in.

Moving as quietly as possible, Shea checked that the front door was locked—it was—then crept towards the back door. Also locked, but as she approached, she heard the soft scraping sound of something being inserted into the lock. Was he trying to pick it? Did he have tools? Had he planned this? How long had he been watching her cottage to know when she'd be alone?

The scraping stopped abruptly, replaced by silence that was somehow worse than the sounds of attempted entry. Where was he now? What was he doing?

Shea pressed herself against the wall beside the back door, trying to control her panicked breathing. She needed to think, needed to make rational decisions, but terror was threatening to overwhelm her capacity for logic. Her phone— where was her phone? Still in the bedroom, charging on the nightstand. Should she risk moving to get it? Risk calling Heath or the police?

A shadow moved past the kitchen window.

Shea bit back a gasp, sliding further along the wall until she was completely out of sight of the window. He was still out there, still moving around her cottage, still looking for a way in. The invasion of her safe space felt almost as violating as if he'd actually entered—knowing that David was out there in her garden, breathing the same night air, studying her home with predatory intent.

The cottage had seemed so secure when she'd rented it, tucked away among the trees with the river as a natural barrier on one side. Now it felt isolated in the worst possible way, too far from neighbours for anyone to hear if she screamed, too remote for casual traffic that might deter an intruder.

Another sound from the back—the soft scrape of something being dragged across wooden decking. Shea realised with growing horror that he was testing the windows now, checking for unlocked latches, looking for any point of vulnerability. The systematic nature of his exploration terrified her more than random violence would have. This wasn't impulsive desperation; this was calculated stalking.

She forced herself to move, creeping back towards her bedroom while staying low and avoiding the windows. Her phone showed 10:47 p.m. when she grabbed it with shaking hands. Should she call Heath first or go straight to the police? Her thumb hovered over Heath's contact, but what could he do from his flat in town? By the time he arrived, David could be inside, could have—

A loud crash from the back deck made her decision for her. Shea dialled 000, her hands trembling so badly she almost dropped the phone.

'Emergency services, which service do you require?'

'Police,' she whispered, barely audible even to herself.

'Police, what's your emergency?'

'Someone's trying to break into my house. I'm alone, and he's been circling the cottage, trying the doors and windows.' The words tumbled out in a panicked rush.

'What's your address?'

Shea gave her River Road address.

'Are you in immediate danger? Is the person inside your home?'

'No, not inside, but he's still out there. I can hear him

moving around, testing the windows.'

'I have a unit dispatched to your location. Can you get to a secure room and lock the door?'

'I'm in my bedroom. I can lock it.'

'Do that now. Stay on the line with me until officers arrive.'

Shea turned the bedroom door lock with fumbling fingers, then grabbed her desk chair and wedged it under the door handle the way she'd seen in movies. The action felt both melodramatic and utterly necessary—if David managed to get into the cottage, she needed every possible barrier between them.

She killed the bedside lamp, plunging the room into darkness, then crouched beside her bed with the phone pressed to her ear. The emergency operator's voice was calm and professional, asking questions about the intruder's description, his behaviour, and whether she knew who it might be. Shea answered in whispers, terrified that David might hear her voice and realise exactly where she was hiding. 'How long until the police arrive?' she asked.

'Units are approximately fifteen minutes out. I know that seems like a long time, but officers are responding with lights and sirens.'

Fifteen minutes felt like fifteen hours when someone dangerous was prowling around your home. Shea strained to hear any sounds from outside, but the cottage had gone eerily quiet. Was David still there, or had he heard her on the phone and fled? Was he waiting somewhere in the darkness, watching for police cars?

The minutes crawled by with agonising slowness. Shea's legs had gone numb from crouching, her fingers cramped around the phone, and she was breathing so hard she was sure David could hear it from outside. Every small sound—the old house settling, wind in the trees, the distant murmur of the river—made her start in terror.

When the police sirens finally wailed in the distance, growing steadily closer, Shea almost sobbed with relief. Blue and red lights flashed through her bedroom curtains as vehicles pulled into her driveway, followed by the slam of car doors and the authoritative voices of responding officers. She quickly changed out of her pyjamas.

'Police are on scene,' the emergency operator told her. 'You can end the call now, but don't leave your room until an officer identifies himself and asks you to come out.'

The next twenty minutes passed in a blur of police activity—officers searching her property with powerful torches, checking for signs of forced entry, taking her statement while she sat wrapped in a blanket on her sofa. They found evidence: footprints in the soft earth around her cottage, scratches on her back door lock where something had been inserted, and most disturbingly, cigarette butts near the tree line where he'd apparently been watching her house for some time before approaching.

'We'll increase patrols in this area,' the senior constable assured her as the officers prepared to leave. 'And we'll follow up on the information you've given us about this David Mason character. You did the right thing calling us immediately.'

After they left, Shea sat alone in her brightly lit cottage, every lamp and overhead light blazing as if illumination could somehow prevent David's return. Eventually, she went back to her bedroom and wedged a chair under the door handle, knowing she had to try to sleep. The familiar space felt contaminated now, violated by his presence even though he'd never actually entered. How long had he been watching her? How much did he know about her routines, her vulnerabilities, her life in Wentworth?

Shea barely slept that night; dawn had never been more welcome. She woke with a start, sunlight streaming through her bedroom curtains, her body stiff from having finally fallen asleep in the armchair beside her window. For a moment, blessed confusion reigned—where was she? Why was she fully dressed? Why did her neck ache from sleeping at such an awkward angle?

Then memory crashed back like a cold wave.

Saturday morning. Her day off. She'd been looking forward to it all week, had even wondered if Heath might be free for a picnic by the river. The normalcy of those thoughts seemed impossible now, like fragments from someone else's life.

Had it really happened? In the bright morning sunlight, with magpies warbling in the garden and the peaceful sound of water lapping at the riverbank, the terror of the previous night felt almost dreamlike. Perhaps her imagination had run wild, perhaps those sounds had been possums or branches or—

Her gaze fell on the chair still wedged under her bedroom door handle.

The makeshift barricade she'd constructed in panicked desperation stood exactly where she'd placed it, solid evidence that the night's terror had been horrifyingly real. David had been here, had circled her cottage like a predator, had tried to get inside while she cowered in the darkness.

Shea pulled the chair away from the door and sank onto her bed, the full impact of her situation finally hitting her. David wasn't going to give up. The week and a half of silence hadn't meant he'd lost interest—it had meant he was planning, watching, escalating from distant threats to physical presence.

Her cottage no longer felt like a sanctuary. It felt like a trap.

# Chapter 21

Shea was nursing her second cup of coffee, still trying to process the events of the previous night, when her phone rang. The sudden sound made her jump, sloshing hot coffee onto her hand. She'd been on edge all morning, every unexpected noise sending adrenaline coursing through her system.

'Ms O'Byrne? This is Senior Constable Matthews from Wentworth Police. I was one of the officers who responded to your call last night.'

'Yes, hello.' Shea set down her mug with a trembling hand. 'Have you found something?'

'Actually, we have. That's why I'm calling. We've apprehended the person responsible for attempting to break into your property, and several others in the area.'

Shea's breath caught. 'Several others?'

'Yes, there were at least four other attempted break-ins in Wentworth last night, all with the same pattern—testing locks, trying windows, looking for easy entry points. You were the only one who called us, which is why we're particularly grateful for your vigilance.'

A wave of uncertainty washed over Shea. 'The only one? But I thought... I mean, it felt so personal, so targeted.'

'I understand why you'd feel that way, especially being alone and isolated out there. But this was an opportunistic crime, not personal targeting. You did absolutely the right thing calling when you did.'

Shea's voice came out smaller than she intended. 'Who was it? Was it...' She couldn't bring herself to say David's name, couldn't voice the fear that had consumed her all night.

'A seventeen-year-old from Balranald. Joshua Turner. He was released from juvenile detention three days ago and appears to have been looking for properties to burgle, probably to fund a drug habit. We picked him up this morning, trying to break into the pharmacy.'

The relief that flooded through Shea was so intense that it made her dizzy. Not David. Not the stalking ex-boyfriend who'd haunted her for months. Just a desperate young person, someone who had no idea who she was or why she might be afraid.

'Ms O'Byrne? Are you still there?'

'Yes, sorry. I'm just... relieved, I suppose. And sad for the boy.'

'That's understandable. Look, I want to reassure you that you didn't overreact. Many people would have ignored those sounds, told themselves it was nothing. Your quick thinking probably prevented several burglaries and possibly saved this young man from making even worse choices.'

Shea nodded, though he couldn't see her. The professional reassurance helped, but she still felt foolish for the terror that had consumed her. 'What happens to him now?'

'He'll be processed through the youth justice system. Given his age and circumstances, he'll likely get support for his addiction issues rather than just punishment. Sometimes getting caught early can be the wake-up call someone needs.'

After ending the call, Shea sat in her kitchen, processing her reaction to last night. The cottage began to feel like her haven again. She smiled as sunlight streamed through the windows, reflecting on the slow-moving river outside.

She thought about Joshua Turner, seventeen and desperate enough to prowl through strangers' gardens in the dark. What had driven him to that point? Her counselling training made her consider the underlying causes, and she felt more compassion than anger for the young man who'd terrified her last night.

Her phone buzzed with a text, and for a second, the old anxiety spiked. Then she saw Heath's name and smiled.

**Hope you slept well. Free for that lunch picnic today? The weather's perfect.**

Shea smiled again; she wasn't used to smiling so much. **I'd love that. Give me an hour to get ready?**

**Perfect. I'll bring lunch. See you soon.**

As she headed to the shower, she caught sight of herself in the hallway mirror. Shadows under her eyes from a sleepless night, but there was something else there too—a glimmer of happy anticipation.

A day of relaxation with Heath.

She turned on the shower, and as steam fogged the mirror in the tiny bathroom, and the hot water touched her skin, her tension eased further. Today was about sunshine and river breezes with Heath and his steady friendship beside her.

But Shea knew that more than friendship was developing on her side, too; she just wasn't ready to examine her feelings yet.

***

The morning sun cast dappled shadows through the river red gums as Shea spread the picnic blanket on the sandy bank. The Darling River moved lazily past them, its surface broken only by the occasional ripple from a fish or water bird. Heath had brought sandwiches from the bakery, and she'd picked two ripe apples from the tree in her back garden—a simple meal that felt perfect for the quiet intimacy of the spot.

'I love this stretch of the river,' Shea said, settling beside him on the blanket. 'It reminds me of home—of *Ceann Mara*. We have similar spots along our section of the Darling, places where the water moves slowly and the red gums lean over like they're trying to touch their reflections.'

Heath stretched out beside her, propping himself on one elbow. 'You miss it? The property?'

'Every day. But I needed to get away for a while, figure some things out.' She pulled her knees up, wrapping her arms around them. 'What about you? Do you have family somewhere missing you?'

'Our parents are still in Melbourne. Eliza is talking about them going into care, but I don't think they're ready yet.' Heath picked up a piece of bark and turned it over in his hands. 'Dad was a cardiologist, and I think he'd like to see me go back to that specialisation.'

'And what do you think?'

Heath was quiet for a moment, still turning the bark in his fingers. 'I used to think I knew exactly what I wanted from life. Had it all planned out.' His voice grew softer. 'But life doesn't always follow our plans, does it? Sometimes the things we think are permanent... aren't.'

'No,' she agreed quietly. 'Sometimes everything changes in an instant.'

They sat in comfortable silence, watching the river flow by. A kookaburra laughed somewhere in the distance, and the breeze stirred the leaves above them.

'Do you know what I've learned?' Heath said eventually. 'That maybe the best we can do is appreciate what we have while we have it. Not worry so much about what comes next. Live each day.'

Heath bit into one of the crisp apples she'd brought, and juice ran down his chin. Without thinking, Shea reached over with her napkin to wipe it away. As she did, his hand came up to gently trap hers against his face for a moment, his eyes meeting hers with unmistakable warmth.

'Thank you,' he said quietly, his thumb brushing across her knuckles before releasing her hand.

'I'm glad you ended up here,' she said softly.

'So am I.' Heath's fingers found hers again, intertwining gently. 'Even if I don't know where "here" leads.'

# Chapter 22

Monday started badly when Shea's phone buzzed at 5:47 a.m. with another message from David. She'd thought—or hoped—his texts had stopped, that he'd eventually get bored or distracted by someone else, but he'd started again. Her eyes widened as she read his message a second time.

**I know you're in Wentworth. Small town, isn't it? If you don't contact me by Friday, I'll have to come there myself. We need to finish our conversation.**

How could he possibly know where she was? She'd been so careful, had told no one in Broken Hill where she was going. But David had always been resourceful when he wanted something, and apparently, what he wanted was to continue the toxic conversation she'd fled from last year.

She deleted the message without responding, as she had with all the others, but the damage was done. The sense of safety she'd built in Wentworth felt suddenly fragile, like a soap bubble that could burst at any moment.

By the time she arrived at the clinic, Shea's nerves were already frayed. Ronald took one look at her face and frowned with concern.

'Are you all right, Shea? You don't look well.'

'I'm fine,' Shea lied, forcing a smile. 'Just tired. What's on the schedule today?'

The first appointment was with the Morrison family and their elderly golden retriever, Patch. Shea had been treating him for kidney disease for the past month, carefully managing his medication and diet, watching him gradually decline despite their best efforts. Today, his laboured breathing and clouded eyes told the story she'd been dreading.

'I think it's time,' she said gently to the family gathered around the examination table. Eight-year-old Emma Morrison was sobbing into her mother's shoulder while ten-year-old Jack stood stoically beside his father, trying not to cry.

'Can't you give him more medicine?' Emma pleaded. 'Please, he's my best friend.'

Shea knelt beside the little girl, her own throat tight with emotion. 'I know he is, sweetheart. And that's exactly why we need to help him now. He's very tired and very sick, and the kindest thing we can do is let him go peacefully.'

The euthanasia was gentle and quick, but watching the children say goodbye to their beloved companion left Shea emotionally drained. She held Emma while the little girl cried, remembering her own childhood losses, the inevitability of heartbreak that came with loving something mortal.

An hour later, she was cleaning up when the Hendersons arrived with their cat, Whiskers—a different Whiskers from the one she'd helped Mrs Patterson mourn in Melbourne, but the name hit her like a punch to the chest. This Whiskers had been hit by a car, with multiple fractures and internal bleeding that no amount of surgery could repair.

'We can't afford complicated treatment,' Mrs Henderson said through her tears. 'But we can't afford to lose him either. He's all we have.'

Shea spent forty minutes explaining options, discussing payment plans, and gently helping the elderly couple understand that some battles couldn't be won with money or determination. By the time Whiskers joined Patch in the sad procession of losses that defined veterinary practice, Shea felt like she was drowning in other people's grief.

The afternoon brought a different kind of challenge. Sixteen-year-old Jessica Cartwright arrived for what was officially a consultation about her rabbit, but within minutes, it became clear she needed counselling support more than veterinary advice.

'I think Binky might be pregnant,' Jessica said, her voice carefully neutral. 'I need to know what options there are.'

Shea examined the rabbit—definitely pregnant, probably about three weeks along—but her attention was focused on the teenager's careful phrasing, the way she wouldn't quite meet Shea's eyes.

'Binky will be fine,' Shea said gently. 'Rabbits are excellent mothers. But I get the feeling you might be asking about more than just your pet.'

Jessica's composure cracked. 'I think I might be pregnant too. I'm scared to take a test, scared to tell anyone. My parents would kill me.'

For the next hour, Shea found herself in familiar territory—holding space for a young woman facing an unplanned pregnancy, offering information without judgement, listening to fears that echoed her own last year. But Jessica's situation was different. She was sixteen, still at school, in a relationship with a boy who'd already started pulling away when she'd mentioned her period was late.

'I don't know what to do,' Jessica whispered. 'I can't have a baby now. I can't even look after myself properly.'

'You have options,' Shea said carefully. 'All of them are valid, all of them are your choice to make. Would you like me to give you some information about support services?'

By the time Jessica left with a handful of pamphlets and

contact numbers, Shea felt emotionally battered. Two family pets lost, a teenager facing the same impossible choices she'd navigated herself—it was too much, too reminiscent of her own losses and fears.

Her phone buzzed again as she locked up the clinic.

**Friday, Shea. I mean it. Don't make me come looking for you.**

This time, she didn't delete the message. Her temper flared, and the anger was powerful. She pushed the speed dial for *Ceann Mara*, and Tom picked up straightaway.

'Hi Dad, it's Shea.'

'Good to hear from you, love. Mum was going to call you later. Everyone's home for the weekend, and we were hoping you were free.'

She bit her lip. 'I'll see.'

'How's everything in Wentworth?'

'I'm fine, but busy. I haven't got much time. Can I just ask a quick question?' She was determined to find out how David had tracked her down.

'Sure, what's up?'

'Dad, has anyone called asking about me? Anyone from Broken Hill, maybe?'

The silence stretched long enough to confirm her suspicions.

'Well,' Tom said finally, 'Cat's still concerned about you. She might have... actually, you'd be better off talking to her.'

Shea's stomach tightened. 'What kind of concerned?'

'Just call your sister. I'm not sure.'

After hanging up, Shea immediately dialled Cat's mobile.

'Cat, it's me. Dad says you've been worried about something?'

'Oh.' Cat's voice went small. 'Sort of.'

'What do you mean sort of?'

'Well, I was talking to Janet at the surgery yesterday, just general chat, and she asked how you were getting on. I said you were doing well, working in a small town...'

'Did you mention Wentworth?' Shea's voice was sharp.

'No, I don't think so. At least... I don't think I did.'

'You don't think so?' Shea's temper flared. 'Cat, this is important. Did you, or didn't you?'

'I honestly don't know, Shea. We were just chatting, and you know how Janet is—she asks lots of questions. She might have asked which town, and I might have said... I'm sorry, I just can't remember our exact conversation. What's happened?'

'Nothing,' Shea snapped, then caught herself. But the damage was done—Cat's uncertainty had confirmed her worst fears. Janet, who'd already betrayed her confidence once by telling David about the miscarriage, might now know where she was living.

'Shea, please don't be angry. If I did say something, it was completely innocent. Janet was just being friendly—'

Shea ended the call without another word, her hands shaking as she set the phone down. She stared out at the peaceful river, but the serenity of the morning had been shattered. Janet's unprofessional gossip had already caused enough damage. If Cat had let slip Shea's location to Janet, she would have blabbed it around the surgery. And David would know.

She was still staring at her phone when Heath appeared beside her on the footpath.

'Hey,' he said gently. 'Rough day?'

Shea startled, quickly closing her phone and shoving it

into her pocket. 'Oh. Hi. Yes, a bit rough.'

Heath studied her face with the care she was growing accustomed to. Over the past three weeks, they'd fallen into an easy routine—shared lunches when their schedules aligned, evening walks along the river, quiet dinners at her cottage or the temporary flat he'd moved into above the chemist. Nothing had been explicitly romantic, but there was something other than friendship that was growing stronger each day.

'Want to talk about it?' he asked.

'Not really.' Shea started walking towards her cottage, needing movement, needing to get away from the clinic where the day's pain wouldn't leave her.

Heath fell into step beside her, not pushing but clearly unwilling to let her retreat entirely. 'Two losses today?'

'How did you know?'

'Ronald mentioned them when I stopped by to check on Mrs Cartwright's blood pressure medication. Also, you have that look.'

'What look?'

'The one you get when you're carrying too much of other people's pain.' Heath's voice was gentle but observant.

They'd reached her cottage now, and Shea stood at the gate, keys in hand but making no move to unlock it. The thought of being alone with her churning thoughts and David's messages felt unbearable, but the alternative—letting Heath see how close she was to falling apart—wasn't going to happen.

'I should probably have an early night,' she said, not looking at him.

'Should, or want to?'

The question caught her off guard. 'What's the difference?'

'Should is what you think you're supposed to do. Want is what might actually help.' Heath moved closer, his presence warm and steady beside her. 'What do you want, Shea?'

The honest answer—to crawl into his arms and let someone else be strong for a while—was too vulnerable to voice. Instead, she unlocked the gate and pushed it open.

'I want to not feel responsible for everyone else's pain,' she said finally.

'That's fair. Mind if I come in? I promise not to try to fix anything, just keep you company.'

Shea hesitated, then nodded. They settled on her small deck overlooking the river, Heath in the wicker chair while Shea curled up on the outdoor sofa, her knees drawn up like a barrier between them.

'Tell me about today,' Heath said quietly.

'Two euthanasias. It was hard for both, especially for the two young children whose family dog had to be put down.' Shea's voice was flat, clinical. 'Then a sixteen-year-old who thinks she might be pregnant and is terrified to find out.'

'That's a lot.'

'It's the job. Animals die, people face difficult choices. I'm supposed to help them through it.'

'You're supposed to provide professional support, not carry their emotional burden,' Heath corrected gently. 'There's a difference.'

'Is there? Because today it didn't feel like there was a difference. It felt like every loss was mine, every fear was mine.' Shea's voice cracked slightly. 'That girl, Jessica—she's the same age I was when I thought I knew what I wanted from life. She's facing choices I had to make, and I wanted to tell her to run. To not trust anyone who makes promises they can't keep.'

Heath was quiet for a moment, watching her carefully. 'Sounds like it brought up some personal stuff for you.'

'Everything brings up personal stuff lately.' Shea laughed bitterly. 'I thought I was healing, thought I was moving forward. But days like today make me realise how fragile it all is.'

'Bad days don't erase progress,' Heath said softly. 'They're just... bad days.'

'How do you know when you're actually better? When you're not just pretending to cope?'

'Maybe when bad days feel manageable instead of catastrophic. When you can sit with pain without drowning in it.' Heath leaned forward slightly. 'Are you drowning right now?'

Shea considered the question honestly. 'Close to it.'

'What's happened?'

The truthful answer was that she needed to tell someone about David's messages, about the fear that he might actually carry out his threats. But admitting that felt like admitting she was still a victim, still controlled by someone who had no right to any part of her life.

'Just a bad day at the surgery,' she said instead.

Heath was quiet for several minutes, seeming to sense that words weren't what she needed. The river murmured past them in the gathering dusk, and gradually Shea's breathing slowed, her shoulders relaxing.

'I rang home today,' she said suddenly. 'All my sisters are going to be home for the weekend. Mum and Dad want me to come home too.'

'That sounds nice.'

'It should be. But I don't want to go.' Shea's voice carried an edge of frustration. 'I'm angry about something Cat's done. Something that's put me back.'

Heath waited, sensing there was more, but when she didn't elaborate, he said gently, 'Do you want to talk about it?'

'Not really.' Shea pulled her knees closer to her chest. 'It's just... sometimes family think they're helping when they're actually making things worse. And then you're the ungrateful one for being upset about it.'

'So, you're not going home because you're angry with her?'

'I'm avoiding going home because I don't trust myself not to say something I'll regret.' Shea's jaw tightened. 'And because I'm tired of having to explain why I'm upset when the answer should be obvious.'

Heath nodded slowly. 'Family dynamics can be complicated, especially when everyone thinks they know what's best for you.'

'Exactly. Sometimes staying away feels safer than dealing with all of that.' Shea looked at him properly. 'When did you get so wise about family dynamics?'

'When I realised that shutting people out doesn't protect them from your pain. It just makes you carry it alone.' Heath's expression grew more serious. 'After Sarah died, I tried to handle everything myself. Convinced myself I was being strong, being independent. Nearly destroyed me.'

'What changed?'

'Eliza. She refused to let me disappear completely. Kept showing up, kept caring, even when I pushed her away.' Heath's smile was soft with memory. 'Sometimes the bravest thing you can do is let people love you through the difficult bits.'

Shea blinked away the tears that threatened. 'I'm not very good at being vulnerable.'

'Few people are. But Shea—' Heath's voice grew more intense, 'you don't have to carry everything alone. Whatever's happening, whatever you're dealing with, there are people who care about you.'

For a moment, Shea considered telling him everything. About David's messages, about her growing fear, about the way the past seemed determined to intrude on the peace she'd built. But the words stuck in her throat, trapped by the desperate need to prove she could handle her own problems.

'I should go home this weekend. I haven't seen all my sisters together since Christmas,' she said finally.

'You should. And maybe while you're there, let them take care of you a little bit.'

As Heath left an hour later, Shea walked him to the gate, reluctant to let the evening end. His presence had been exactly what she needed—steady, understanding, undemanding. For a moment, she considered asking him to stay, to not leave her alone with her churning thoughts and David's threatening messages.

'Thank you,' she said quietly. 'For sitting with me, for listening. It helped more than you know.'

'Any time,' Heath replied, his hand resting on the gate latch. 'You don't have to face the difficult days alone, Shea.'

She almost reached for him then, almost asked him to come back inside, to hold her until the fear receded. But something held her back—a memory of another night when she'd made a poor decision based on need and loneliness. The night with David that had changed everything, that had led to the pregnancy and heartbreak and all the pain that followed.

She'd been vulnerable then, too, had let someone close when her judgement was clouded by emotion.

'Goodnight, Heath,' she said instead, stepping back from the gate.

If he noticed her withdrawal, he didn't comment on it.

'Sleep well. And Shea—consider going home this weekend. Your family sounds like they love you very much.'

As his footsteps faded down the quiet street, Shea walked inside, reflecting on her strong attraction to Heath. She'd let her guard down, had given in to need and attraction, and look where that had got her.

She wouldn't make the same mistake again, no matter how different Heath seemed, no matter how much she wanted to believe he would never hurt her the way David had.

On Friday, she would pack for the drive to *Ceann Mara*.

But tonight, she would sit with her fear and her uncertainty, giving thought to Heath's words about letting people love you through the difficult bits.

He'd been through hard times, and she was going to take his advice. Cat was only trying to support her, and she would let her anger go.

# Chapter 23

*Friday*

The red dirt road stretched endlessly ahead, shimmering in the late morning heat as Shea's ute ate up the kilometres between Wentworth and home. She'd left early, wanting to arrive at *Ceann Mara* in time for lunch at the homestead, but also needing the six-hour drive to sort through the tangle of thoughts that had kept her awake most of the night.

David's latest message sat unanswered on her phone; his Friday deadline was now here. But it wasn't just his threats occupying her mind during the long stretches of highway—it was Heath, and her deepening feelings for him.

Three weeks. It had been exactly three weeks since he'd arrived in Wentworth, and she'd learned so much more about him. Three weeks of careful conversations, shared meals, and the gradual rebuilding of trust when she'd accepted his reason for not telling her everything when they'd met.

She thought about the other night, how desperately she'd wanted to ask him to stay, to not face her fears alone. The pull towards him was becoming harder to resist—not just physical attraction, though that was definitely present, but something deeper. The way he listened without trying to fix things. His understanding of grief and trauma from personal experience. The gentle persistence that respected the barriers she put up while making it clear he cared about her well-being.

But was it too soon? Three weeks of rediscovering each other, almost a year after she'd fled the disaster with David. Was she ready for something real, or was she simply projecting her need for comfort onto the first kind man who'd shown genuine interest?

The question had circled in her mind all morning: should she have asked Heath to come with her this weekend? Part of her had wanted to, had imagined introducing him to her family, watching him talk to her family with the same easy warmth that had drawn her to him in Melbourne. But she knew it was too soon, too complicated, too risky to merge her carefully separate worlds.

What would she even say? "This is Heath, the man I've been seeing for three weeks. I thought he was a barman when we became friends last year, and then he told me he's a doctor." The explanation alone would raise Dad's eyebrows.

A wedge-tailed eagle circled overhead as she passed through Menindee, and Shea thought about being at home. All five sisters would be home—Cat and Logan from their property next door, Róisín and Seth driving up from Bourke, Erin and Jack back from their latest photography expedition, and even Bridget taking a break from her university studies. She was looking forward to seeing everyone, but the thought of facing Cat's pregnancy again brought an ache to her chest. Cat was getting close to full term; Shea had been practising her responses, her expressions of excitement and joy, the questions she should ask about nursery preparations and baby names.

It wasn't that she wasn't happy for her—she genuinely was. But being around obvious pregnancies still felt like pressing on a bruise, a reminder of what she'd lost, what she might never have again.

Would it be easier if Heath was there with her? Someone who understood loss, who wouldn't expect her to display unqualified happiness? Or would his presence just add another layer of complexity to an already emotional situation?

She pulled over at a roadside stop near Broken Hill—too close to where her disaster with David had unfolded, but she needed fuel and coffee. As she waited for the tank to fill, Shea found herself scanning the small crowd of travellers, half-expecting to see David's familiar figure among them. The paranoia was probably irrational, but his knowledge of her location had shaken her more than she'd admitted to herself.

How had he found her? Wentworth wasn't exactly on any major travel routes; it wasn't the kind of place you'd stumble across by accident. Someone must have told him, or he'd hired someone to find her, or... the possibilities were endless and none of them were pleasant.

Maybe she should tell her family about David and his messages this weekend. The thought both relieved and terrified her. They'd want to help, would probably insist on involving the police or confronting David directly. Part of her craved that protection, that sense of not facing this alone. But another part recoiled from the idea of being seen as a victim again, of admitting that she still hadn't fully escaped the chaos David had brought to her life.

The coffee was terrible, but it gave her something to do with her hands as she considered her options. She could tell them about David, but not about the pregnancy and miscarriage—keep some secrets while sharing others. She could mention Heath casually, as a friend, without getting into the details of their developing relationship. She could focus on her work, her growing confidence in the counselling role, and the positive aspects of her new life in Wentworth.

Or she could be completely honest. Tell them about the

baby she'd lost, about David's ongoing harassment, about Heath and her conflicted feelings about getting involved with someone new.

Shea pulled back onto the highway with several hours still to go. The landscape was becoming more familiar now—the red of the soil, the way the river red gums clustered along watercourses, the vast openness that had shaped her childhood. This was her home country, the place that had formed her understanding of resilience and family loyalty and the kind of quiet strength that came from working the land.

Would Heath love this landscape the way she did? He'd said how much he'd loved his time in the remote outback of the Northern Territory. Would he see the beauty in the sparse vegetation, the endless sky, and the profound silence that always soothed her?

*Stop it. I'm not bringing him home this weekend, so it doesn't matter whether he'd understand the country or get along with the family. I'm not ready for that, and he probably isn't either.*

But the thought persisted as she turned onto the familiar dirt road that led to *Ceann Mara*. What would it be like to share this part of herself with Heath? To show him the river where she'd learned to swim, the paddocks where she'd helped with mustering, the homestead that had sheltered five generations of O'Byrnes? To watch him meet her father and see how they got on?

The mailbox was empty, and she continued along the road until the homestead came into view. Smoke rose from the chimney despite the warm day, probably from the Aga that Mum kept going year-round. The vegetable garden was green and flourishing, the pepper trees cast their familiar shadows across the front yard, and several cars were already parked near the house.

Everyone was here, and there would be enough chaos and conversation to distract her from David's messages and Heath's absence and the complicated emotions that came with being home.

As she pulled up beside Logan's ute, Shea took a deep breath and made her decision. This weekend would be about family, about reconnecting with the people who'd loved her longest and best. She wouldn't mention David's escalating threats—not yet. She wouldn't complicate things by talking about Heath or the growing feelings she wasn't sure how to navigate. She would simply be present, enjoy the rare opportunity to have all her sisters together, and try to push aside the anxiety about what Monday would bring.

The back door opened before she'd even turned off the engine, and Bridget came flying down the steps.

'Shea! You're here!' Her youngest sister looked more grown-up than she had at Christmas, her first year of university clearly agreeing with her. 'Mum's been cooking all morning, and Cat looks so pregnant, and it's so exciting, and Jack brought his new camera equipment to show us—'

Shea laughed, accepting Bridget's enthusiastic hug. 'Slow down, Bridge. I'm not going anywhere.'

But even as she spoke, part of her mind was already back in Wentworth, wondering what Heath was doing and whether he was thinking about her.

The weekend stretched ahead, full of family and conversation and the comfort of being home. It would be good, she told herself. Exactly what she needed. And if she found herself wishing for Heath's quiet presence beside her, well, that was probably just proof that what they had was becoming real enough to miss.

# Chapter 24

*Saturday - late August*

The billabong stretched before them like a mirror, reflecting the late afternoon sky in its still surface. River red gums leaned over the water's edge, their ancient branches creating dappled shadows that danced with each gentle breeze. Shea had always loved this place—the quiet heart of *Ceann Mara* where generations of O'Byrne children had learned to swim, where family picnics had been held, and where the sisters always met.

The five of them sat scattered around the grassy bank, Cat was stretched out on a rug, one hand resting on her huge bump, while Bridget skipped stones across the surface with the same enthusiasm she'd shown as a child. Róisín and Erin sat close together on a fallen log, shoes kicked off, toes dangling in the cool water. Erin kept glancing at her sisters with barely contained excitement.

'I can't keep it in any longer,' Erin burst out suddenly, her face glowing with happiness. 'Jack and I have news.'

'Let me guess,' Bridget grinned, abandoning her stone-skipping. 'You're pregnant!'

'How did you know?' Erin laughed, accepting hugs from her sisters.

'Because you've been practically vibrating with excitement all afternoon, and I recognised that look,' Cat said warmly. 'When are you due?'

'Six months after you. March.' Erin's smile was radiant. 'We wanted to wait until we were all together to tell everyone.'

Shea felt the familiar pang of loss mixed with genuine joy for her sister. 'That's wonderful news, Erin. Really wonderful.'

As the congratulations and excited chatter continued, Shea noticed Róisín's expression—a particular look she knew well after twenty-four years of sisterhood. There was something in her sister's eyes, a mix of anticipation and rare nervousness that made Shea look at her closely.

'Róisín?' Shea said, her tone half-joking but with genuine curiosity. 'You've got that look.'

Róisín took a deep breath. 'Seth and I are expecting too. Due in April.'

The squeals of excitement from Bridget could probably be heard back at the homestead. More hugs, more tears, more rapid-fire questions about morning sickness and due dates and nursery plans. Shea found herself swept up in the celebration, genuinely delighted for her sisters while trying to push down her own complicated emotions.

'Mum already knows about you two, doesn't she?' Cat said, gesturing at Erin and Róisín. 'I could tell by the way she was smiling this afternoon.'

'She made us promise to wait until we were all together,' Erin admitted. 'Said it was too important for sharing in phone calls.'

Bridget looked around at her sisters with wonder. 'Three babies! I'm going to be an auntie three times over!'

'Well, kiddo,' Shea said, trying to keep her voice light, 'the pressure will be off us for a while.'

Cat looked at her with curious eyes. 'You seem a lot happier than last visit, Shea.' They hadn't talked about the phone call earlier in the week, but Shea had hugged Cat extra close when she'd arrived.

'There's... a friend. Heath.' Her honesty surprised her, but she couldn't hold it back. 'He's doing a placement at the medical centre in Wentworth.' She pulled at the grass beside her, not meeting their gazes. 'He's nice. We've become quite close.'

'Just a friend?' Róisín asked with the knowing tone that came from years of sisterly interrogation.

'It's complicated. He's only there for another three weeks, then he goes back to Melbourne to finish his specialisation.' Shea finally looked up at her sisters. 'We actually met in Melbourne. We're taking it slowly. Seeing what develops.'

'What's he like?' Erin asked, leaning back on her hands on the soft grass.

'Intelligent. Kind. He's a doctor specialising in rural medicine, so he understands country life. We met at a pub where he worked part-time in Melbourne.' Shea found herself smiling as she talked about Heath. 'He has this way of listening that makes you feel heard, you know?'

'You're glowing when you talk about him,' Cat observed quietly.

'Am I?' Shea touched her cheek self-consciously. 'It's still early days. I'm not sure what will happen when his placement ends.'

'Long-distance relationships can work,' Bridget said earnestly. 'If you both want them to.'

'Maybe. We'll see.' Shea changed the subject before her sisters could probe deeper. 'Tell me about the nursery plans. Is it ready yet, Cat?'

The conversation flowed back to babies and preparations, and Shea let herself relax into the familiar comfort of family chatter. As the sun began to set, and the birdlife around the billabong quietened, a deep sense of peace filled her.

The water reflected the darkening sky like black glass, and the first stars appeared overhead. Insects hummed in the reeds, and somewhere in the distance, a single curlew called its haunting cry across the plains.

'We should head back,' Cat said eventually. 'Mum will have dinner ready soon.'

As they gathered the rugs and prepared to leave, Erin walked over to a small stone memorial near the water's edge. She knelt and touched the weathered stone gently, her fingers tracing the inscription: 'Gilbert O'Byrne, 1895-1918, Finally Home.'

'Hello, Great-Great-Uncle Gilbert,' she whispered. 'We found you, didn't we? Dad will be so pleased we're all here together.'

The others stood quietly, respecting the moment. Gilbert's story had become part of their family narrative—the young man who'd never returned from France, whose body had been lost for over a century before finally being identified and given a proper burial. His memorial here at the billabong felt right, connecting past and present in the place that meant most to their family.

As they walked back towards the homestead, Cat linked her arm through Shea's, letting the others move ahead.

'I'm happy you have Heath in your life,' Cat said quietly. 'Even if it's just friendship for now. You deserve someone who sees how special you are. I'm sorry I upset you.'

Shea squeezed her sister's arm. 'All good. And thank you. It's good to have someone to talk to, someone who understands...' She trailed off, not sure how to explain Heath's own experience with loss without revealing too much.

They were still fifty metres from the house when service kicked in. Shea's phone erupted with notification sounds—message after message arriving in rapid succession. Her stomach dropped as she pulled it from her pocket, already knowing who it would be from.

'Heath?' Cat asked with a knowing smile. 'He must miss you.'

'No, it's not him.' Shea's voice was tight with anxiety as she scrolled through the messages.

Cat saw the distress on her sister's face immediately. 'What's wrong?'

Without answering, Shea veered away from the path, pulling Cat with her towards the wooden bench that faced the river. Erin followed them, and Róisín and Bridget went back to the house, unaware of the sudden drama. The three sisters sat down, and Shea handed over her phone with shaking hands.

Cat read through the messages, her expression growing increasingly concerned. **Where are you? Your car isn't at your cottage. I know you're hiding from me. This is ridiculous, Shea. We need to talk. I'm coming to find you. Don't make this harder than it needs to be.**

'Tell me,' Cat said quietly, her protective instincts clearly activated.

'It's the guy I dated briefly in Broken Hill last year. When I broke it off, he... David wouldn't accept it. He kept saying we belonged together, that I was making a mistake.' Shea's voice was barely above a whisper. 'I moved to Melbourne to get away from him, but he's been texting me for months.'

'Are you scared of him?'

'He was strange, Cat. Intense. When I said I didn't want to see him again, he got angry. Said I was being dramatic, that I owed him more consideration.' Shea wrapped her arms around herself. 'He wouldn't leave me alone. At work, at my flat, always wanting to talk, to explain why I was wrong.'

'And that's why you moved to Melbourne.'

'Yes.'

'And why you moved to Wentworth?'

'Partly, yes. But also, to put my counselling knowledge into practice.' Shea's phone buzzed again, and she looked down to see the most frightening message yet: **I know you're at your family's place. Pretty isolated out there, isn't it?**

Shea's hand flew to her mouth, her face going white. Cat leaned over and read the text.

'You need to go to the police. He must be watching you, or tracking your car or something. And Janet must have told him,' Cat said firmly. 'This is stalking, Shea. This is threatening behaviour.'

'I've been so careful—'

'It doesn't matter how. What matters is that he's escalating.' Erin had faced her own dangerous situation the previous year. 'Look what happened to me when I didn't take threats seriously. I didn't see it coming with Miles. You never know when someone is truly dangerous. Mental health issues can make people unpredictable.'

Shea stared at the phone screen, fear and anger warring in her chest. 'He knows I'm here, Cat. He knows where our family lives.'

'All the more reason to involve the police.' Cat stood up, her protective instincts in full force. 'Does Heath know about

David?'

Shea shook her head. 'I haven't told him.'

'Shea, look at me.' Cat's voice was gentle but firm. 'You have to report this.'

'We need to tell Mum and Dad too,' Erin said. 'And you need to call the police. This can't wait until you get back to Wentworth.'

Shea shook her head. 'No, not yet.' The weekend she'd hoped would be about family celebration and healing had suddenly become about protection and fear. 'I'll call the police when I get home, and I don't want Mum and Dad involved.'

Her phone buzzed one more time: **See you soon, Shea.**

She put her phone in her pocket without sharing that message.

The message sent a shiver down her back, and for the first time, she truly understood that David wasn't going to leave her alone. He *was* escalating, becoming more dangerous, and she could no longer handle this by herself.

'Let's go inside,' she whispered. 'But I'm not telling them yet. I'll deal with it. Can I trust you both with that? Cat? Erin? Promise me.'

After her sisters reluctantly gave their word, they walked back to the homestead together. Shea thought about Heath, wishing desperately that she'd asked him to come with her. His steady presence, his understanding of trauma, his quiet strength, not to mention company on the drive home—she needed all of it now. The decision to keep their worlds separate suddenly felt like a mistake rather than wisdom.

But it was too late to change that now.

# Chapter 25

*Sunday*

The study at *Ceann Mara* had always been Dad's sanctuary, lined floor to ceiling with leather-bound books, station records, and now, boxes of genealogical research that had consumed him for the past three years. Afternoon sunlight streamed through the tall windows, illuminating dust motes that danced above stacks of photocopied documents, birth certificates, and shipping manifests spread across his mahogany desk.

Shea curled up in the old leather armchair beside the window, grateful for this quiet moment with Dad and Cat before she had to drive back to Wentworth. The rest of the family had left that morning—Róisín and Seth back to Bourke, Erin and Jack continuing their photography expedition, Bridget returning to university. Only Cat remained, having decided to stay here to help with the David situation and spend time on family research. Shea had planned the report she would make to the police, both in Wentworth and Broken Hill, and some of the tension had left her.

'I've made some real progress on Samuel's story,' Tom said, his eyes bright with the enthusiasm that always accompanied his historical discoveries. 'But Catherine remains a mystery. She simply vanishes from all official records after 1874.'

'Show Shea what we found last week,' Cat suggested, settling on the small sofa with a cup of tea balanced on her bump.

Shea looked away, and Tom picked up a manila folder

and extracted several photocopied pages. 'These are letters from the State Library archives—correspondence between Samuel and his wife, Breda, during the 1870s. Most of it is standard family news, but this one...' He handed Shea a carefully preserved photocopy. 'This one in 1880 mentions Catherine directly.'

Shea adjusted her reading glasses and studied the faded script:

*My Dearest Samuel,*

*I received your letter regarding the wool contracts in London with gratitude and relief. The Melbourne house seems so empty without you and the girls, but I understand the necessity of these extended river journeys for the business.*

*I must tell you that I received another letter from Catherine last week. As always, she writes with such warmth about her life by the rivers, and I am increasingly convinced that we were right to respect her choice to build something of her own, away from Melbourne society's expectations.*

*She mentions that the paddle steamer trade has been exceptionally busy this season, with Captain Morrison's vessel stopping at her town twice weekly. She speaks fondly of the various captains and their crews, and it seems she has become something of a fixture in their community. Her work as a healer continues to flourish—she attended three births this month alone, all successful thanks to her gentle skill.*

*What strikes me most in her letters is her contentment. She writes of evening walks by the confluence where two rivers meet, of her small garden flourishing beside the water, and of the sense of belonging she has found among people who ask no questions about her past. She named her daughter Elizabeth.*

*Samuel, she has built herself a life of purpose and dignity, and while I miss her terribly, I cannot help but admire her courage. I do want to meet our granddaughter. I miss Róisín so much.*

*She enclosed a pressed flower with her letter—some native bloom I don't recognise—and wrote that the river country is ablaze with wildflowers this spring. She says the land speaks to her in ways that Melbourne never did, that she understands now why the river trade called to you so strongly in your younger days.*

*I hope you will consider visiting her when next your business takes you to that region. I believe she would welcome the chance to show you the life she has made, the community that has embraced her so fully. Our daughter has found her place in the world, my love, and perhaps it is time we celebrated that rather than mourning what might have been. I look forward to your return,*

*Your devoted wife, Breda*

*Post scriptum: Catherine sends her love and asks me to tell you that she thinks of you whenever she hears the steam whistles echoing across the water.*

Shea looked up from the letter, her throat tight with emotion. 'She sounds happy. Truly happy.'

'Doesn't she?' Tom leaned back in his chair. 'The letter is dated 1880, so Catherine would have been thirty-three then.'

'But which river town?' Cat asked. 'There were dozens of settlements along the Murray-Darling system in the 1870s.'

'That's what I've been trying to work out.' Tom pulled out a large map, spreading it across the desk. Red pins marked various locations along the river network. 'The clues are limited—a confluence where two rivers meet, regular paddle steamer service, a place where someone could work as a healer without formal qualifications.'

Shea studied the map, her finger tracing the river systems. 'Where the two rivers meet... that has to be the Murray-Darling confluence, doesn't it? That's the only place that would be described that way.'

'That's exactly what I thought,' Tom said, his excitement building. 'Which means Catherine was living in Wentworth.'

The coincidence hit Shea like a physical blow. 'Wentworth? Really?'

'It fits perfectly,' Cat said, leaning forward despite her awkward position. 'The confluence, the paddle steamer trade, the size of the community where someone could establish themselves as a healer. And the timing works—Wentworth was just becoming established as a major river port in the 1870s.'

Shea stared at the map, overwhelmed by the implications. 'I've been living in Catherine's town. Working where she worked, walking where she walked.'

'More than that,' Tom added quietly. 'If our calculations are correct, you might be living very close to where she built her life. The river cottage you're renting—that whole area was developed during the 1870s and 1880s.'

The room fell silent as they all contemplated this revelation. Shea thought about her daily walks to the confluence, the sense of peace she'd found by the water, the way Wentworth had felt like home from the moment she'd arrived. Had she been drawn there by more than coincidence? Was there something in the family bloodline that called O'Byrne women to that particular stretch of river?

'Have you found any official records of her in Wentworth?' Shea asked.

'That's the problem,' Tom said, frustration creeping into his voice. 'Official records from that period are patchy at best. The town was still quite small, record-keeping was informal, and if Catherine was living under an assumed name or simply didn't register officially...'

'She might have had reasons to stay off official records,' Cat observed. 'A young unmarried woman in the 1870s, setting up independently—that would have raised questions.'

Shea thought about her own reasons for seeking anonymity, for choosing places where questions weren't asked and pasts could be left behind. 'Maybe that's exactly what she wanted. A place where she could reinvent herself.'

'The letter mentions her work as a healer and a child,' Tom continued. 'If she was attending births, treating illness, she would have been well known in the community, even if she wasn't officially documented. Her reputation would have spread through word of mouth.'

'Is there any way to find local records from that period? Church registers, newspaper accounts, anything that might mention her work?'

'I've been in contact with the Wentworth Historical Society,' Tom said. 'They have some archived newspapers from the 1870s, but they're not digitised yet. Someone would need to go through them manually.'

Shea felt a spark of excitement cut through her anxiety about David and the uncertain situation with Heath. 'I could do that. I'm right there, I have access to the historical society, and I understand the family history well enough to know what to look for.'

'Would you?' Tom's face lit up. 'That would be

incredible, love. To think that Catherine's story might be sitting in some dusty archive, waiting for the right person to find it.'

Cat reached over and squeezed Shea's hand. 'It's perfect, really. You following in Catherine's footsteps, literally and figuratively. Building a new life in the same place she did, using your healing skills to help people just like she did.'

The parallel hadn't escaped Shea's notice. Both of them had fled to Wentworth seeking a fresh start. Both had found ways to use their skills to help others. Both had discovered something by the rivers that they couldn't find anywhere else.

'There's something else,' Tom said, pulling out another document. 'This is a passenger manifest from 1876—the paddle steamer *River Queen*, Captain Morrison commanding. Look at this entry.'

Shea leaned closer to see where his finger pointed: *Miss Catherine O'B, Wentworth to Echuca.*

'Catherine O'B,' she whispered. 'She was still using the family initial. If it is her.'

'Just that once, as far as we can tell. But it proves she was in Wentworth in 1876, and maybe that she was confident enough in her position there to travel to Echuca under something close to her real name.'

'What was she doing in Echuca, I wonder?' Cat asked.

'Medical supplies, perhaps?' Tom suggested. 'If she was working as a healer, she might have needed items that weren't available in smaller river towns.'

Shea studied the manifest, imagining Catherine aboard the paddle steamer, watching the riverbanks slide past, perhaps thinking of the father she'd left behind in Melbourne. 'She must have been so brave. To start over completely, to build a reputation from nothing.'

'Like someone else I know,' Cat said pointedly.

The comparison made Shea uncomfortable, but she couldn't deny the similarities. Both had helped others. Perhaps Catherine, too, had discovered strength she didn't know she possessed.

'I'll start researching as soon as I get back to Wentworth,' Shea promised. 'If Catherine's story is there, I'll find it.' She needed to leave soon to make the drive home tonight.

Laura and Tom stood on the veranda as Cat walked with her to her car. Shea hugged her sister and then briefly rested her hands on Cat's growing belly. 'Take care of yourself,' Shea murmured. 'And call if you need anything.'

'I will. The same goes for you, too, remember? Drive safely and be aware. Make that report and tell Heath what's happening. Okay?'

Shea nodded.

***

After Shea's car disappeared down the drive, Cat made her way home to Logan, trying to deal with the worry about Shea's situation. She of all people, knew how bad things could get. The scars on her legs from the attack on her when she was at university reminded her of that every day. She had tried to persuade Shea that Heath needed to know—both for support and protection—and Cat and Erin had both promised not to interfere or share her knowledge with their parents. Cat still knew that she was responsible for David finding out where Shea lived.

The late afternoon sun cast long shadows across the paddocks as she walked up to their temporary cottage, noting the progress Logan had made on the landscaping around the house. Native grasses had been planted along the new pathways, and the concrete foundations for their new house were finally finished.

Logan appeared from the direction of the machinery shed, his grin wide. 'Good day?' He opened his arms, and she stepped into his embrace, clinging to him for a moment. 'Everything okay?'

Cat swallowed and took a step back. 'Fabulous, we discovered more about Catherine and—'

'Tell me all about it later. I found something in the small shed today—you know, the one full of old bits of machinery?'

'What is it?' Cat asked, but Logan was already leading her across the yard, his excitement infectious.

'I won't tell you. You have to see it.' He guided her to stand near the door. 'Wait here and close your eyes.'

Cat obeyed, hearing him disappear back towards the shed, then return with something that clanked softly as he walked.

'Open them now.'

She opened her eyes and gasped. Logan was holding a large metal sign, weathered but still readable: '*Wambool*' in elegant script lettering.

'Oh my God, is that the original sign from last century?' Her voice caught in her throat. 'Before it became *Dunleavy*? When Matilda and her family were here?'

Logan's smile widened. 'I knew you'd have the history in your head. And yes, it must be.'

'Oh, that is amazing. Wait until Dad sees it. What else is in there?'

'Whoa, slow down. That's the only thing I've found so far.'

'Can we?' Cat said slowly.

'Can we use that as the new name for our place? I don't

see why we can't.'

So now we know what we're going to call the property. Put it back to what it was.'

Cat blinked away sudden tears, reaching out to trace the letters with her fingertips. 'It must have been here when Matilda lived here. She would have seen this sign every day.' The metal was cool under her touch, solid proof of the lives that had been lived here before them. 'It feels so real suddenly. All those stories we've been researching—they happened right here.'

'I think I could do this one up, so we can use the original,' Logan said, his voice gentle. 'What do you think?'

Cat wiped her eyes with the back of her hand, smiling through her tears. 'I think Matilda would approve. And Gilbert.'

# Chapter 26

*September 1877 - Wentworth*

The morning sun filtered through the lace curtains of the small cottage as Catherine Morrison—for that was the name she'd taken—watched her three-year-old daughter Elizabeth chase butterflies in their garden. Her little girl's laughter rang across the quiet morning air, a sound that never failed to fill Catherine's heart with fierce joy and protective love.

'Mama, look!' Elizabeth called, her dark curls bouncing as she pointed to a cluster of native flowers blooming beside the river red gum. 'Pretty flowers!'

'Very pretty, darling,' Catherine replied, continuing to hang washing on the line. The domestic routine had become second nature over the past three years, but she never took it for granted. This life—this cottage, this garden, this precious child—represented everything she'd fought to build for them.

Mrs Catherine Morrison. The name still felt foreign on her tongue sometimes, but it had served its purpose well. After she'd settled in Wentworth with her swelling belly, she'd quietly let it be known that she was a young widow whose husband had died in an accident on the river. Poor Mrs Morrison, people said with sympathy, so young to be left alone with a child coming. The story had been accepted without question in a frontier town where tragedy was common and personal histories were rarely examined too closely.

The irony of her chosen surname wasn't lost on her. Captain Thomas Morrison of the paddle steamer *Murray Star* had been one of the first people to show her kindness in

Wentworth, had helped arrange the purchase of her cottage, had always treated her with gentle respect. When she'd needed a surname for her new identity, his had seemed like a fitting tribute to the man who'd helped her build this life.

Elizabeth ran towards her, arms outstretched, and Catherine scooped her up, smiling as she always did at her child's perfect health and spirited nature. Elizabeth had her father's dark hair but Catherine's green eyes. She was bright, curious, affectionate—everything Catherine had hoped for during those long months of pregnancy when the future had seemed so uncertain.

'Mama, can we go to the river today?' Elizabeth asked, settling on Catherine's hip.

'After I finish my work, sweetheart. Mrs Chen is coming this morning with her new baby, and then I need to prepare medicine for old Mr Fletcher's chest.'

Elizabeth nodded solemnly. At three, she already understood that Mama helped people when they were sick or hurt, and that this work was important. The cottage had a steady stream of visitors—women seeking advice about difficult pregnancies, families needing treatment for everything from broken bones to winter fevers, even the occasional emergency that required Catherine's quick thinking and gentle hands.

Her reputation as a healer had grown steadily over the years. Word had spread along the river network about the young widow in Wentworth who possessed an almost magical ability to ease suffering and bring life safely into the world. Paddle steamer captains brought patients to her from towns fifty miles away, and more than once she'd been summoned to isolated stations to attend difficult births or treat serious injuries.

The work gave her life meaning and purpose, but it also served another function: it made her too valuable to question. People in need of healing didn't ask uncomfortable questions about backgrounds or qualifications. They simply thanked God for Mrs Morrison's skill and paid her well for services that might otherwise be unavailable for hundreds of miles.

A familiar steam whistle echoed across the water, and Catherine instinctively tensed. Even after three years, the sound of approaching paddle steamers still sent a flutter of anxiety through her chest. She moved to the window, careful to stay behind the curtain as she watched the vessel approach the Wentworth wharf.

It wasn't one she recognised—*River Queen* according to the name painted on her wheelhouse. A newer vessel, probably carrying wool down from the northern stations. Still, Catherine waited until the steamer had tied up and she could assess the passengers before emerging fully from her cottage. The habit had become automatic: watch, evaluate, ensure that no familiar figures from her Melbourne past were aboard before showing herself in town. Especially her father. She missed him so much, but she was not going to jeopardise his standing.

The precaution was probably unnecessary. Captain Morrison's anecdotes suggested that her father was indeed too important these days to personally supervise river journeys. His wool empire had grown so large that he remained in Melbourne, directing operations from his Toorak mansion while trusted employees managed the day-to-day transport and trade.

But there was one journey he might still make personally: visits to his brother Thomas at *Ceann Mara*. Catherine remembered childhood trips to the family station, how Samuel had always insisted on accompanying the wool shipments to ensure their safe passage to Adelaide. If he ever decided to visit Uncle Thomas again, he might well travel on one of his own steamers, might pass right through Wentworth where she'd built her hidden life.

The risk felt manageable most days, but it was always there—a low-level anxiety that kept her watchful and ready to retreat if necessary.

'Miss Catherine?' A gentle voice called from her front gate.

Catherine looked out to see Mrs Chen approaching with her week-old son wrapped in soft blankets. Behind her walked Dr James Sterling, the new doctor who'd arrived in Wentworth the previous month. Catherine had been wary of his presence at first—a formally trained physician might question her methods or challenge her authority—but he'd proven to be a thoughtful, collaborative man who seemed genuinely interested in learning from her experience with her patients in the small town.

'Good morning,' Catherine called, settling Elizabeth on the ground and moving to open the gate. 'How is young Master Chen today?'

'Andrew is not feeding properly,' Mrs Chen replied, with worry evident in her voice. 'Dr Sterling thought perhaps you might have some suggestions.'

Catherine glanced at the doctor, noting his careful expression. He was perhaps her age, with kind brown eyes and prematurely grey temples that gave him an air of distinguished competence. In the month since his arrival, they'd worked together on several cases, and she'd found his approach refreshingly free of the arrogance she might have expected from a university-trained physician.

'Of course. Please, come inside.' Catherine led them into her sitting room, which doubled as her consultation space. Shelves lined the walls, filled with carefully labelled jars of herbs and tinctures, while a small examination table sat positioned to catch the best light from the windows.

As she examined the infant with gentle hands, Catherine was aware of Dr Sterling watching her technique with professional interest rather than criticism. He'd already learned not to question her methods when they proved effective, and she'd begun to appreciate having someone with formal medical training to consult on the more complex cases.

'He's healthy,' she pronounced after her examination. 'But Mrs Chen, you're anxious about feeding, and babies sense that anxiety. Here...' She prepared a mild herbal tea known to promote relaxation and milk production. 'Drink this twice daily, try to rest when you can, and remember that every baby learns at their own pace.'

As Mrs Chen departed, looking visibly relieved, Dr Sterling lingered.

'I've never seen anyone read the emotional dynamics of new mothers quite so accurately.'

'Experience,' Catherine replied, though she felt a flush of pleasure at his professional recognition. 'And perhaps an understanding of what it feels like to be frightened and alone with a new baby.'

The words slipped out before she could stop them, revealing more than she'd intended. Dr Sterling's expression grew more thoughtful, but he didn't press for details.

'Would you...' He paused, seeming to gather courage. 'Would you be willing to work with me more formally? I've been thinking about establishing a proper medical practice here, and I believe your skills would complement my training perfectly.'

Catherine felt her heart skip. The offer was tempting—official recognition of her abilities, steady income, the chance to help even more people. But it would also mean scrutiny, questions about her background and training that she wasn't prepared to answer.

'That's very kind of you, Dr Sterling. May I think about it?'

'Of course. And please, call me James. I hope we can be friends as well as colleagues.'

Catherine felt a familiar flutter of attraction mixed with wariness. James Sterling was exactly the sort of man she might have been interested in, in another life. Educated, compassionate, respectful—everything Daniel McKenzie had not been.

But Miss Catherine, supposed widow and mother, could not afford romantic entanglements with a man who might ask too many questions about her past.

After he left, Catherine sat in her garden watching Elizabeth play, deep in thought. She'd built something good here, something worthwhile. Her child was thriving, her work was valued, and their future seemed secure.

But sometimes, on quiet afternoons like this one, she wondered what it would be like to share her life with someone who truly knew her and who could share raising her child. Not the sad widow who helped sick people, but Catherine O'Byrne—the woman who'd made a difficult choice. Sometimes she let herself wonder if life would be easier in Toorak, but then she remembered the damage it would have done to her father and his business.

The steam whistle sounded again as the *River Queen* prepared to depart, and Catherine automatically glanced towards the wharf. Safe for another day, another week, until the next vessel arrived.

'Mama,' Elizabeth said, climbing onto her lap. 'Tell me the story about the brave lady by the river.'

Catherine smiled, settling her daughter more comfortably against her chest. The story had evolved over the years—a tale of a woman who'd found her way to the rivers and built a life of helping others. Elizabeth loved the story, never seeming to realise that she was hearing her mother's own carefully edited history.

'Once upon a time,' Catherine began, 'there was a lady who came to live by the confluence where two great rivers met. She was very sad at first, but the rivers whispered to her that she could be happy again if she was brave enough to try...'

As she spoke, Catherine gazed out over the water that she had come to love. Tomorrow would bring new patients, new challenges, and the need for an answer to Dr Sterling's offer. But tonight, she would simply hold her daughter close and be thankful for this moment of peace beside the rivers that had given them a home. She was always mindful of the contribution her father had made, and she gave her thanks for his love in her prayers each night.

Now, to give thought to Dr Sterling's offer. Catherine sighed as she stood, carrying a sleepy Elizabeth inside for her nap.

# Chapter 27

*Ceann Mar - early September*

Tom was staring at the computer screen, and he looked up when Cat looked around the door.

'I thought I'd find you in here,' she said. 'What are you looking at today?'

Her father turned back to the screen, and Cat put a hand to her back. It was aching, and she was tired; her sleep was being interrupted by the baby pressing against her ribs. Not to mention her constant worry about Shea. She hadn't been able to reach her, but Shea had sent a text message saying all was well. *Whatever that meant.* Cat didn't know.

Tom absently reached for his cup and pulled a face before he put it on the desk again. 'Yuck, that's cold. I've been looking through digitised newspaper records from the New South Wales State Library. Come and look at this.' Tom gestured to his computer screen. 'I think I might have found a lead about Catherine, but I need another pair of eyes.'

'Mum's making lunch—are you planning to eat with the living today? What have you found?'

'Yes, I'll just show you this. It's from the *Wentworth Telegraph*, March 1878.' Tom read from the screen: 'Mrs Morrison of River Street continues to provide invaluable service to our community in matters of health and healing. This week alone, she successfully delivered the Henderson twins and treated young Tommy Fletcher for a grievous fever that had baffled his family for days.'

Cat frowned thoughtfully. 'Mrs Morrison... that's not

Catherine's name, though.'

'No, but think about it. We know Catherine disappeared from all official records and social commentary after 1874. If she was starting a new life, especially if there was a reason for her to leave Toorak, she'd need a new identity.' Tom leaned back in his chair. 'The timing could work—this article is from 1878, four years after Catherine vanished. And Wentworth is in the right region based on Breda's letter about Catherine living by a river confluence.'

'It's a big jump, Dad. Morrison could be anyone. It's not an uncommon name.'

'That's exactly what I thought. But look at this.' Tom pulled up another window showing a hand-drawn map of 1870s Wentworth. 'River Street ran directly along the Murray, in exactly the area where Shea's cottage is located now. And I found two more brief references to Mrs Morrison in the local papers between 1878 and 1879—always described as a widow, always working as a healer.'

Cat studied the screen more carefully. 'It's interesting, but pretty circumstantial. We'd need evidence to be certain.'

'Exactly. Which is why I'm thinking about calling the historical society there, to see what local records they might have that aren't digitised yet. Church registers, burial records, maybe personal accounts from that period. Hea said they have a good collection.' Tom was already reaching for his phone. 'I found their contact details online. Worth a try to see if they know anything about this Mrs Morrison.'

The phone rang several times before a cheerful voice answered. 'Wentworth Historical Society, Maureen speaking.'

'Hello, Maureen, my name is Tom O'Byrne, and I'm researching my family history. I've come across some newspaper references to a woman known as Mrs Morrison who worked as a healer in Wentworth during the 1870s. I'm wondering if you might have any additional local records about her.'

'Oh, Mrs Morrison! Yes, she's mentioned in several of our archived documents. Quite a respected figure in the early community, from what we can tell. We have some newspaper clippings, and I believe there might be a few other references in church records or personal diaries from that period.'

Cat raised her eyebrows as she listened to her father's side of the conversation.

'That's very encouraging,' Tom said carefully. 'Would it be possible for me to visit and examine your archives? I'm particularly interested in any details about her background or family.'

'Of course! We're open Tuesday through Saturday, and I'd be happy to help you with your research. Though I should mention that our records from that period are somewhat patchy—it was a small frontier town, and record-keeping wasn't always systematic.'

'I understand completely. I'm just following up on leads at this point. When would be a good time to visit?'

'Any time next week would work well. We're not usually too busy, so I could spend some time helping you go through the archives.'

After ending the call, Tom and Cat sat quietly for a moment.

'So,' Cat said slowly, 'it's possible but far from certain.'

'Exactly. Could be a complete dead end, or it could be the break we've been looking for.' Tom rubbed his chin thoughtfully. 'I think it's worth a trip to investigate properly. At the very least, I'd learn more about the period and the region.'

'Mum would probably like to go too. She's been just as invested in this mystery as you are. And she'd love to see where Shea is living.'

'True, but I don't think she'd go that far from you with the baby due so soon.' Tom frowned, then looked at her. 'Me either. We might have to put it off, although to be honest, your mother's been worried about Shea. She says everything seems fine on the surface, but she has this feeling that there's still more going on than Shea's telling us.'

'I agree.' Cat nodded slowly as guilt tugged at her. 'Mum's intuition about us girls is usually pretty accurate.'

'She keeps saying she'd like to see Shea in her own environment, get a better sense of how she's really doing. This trip would give her a perfect excuse.'

After lunch and after running the idea past Laura, Tom called Shea.

The phone rang four times before Shea's voice answered, slightly breathless as if she'd been running.

'Dad! Is everything all right? Cat? It's not baby news, is it?'

'Everything's fine, love. Actually, I'm calling because I've made some discoveries about Catherine's story, and I think it's time for a research trip to Wentworth.'

'Really? What kind of discoveries?'

Tom could hear the interest in his daughter's voice as he described the newspaper clippings, the street map, and the evidence that Catherine had not only lived in Wentworth but had been a respected member of the community.

'Dad, this is incredible,' Shea said when he finished. 'I've been working my way through the historical society archives, but I haven't found anything this specific. When were you thinking of coming?'

'Maybe next week, if that suits you. Mum would come too.'

There was a pause before Shea responded. 'Next week might be... well, it's a bit soon for me. I've got some things I need to sort out first. Could we maybe look at the week after?'

Cat, who was listening on speakerphone, frowned at something in her sister's voice—a hesitation that hadn't been there moments earlier when she'd been enthusiastic about the research.

'Of course, love,' Tom said. 'Whatever works best for you.'

Laura leaned towards the phone. 'Actually, that's probably better anyway, Shea. Cat's getting close to her due date, and I'd rather not be too far from home right now.'

'Right, yes,' Shea said, though her relief was evident. 'That makes sense. The week after would be perfect, actually. I can arrange to take a few days off work, show you around the town, and introduce you to the historical society volunteers. Oh, and Dad, Mum—there's someone I'd like you to meet while you're here.'

Tom exchanged a meaningful glance with Laura. 'The doctor fellow?'

'Heath, yes. I think you'd like him.'

'Then we'll look forward to meeting him,' Tom said warmly. 'I'll make accommodation bookings and let you know the exact dates.'

After ending the call, Tom turned to Laura with a puzzled

expression. 'Did Shea sound strange to you? She went from excited to... I don't know, evasive.'

'I noticed that too,' Laura said thoughtfully. 'Something about next week not suiting her. I wonder what's going on that she doesn't want to tell us about.'

Cat sat there and didn't say a word.

# Chapter 28

*October 1877 - Wentworth*

Catherine woke to the sound of whimpering from Elizabeth's small bed across the room. In the grey pre-dawn light, she could see her three-year-old daughter tossing restlessly, her usually rosy cheeks flushed with fever. Catherine was beside her in an instant, pressing the back of her hand to Elizabeth's burning forehead.

'Mama,' Elizabeth whispered, her voice hoarse and frightened. 'I'm sick.'

'I know, darling. Mama's here.' Catherine's stomach clenched as she examined her daughter with as much clinical detachment as she could summon. High fever, laboured breathing, the particular flush that spoke of serious illness rather than simple childhood malaise.

Elizabeth had been perfectly healthy the evening before, laughing and playing in the garden, chattering about the ducklings she'd seen at the river's edge. Children could sicken quickly, Catherine knew, but the speed of this onset was alarming.

'My throat hurts,' Elizabeth whimpered, trying to swallow and wincing with the effort.

Catherine lit the oil lamp and examined Elizabeth's throat as gently as possible. What she saw made her blood run cold— angry red inflammation with white patches that could only mean one thing: diphtheria. The disease that had claimed more children in frontier towns than any other, the nightmare that haunted every parent in communities far from proper medical care.

For a moment, panic threatened to overwhelm her professional composure. This wasn't someone else's child, someone else's crisis to manage with calm efficiency. This was Elizabeth, her precious girl, the centre of her world, the reason she'd fought so hard to build this life by the rivers.

'I need to make you some medicine, sweetheart,' Catherine said, forcing her voice to remain steady. 'Can you be brave for Mama?'

Elizabeth nodded weakly, her trust absolute despite her discomfort. That unwavering faith in her mother's ability to fix anything strengthened Catherine's resolve. She was not just a frightened parent—she was a healer, someone who'd successfully treated dozens of cases of childhood illness. If anyone could save Elizabeth, she could.

Catherine lit the kitchen fire and set water to boil despite the tremor in her hands. Diphtheria was often fatal, especially in young children, but she'd seen cases where early intervention with the right treatments could turn the tide. Everything depended on acting quickly and decisively.

She prepared a steam tent first, adding eucalyptus oil to boiling water and positioning Elizabeth where she could breathe the medicated vapour. Her little girl submitted without complaint, though Catherine could see the effort it cost her to draw each breath.

'That's my brave girl,' Catherine murmured, smoothing damp curls from Elizabeth's forehead. 'This will help your throat feel better.'

While Elizabeth breathed the steam, Catherine prepared a throat wash of salt water and honey, along with a tincture of echinacea and goldenseal that might boost her natural defences.

Every remedy she'd learned, every technique she'd observed, every instinct honed through years of practice—all of it focused now on the single most important patient she would ever treat.

As the hours passed, Catherine maintained a careful vigil, monitoring Elizabeth's temperature, encouraging small sips of fluid, and adjusting treatments based on her response. She sent word to her usual patients that she would be unavailable for several days, unable to leave Elizabeth's side even for emergencies.

Dr Sterling appeared at her door that afternoon, having heard about Elizabeth's illness from Mrs Chen.

'Let me examine her,' he said quietly, his professional demeanour masking obvious concern for both patient and mother.

Catherine hesitated, her protective instincts warring with recognition that Elizabeth needed every possible advantage. She stepped aside, watching with hawk-like intensity as James conducted his examination with gentle thoroughness.

'You've diagnosed correctly,' he said when he finished. 'And your treatment approach is exactly what I would have recommended. How is she responding?'

'The fever broke briefly this morning, but it's rising again. She's managing to take fluids, but her breathing... It's laboured.' Catherine's voice caught. 'I've seen children die from this, James. I know the signs.'

'So have I,' he said honestly. 'But I've also seen children recover, especially when they have skilled care and someone who loves them absolutely.' He placed a gentle hand on Catherine's shoulder. 'She has both of those things.'

'What if it's not enough? What if I lose her?' The words

came out as barely a whisper, carrying all the terror she'd been holding at bay.

'Then you'll know you did everything humanly possible,' James said firmly. 'But don't prepare for defeat, Catherine. Elizabeth is strong, and she has the best healer in the region caring for her. Fight with everything you have.'

For three days and nights, Catherine barely left Elizabeth's bedside. She administered treatments regularly while her heart broke a little more each time Elizabeth struggled for breath. Her fever climbed higher, her breathing became more laboured, and there were moments when Catherine feared she was losing the battle that mattered more than any other fight of her life.

On the third night, as Catherine dozed fitfully in the chair beside Elizabeth's bed, she was woken by silence. The laboured breathing that had filled the cottage for days had stopped. Catherine's heart nearly stopped as she reached desperately for her daughter.

Elizabeth's skin was cool to the touch—not the burning heat of fever, but the blessed coolness of a temperature that had finally broken. Her breathing was deep and regular, the first peaceful sleep she'd had since falling ill.

Catherine sank to her knees beside the small bed, tears of relief streaming down her cheeks. The crisis had passed. Elizabeth would live, would recover, would continue to be the bright, spirited child who made every sacrifice worthwhile.

'Thank you,' Catherine whispered to whatever force had seen them through this trial. 'Thank you for giving her back to me.'

As Elizabeth's recovery progressed over the following days, Catherine found herself looking at her life very differently.

The absolute terror of perhaps losing her daughter had made everything very clear—her understanding of what truly mattered in their lives.

When James Sterling stopped by to check on Elizabeth's progress, he found mother and daughter sitting in the garden, Elizabeth weak but alert, Catherine reading aloud from a book of fairy tales.

'How are you feeling, little one?' James asked, kneeling beside Elizabeth's chair.

'Much better,' Elizabeth replied solemnly. 'Mama made me well again.'

'Your mama is very clever,' James agreed, his eyes meeting Catherine's over the child's head. 'She loves you very much.'

'I know,' Elizabeth said with the simple certainty of a loved child. 'Mama always takes care of me.'

That evening, after Elizabeth had fallen into another healing sleep, Catherine sat on her veranda watching the rivers flow together in the distance. She thought of the letter she'd written to Breda months earlier, describing her contentment in the small town. That happiness felt even more precious now, deepened by the knowledge that she'd nearly lost it, strengthened by the proof that she possessed whatever it took to protect it.

Elizabeth stirred in her sleep, murmuring, and Catherine smiled.

It was time for Elizabeth to meet her grandparents.

# Chapter 29

*Early September - Wentworth*

The early spring sun felt like a gift after a week of cold, grey weather since Shea had come home from *Ceann Mara*. Shea and Heath spread a blanket on the grassy bank near her cottage, close enough to the river that they could hear the gentle murmur of water flowing towards the confluence. The afternoon warmth encouraged them to shed their jackets, and they lay side by side, faces turned towards the pale blue sky.

'This might be my favourite spot in all of Wentworth,' Heath said, his eyes closed against the gentle sunlight. 'You can see why your Catherine chose to settle here.'

'Speaking of which, I have news.' Shea turned onto her side, propping her head on her hand. 'Dad rang yesterday. He and Mum want to come visit next week. Dad thinks he might have found another lead about Catherine—some references to a Mrs Morrison who worked as a healer here in the 1870s.'

'That's wonderful. When are they coming?'

'They're not. I put them off.' Shea's voice carried a note of reluctance. 'I told them next week didn't suit me.'

Heath opened his eyes and looked at her with concern. 'Why? You love your family.'

'I do. But there's something I need to tell you first, Heath. Something that's been happening that I should have told you about before now.' Shea sat up, drawing her knees to her chest. 'I've been getting text messages. From David.'

Heath sat up as well, his expression immediately serious. 'What kind of messages?'

Shea pulled out her phone with trembling fingers and showed him the screen. 'Threatening messages. They've been getting worse. Look.'

Heath read the messages, his jaw tightening with each one:

**You can't hide forever, Shea. We need to finish our conversation.**

**Wentworth's a small town. People talk. I know you're there.**

**You murdered my child and you think you can just run away?**

**I'm coming to find you soon. We belong together.**

'How long has this been going on? And what child?' Heath's voice was carefully controlled, but Shea could see the distress in his eyes.

'Months. Since I left Melbourne. He threatens, but he never follows through. His texts are getting more frequent, more... intense.' Shea's voice shook. 'I promised my sisters I'd call the police, but I've kept putting it off. I thought I could handle it myself.'

'Why didn't you tell me? We've been spending time together, growing closer, and you've been dealing with this alone?'

'I didn't want you to think I was weak, or bringing drama into your life.' Tears filled her eyes. 'I didn't tell you about the baby because I was so guilty. David and I... we only had one night together. I was horrified when I realised I was pregnant. I lost the baby early on, and I felt like it was my fault somehow. I thought I could handle the grief alone, but then someone at the veterinary surgery told him about the pregnancy, about the miscarriage. I thought I could cope with the situation, but it's gotten completely out of hand.'

Heath's expression softened with understanding. 'I'm glad you've told me, Shea. This isn't drama, this is harassment. This is serious, and something that you don't have to deal with alone.' Heath stood up, extending his hand to her. 'Come on. We're going to the police station right now.'

'Now?'

'Yes, now. These messages are threats, Shea. He's talking about coming to find you. You can't wait any longer.'

##

An hour later, they sat in the small Wentworth police station while Senior Constable Williams took Shea's statement and photographed the messages on her phone.

'How long since the last contact?' Constable Williams asked.

'Two days ago,' Shea replied, her voice steady now that she was finally taking action.

'And he's definitely located you here in Wentworth?'

'He mentions the town by name. He says people talk, that he knows I'm here.'

Constable Williams nodded grimly. 'I'm going to contact Broken Hill police—that's where he's based, correct? We'll have them visit him, make it clear this harassment needs to stop immediately, or charges will be laid.'

While the constable made the call, Heath sat beside Shea, his hand covering hers.

'I'm sorry I didn't tell you sooner,' she whispered.

'I'm sorry you felt you had to carry this alone,' he replied. 'But you're not alone anymore.'

The phone call to Broken Hill took twenty minutes. When

Constable Williams returned, she looked satisfied.

'They're going to see him today. Make it very clear that continued contact constitutes criminal harassment. We're also putting a note on our system here—if he shows up in Wentworth, call us immediately.'

As they walked back to Shea's cottage, the worry that had consumed her for months finally began to lift.

'Thank you,' she said quietly. 'For making me do the right thing.'

'Thank you for trusting me with it.' Heath stopped walking and turned to face her. 'Shea, I need you to know something. What you've been dealing with, what you've survived—it doesn't make you damaged or complicated. It makes you incredibly strong.'

They stood facing each other in the garden, the golden light of sunset surrounding them. Shea looked up into Heath's eyes, and her heart skipped as he looked at her—not with concern or friendship, but something much deeper.

'I care about you,' she said softly. 'More than I should, probably.'

'Why more than you should?'

'Because I'm still figuring out who I am without all this fear hanging over me. Because I don't want to drag you into my mess.'

Heath stepped closer, his hands gently framing her face. 'Shea, you're not a mess. You're one of the strongest, most compassionate people I've ever met. And I don't care how complicated things get—I want to be here with you, for all of it.'

The kiss they shared was gentle at first, tentative, then deepened as Shea leaned into Heath. When they separated, both were breathing unsteadily.

'Stay with me tonight?' she whispered. 'I don't want to be alone.'

'Are you sure?'

'I've never been more certain of anything.'

They cooked dinner together and then spent the evening talking quietly on her small sofa, sharing stories and gentle kisses. When they went to her bedroom, it was gentle and unhurried, both of them knowing how much this meant to each of them.

Shea watched Heath sleep in the early morning light, his face peaceful against the pillow. She smiled, realising she was no longer alone as the river murmured past her window, and she felt hopeful for the first time in months.

# **Chapter 30**

*Two weeks later*

Shea checked her appearance in the bathroom mirror for the third time that morning, smoothing down her hair and adjusting her blouse. Her parents' car would arrive any moment, and she felt the flutter of nerves caused by her eagerness to introduce Heath, and she hoped they liked him.

How could they not?

Her feelings for Heath were getting deeper every day, and she couldn't imagine not having him in her life.

The sound of tyres on gravel sent her hurrying to the front door. Tom's familiar Land Cruiser pulled up beside her cottage, dust settling around the wheels as he switched off the engine. Through the windscreen, she could see her mother already reaching for the door handle.

'Shea!' Laura was out of the car and up the path before Tom had even opened his door, enveloping her daughter in a fierce hug that smelled of home and lavender soap. 'Oh, love, you look so much better.'

'Thanks, Mum.' Shea returned the hug. 'How was the drive down?'

'Long but worth it,' Tom said, joining them with a travel bag in each hand. 'This place is even more beautiful than you described. I can see why Catherine would have chosen to settle here.'

Shea led them inside, watching her parents take in her small cottage on the river. Laura moved immediately to the French doors that opened onto the deck, her face lighting up at the view of the river beyond.

'The rivers,' she breathed. 'They're just as you said—so peaceful.'

'The confluence is about a five-minute walk downstream,' Shea said. 'I go there most mornings. It's where I do my thinking.'

Tom was already unpacking a folder of documents from his briefcase. 'I brought copies of everything I've found about the Morrison references. I'm hoping the historical society can help us determine whether there's a real connection to Catherine or just wishful thinking on my part.'

'Maureen at the historical society is lovely—she's expecting us this afternoon. But first... I'll put the kettle on.' Shea glanced at her watch. 'Heath should be here soon. He's very much looking forward to meeting you both.'

'And we're looking forward to meeting him. A rural placement, you said on the phone?'

'Yes. He's been in Wentworth for about six weeks now. The community here has really embraced him. He's kind and thoughtful, and very good at his work.'

'And you?' Tom asked gently. 'It sounds like you're impressed too.'

Before Shea could answer, a knock at the front door saved her from having to talk about her feelings for Heath.

'That'll be him now,' she said, moving to answer the door.

Heath stood on her doorstep wearing dark jeans and a crisp blue shirt, his hair still slightly damp from the shower. He was holding a small bunch of native wildflowers and looked nervous.

'For your mum,' he said quietly, handing her the flowers.

'Seemed like the right thing to do.'

'Perfect choice,' Shea smiled, standing on her tiptoes to kiss his cheek. 'Come and meet the parents.'

She led Heath into the kitchen, where Laura had already filled the kettle.

'Mum, Dad, this is Heath McGregor. Heath, my parents, Tom and Laura O'Byrne.'

Heath stepped forward with the easy warmth that had attracted Shea to him in Melbourne, extending his hand to Tom first. 'Mr O'Byrne, it's a pleasure to meet you. Shea's told me so much about your family.'

'Call me Tom, please. And this is Laura.' Tom's handshake was firm, his assessment obvious but not unfriendly. 'We've been looking forward to meeting you.'

'Mrs O'Byrne.' Heath offered the flowers with a slight smile. 'Shea mentioned you have beautiful gardens at home—I thought you might appreciate some local native varieties.'

Laura's face lit up as she accepted the bouquet. 'How thoughtful! And please, call me Laura. These are lovely—is this Sturt's desert pea?'

'Among others, yes. I asked at the nursery for flowers that represented the region well.'

'Bonus points for doing your homework,' Tom said with approval. 'Sit down, lad. Tell us about this rural medicine training.'

As Heath settled at the kitchen table, Shea busied herself making tea, listening to the conversation flow around her. She'd been nervous about this meeting, worried that they might overwhelm him, but Heath handled their questions with thoughtful honesty.

'So you're from Melbourne originally?' Laura asked, settling into the maternal interrogation mode that all five O'Byrne daughters knew well.

'Born and raised in Camberwell.'

'And what drew you to rural medicine?' Tom leaned forward with genuine interest. 'It's a challenging specialty.'

Heath's expression grew more serious. 'Personal experience, partly. I began specialising in cardiology, but when I did my first rural placement in the Northern Territory, I saw how different healthcare delivery is when you're hundreds of kilometres from the nearest specialist. People need doctors who can handle a wide range of conditions, who understand the community context. I realised where I wanted to be.'

'That must have been quite an adjustment from cardiology,' Laura observed.

'It was. And it taught me that medical training only gets you so far—you need to understand the people and the place to really be effective.' Heath glanced at Shea. 'Coming to Wentworth has reinforced that lesson. The community here has its own rhythms, its own needs.'

'And you're enjoying the placement?' Tom asked.

'Very much. The work is varied, the people are welcoming, and...' Heath's eyes found Shea's across the table, 'I've discovered some unexpected benefits to small-town life.'

Heat rose in Shea's cheeks, but she couldn't hide her smile. Mum, she noticed, was watching this exchange with a satisfied expression.

'What happens when your placement ends?' Laura asked the question Shea had been dreading.

'That's still being determined,' Heath replied carefully. 'There are several options on the table—further placements, potential permanent positions, continuing my research. A lot depends on what opportunities arise.'

Tom nodded approvingly. 'Sensible approach. No point making hasty decisions about career direction.'

'Speaking of careers,' Shea interjected, 'Heath's been very supportive of my counselling work. He understands the value of different approaches to healing.'

'That's wonderful, love,' Laura said warmly. 'You always did have a gift for helping others through difficult times.'

'She's exceptional at it,' Heath said simply. 'The combination of clinical knowledge and emotional intelligence—it's exactly what people need when they're facing loss or trauma.'

The conviction in his voice made Shea's chest tighten with emotion. Hearing Heath describe her work with such respect, and feeling her parents' pride—it felt like pieces of her life finally clicking into place.

'Right then,' Tom said, checking his watch. 'Let's have this cup of tea, and then head to the historical society. I'm eager to see what they've got in their archives.'

Shea went to the cupboard with another smile and produced a Tupperware container with a flourish. 'Look, Mum, I made a cake.'

Laura pretended to fan herself. 'Oh, my goodness, Heath. You are a good influence. For all Shea's talent, I could never interest her in baking.'

The look that Heath exchanged with her over her mother's head made Shea's heart beat a little faster.

# Chapter 31

*May 1879 - Wentworth*

Catherine stood at her kitchen window, watching five-year-old Elizabeth chase butterflies through the vegetable garden with the boundless energy that showed her health and happiness. The morning sun caught the copper highlights in Elizabeth's dark curls—so like her father's colouring, though thankfully nothing else seemed to have been inherited from Daniel McKenzie.

'Mama, look!' Elizabeth called, pointing to a cluster of orange and black butterflies hovering over the native grevilleas. 'They're having a tea party!'

'What lovely guests for our garden,' Catherine replied, smiling at her daughter's vivid imagination. At five, Elizabeth had developed into a bright, confident child who charmed everyone she met with her quick wit and natural curiosity. The early years of uncertainty and fear seemed like another lifetime now.

A gentle knock at the front door interrupted Catherine's morning observations. She opened it to find Mrs Chen standing on her doorstep, cradling her new baby with the careful exhaustion of a new mother.

'Mrs Morrison, I'm so sorry to bother you, but little Douglas won't settle. It's the same problem I bothered you with, with my Andrew when he was born, and I wondered if I could trouble you again?'

'Of course, come in.' Catherine led her into the sitting room that had long since been converted into her primary consultation space.

As Catherine examined the baby with gentle hands, she was aware of Elizabeth hovering in the doorway, watching the proceedings with the focused attention she always showed when Mama was helping people.

'Douglas is perfectly healthy,' Catherine pronounced, settling the infant back into his mother's arms. 'But I suspect he's picking up on your anxiety about feeding like your last baby did. Mothers often worry that they're not producing enough milk, and babies sense that tension.'

'Dr Sterling said something similar,' Mrs Chen admitted. 'But it's hard not to worry when he seems so fretful. I'm so tired with a two-year-old, and now the new baby.'

The mention of James Sterling sent a familiar flutter through Catherine's chest. Over the past year, their professional relationship had deepened into something that was becoming more personal, though neither had acknowledged it directly. He consulted her on difficult cases, she referred patients who needed formal medical intervention, and their professional interactions had led to a deepening friendship.

'Dr Sterling is very wise,' Catherine said carefully. 'Perhaps some chamomile tea might help calm your nerves, which in turn will help Douglas settle.'

As she prepared the herbal remedy as she had last time, Catherine heard the familiar sound of horse hooves on the road outside, followed by James's voice calling a greeting to Elizabeth in the garden. The child's delighted response—'Dr James! Come see the butterfly tea party!'—made Catherine smile despite the sudden nervousness that accompanied his unexpected visits.

James appeared in the doorway a few minutes later, his medical bag in hand and his hair slightly dishevelled from the morning ride. At thirty-two, he'd grown into his role as Wentworth's doctor with a combination of professional competence and genuine compassion that had won over even the most sceptical residents.

'Good morning, Catherine. Mrs Chen.' He nodded to both women with the careful courtesy that marked all his interactions with Catherine. 'I was making rounds and thought I'd check on young Douglas' progress.'

Mrs Chen looked relieved to see him. 'Mrs Morrison was just explaining about anxiety affecting feeding. It makes so much sense when you both say it.'

'Mrs Morrison has an excellent understanding of how emotional state affects physical wellbeing,' James said, his eyes meeting Catherine's briefly. 'It's one of the reasons our collaboration works so well.'

The word "collaboration" seemed to intimate more than a professional relationship, and Catherine felt heat rise in her cheeks.

After Mrs Chen departed with her baby and a small bottle of calming tea, James lingered in Catherine's sitting room, seemingly in no hurry to continue his rounds.

'You have a wonderful gift for reading people,' he said quietly. 'The way you understood immediately that her anxiety was affecting the baby—that's not something medical school teaches.'

'Experience teaches it,' Catherine replied, beginning to tidy her consultation area. 'When you've seen enough mothers struggle with the same issue, causes become clear.'

'As well as your own experience as a mother?'

The question was gently asked, but Catherine felt the familiar tension that came with any reference to her personal history. 'That too, perhaps.'

James was quiet for a moment, watching her carefully replace jars on their shelves. 'Catherine, may I ask you something personal?'

Her hands stilled on a bottle of lavender oil. 'You may ask.'

'Are you happy here? In this life you've built?'

The question caught her off guard with its directness and genuine concern. 'That's... an unexpected question.'

'I've watched you work. You're respected, valued, and clearly find fulfilment in helping others. But sometimes I notice you watching the paddle steamers arrive with such wariness, and I wonder if you're hiding from something rather than simply living a life you chose.'

Catherine set down the bottle carefully, considering how much truth she could safely share. 'I suppose I'm doing both. This life—my work, Elizabeth, this community—it's real and meaningful. But yes, there are aspects of my past that I prefer to keep private.'

'Because you're protecting Elizabeth?'

'Partly. And partly because some mistakes are better left unspoken.'

James stepped closer, his expression serious but not judgmental. 'Catherine, I want you to know that whatever brought you here, whatever circumstances led to you building this life, none of it changes how I see you. You're an exceptional woman, an extraordinary mother, and a healer whose skills rival any formally trained physician I've known.'

The honesty in his voice made Catherine's throat tighten with emotion. 'James...'

'I'm not asking you to share your secrets. I'm simply saying that if you ever want to stop watching the river for threats, if you ever want to trust that you're safe here, permanently—I'd like to be part of that future.'

Catherine's heart raced as she realised what he was offering—not just romantic interest, but acceptance, partnership, the kind of future she'd stopped allowing herself to imagine.

'I have Elizabeth to consider,' she said quietly.

'Elizabeth is delightful, and I'd be honoured to be part of her life if you'd allow it.'

Through the window, they could see Elizabeth playing with a family of ducklings that had wandered up from the river, her laughter carrying on the warm morning air.

'I care for you very much, James,' Catherine admitted. 'More than I expected to care for anyone again. But my situation is... complicated.'

'Most things worth having are.' James reached out tentatively, taking her hand in his gentle grip. 'I'm not asking for immediate answers, Catherine. I'm simply letting you know that when you're ready to trust again—completely, without reservations—I'll be waiting.'

Catherine looked down at their joined hands, knowing how right it was to have someone else's strength supporting her own. For six years, she'd managed alone, and the possibility of sharing her life with James was very tempting.

'May I think about it?' she asked.

'Of course. Take all the time you need.'

Elizabeth's voice called from the garden: 'Mama! Dr James! Come see what the ducklings are doing!'

James smiled, releasing Catherine's hand. 'Shall we go admire the ducklings? I find Elizabeth's nature observations are usually quite enlightening.'

For the first time since Daniel McKenzie had broken her trust, Catherine allowed herself to imagine a future with a man. A man she suspected she was falling in love with.

The ducklings waddled importantly around Elizabeth's feet while she provided detailed commentary on their behaviour. She looked up at the two adults, her green eyes bright with mischief. 'Dr James, are you going to marry Mama?'

Catherine felt her face burn with embarrassment as James knelt to Elizabeth's level with perfect seriousness.

'That would be up to your mama, Miss Elizabeth. But if she said yes, would you mind having me around more often?'

Elizabeth considered this gravely. 'Would you still let me help with sick animals?'

'I think that could be arranged.'

'Then I wouldn't mind,' Elizabeth announced, then turned her attention back to the ducklings as if the matter was settled.

Catherine met James's eyes over Elizabeth's head, seeing warmth, patience, and the quiet confidence of a man who seemed to share her feelings.

# Chapter 32

*Murray-Darling Historical Museum - Wentworth*

Maureen Carter led them through the archive room where boxes of documents lined metal shelving units, each carefully labelled with dates and categories spanning more than a century of the Murray-Darling early settlers' history.

'The Morrison materials are in this section,' she explained, pulling a modest cardboard box from a middle shelf. 'As I mentioned on the phone, they were donated in the 1960s when the Henderson family renovated the old cottage on River Road.'

Tom's hands trembled slightly as Maureen opened the box, revealing a collection of items wrapped in acid-free tissue paper. The first item she unwrapped was a small leather medical kit, its brass clasps tarnished with age but still functional.

'This appears to be a midwife's or healer's kit from the 1870s,' Maureen said, opening it carefully. Inside, nestled in faded velvet, were small glass vials, surgical instruments, and a leather-bound notebook with 'Mrs C. Morrison' embossed on the cover in faded gold lettering.

'C. Morrison,' Shea whispered. 'Catherine Morrison.'

'The notebook contains what appear to be medical notes and recipes for various remedies,' Maureen continued, gently opening the journal. 'But look at this—there's an inscription on the first page.'

She turned the book towards them, and Tom adjusted his reading glasses to read out the faded ink: 'For my darling daughter Elizabeth, may you always remember that healing comes from the heart as much as the hands. All my love, Catherine O'Byrne Morrison, Christmas 1884.'

The silence in the archive room was profound. Tom reached out with trembling fingers to touch the page, this tangible proof that their lost ancestor had not only survived but thrived.

'Catherine O'Byrne Morrison,' Shea breathed. 'She kept part of her real name.'

'And she signed it in 1884, which means she lived at least ten years after arriving in Wentworth,' Heath observed quietly.

Maureen nodded enthusiastically. 'We always wondered about the O'Byrne connection. And there's more.' She unwrapped another item—a small silver locket, tarnished but intact. 'This was with the medical kit.'

Inside the locket was a miniature photograph of a young woman who could only be Catherine, her eyes serious but kind, wearing the dark dress typical of the 1870s. Opposite the photograph was a lock of dark hair tied with a faded blue ribbon.

'Elizabeth's hair,' Tom said with certainty. 'A mother's keepsake.'

'There's something else that might interest you,' Maureen said, moving to another section of the archives. 'Elizabeth Sterling—Catherine's daughter—left her own papers to the historical society when she died in 1966.'

Tom carefully turned the pages of Elizabeth Sterling's personal journal, donated to the historical society in 1955. The faded brown ink told the story Catherine's gravestone couldn't—the final years of a woman who'd built purpose from loss.

'Listen to this,' he said to Laura, who was examining a

collection of pressed wildflowers found between the journal pages. 'Elizabeth writes, "Mother always said the rivers called to O'Byrne women, that we were drawn to water because it taught us how to flow around obstacles instead of breaking against them".'

Laura looked up from the flowers. 'She knew about the family name.'

'There's more.' Tom adjusted his reading glasses again. '"Dr Sterling and his wife adopted me formally when I was eleven, but they never let me forget where I came from. Mother's grave overlooks the confluence, and every Sunday we would visit together. Mrs Sterling would bring fresh flowers, and Dr Sterling would tell me stories about Mother's healing work, how she'd helped bring dozens of babies safely into the world".'

Maureen leaned forward with interest. 'We always wondered about the Sterling family's connection to that grave. They maintained it for decades.'

Tom turned more pages, his excitement building. 'Here—Elizabeth describes her mother's final illness. "Mother knew she was dying, but she wasn't afraid. She said she'd found her purpose by the rivers, that she'd turned her mistake into meaning. The night before she passed, she made me promise to carry forward the healing tradition, to help other women who faced impossible choices".'

'Did she?' Shea asked.

'Oh yes.' Maureen pulled out another folder. 'Elizabeth Sterling became the most respected midwife in the region. Delivered over three hundred babies and never lost a mother or child.'

# Chapter 33

*November 1884 - Wentworth*

Catherine O'Byrne Morrison lay in her narrow bed, listening to the familiar sounds of the river town that had become her sanctuary. Ten years had passed since she'd arrived in Wentworth, pregnant and desperate, and in that time, she'd built a life of purpose and meaning. But the persistent cough that had plagued her for months, the weight loss that no amount of her own remedies could reverse, told her clearly that her time was ending.

'Mama?' Elizabeth appeared in the doorway, her face pinched with worry. 'Dr Sterling is here to see you.'

'Send him in, darling. And perhaps you could make us some tea?'

Elizabeth nodded and disappeared, her footsteps echoing through the cottage that had been their haven for so many years. Catherine struggled to sit up straighter as James Sterling entered, his medical bag in hand and his face grave with professional concern and personal grief.

'Catherine.' He settled in the chair beside her bed, taking her hand in his gentle grip. 'How are you feeling today?'

'We both know the answer to that question,' Catherine replied with a weak smile. 'How much longer, James?'

'Days, perhaps a week.' His honesty was one of the things she'd always valued about him, even when it hurt. 'I'm sorry, Catherine. I wish...'

'Don't apologise for what can't be changed. You've been a good friend to me, to Elizabeth. More than I deserved, perhaps.'

James's grip on her hand tightened. 'You deserved so much more than you allowed yourself to accept.'

They sat quietly for a moment, both remembering the proposal he'd made five years earlier, Catherine's gentle refusal, his subsequent marriage to Flora Whitman, a kind young woman who'd come to Wentworth to teach at the new school. Catherine had never regretted her decision—James and Flora were well-suited, and Catherine's complicated past would have brought nothing but trouble to his life.

'James, I need to ask something of you,' Catherine said, her voice growing weaker with the effort of speaking. 'Elizabeth. When I'm gone, she'll have no one.'

'Flora and I have already discussed it. We'll adopt her formally, raise her as our own. You have my word, Catherine. She'll be loved and cared for as if she were our daughter by birth.'

Tears of relief slipped down Catherine's cheeks. 'Thank you. She's everything to me, James. Everything good that came from...'

'She's extraordinary because she's your daughter. Your love, your strength, your values—they're all part of who she is.'

Elizabeth returned with a tea tray, her movements careful and solemn. At ten, she was already showing signs of the woman she would become—intelligent, compassionate, with her mother's understanding of others' pain.

'Dr Sterling says he and Mrs Sterling will take care of me when you go to heaven,' Elizabeth said with the direct honesty of childhood.

Catherine felt her heart break. *How can I leave my beautiful girl?* 'Would you like that, darling?'

'I'd like to stay here, where your garden is. Where the rivers sing to us at night.' Elizabeth climbed carefully onto the bed, settling beside Catherine. 'Will you tell me the story about the brave lady by the river one more time?'

'Of course, sweetheart.' Catherine's voice was growing fainter, but she gathered her strength for this final gift. 'Once upon a time, there was a lady who came to live by the confluence where two great rivers met...'

As Catherine spoke, James watched this final telling of the story that had defined Elizabeth's childhood. It was Catherine's own story, edited and transformed into something a child could understand and find strength in.

'James,' Catherine whispered when Elizabeth had fallen asleep beside her. 'There's something else. My parents... they live in Melbourne. Samuel and Breda O'Byrne, in Toorak. They need to meet Elizabeth; I didn't ever take her there. They loved me, but I let them down. If she ever needs...''

'Catherine?' James leaned closer as her voice faded to barely a whisper.

'Tell her... tell her she comes from a long line of strong women. Tell her the O'Byrne women survive whatever life throws at them, and they find ways to help others survive, too.'

'I will. I promise.'

Catherine's eyes found his one last time. 'Thank you for believing I was worth saving, even when I couldn't believe it myself.'

Those were her last words. She passed peacefully in the early hours of dawn, with Elizabeth sleeping beside her and James keeping vigil in the chair, honouring his promise to ensure she wasn't alone.

# Chapter 34

*Murray-Darling Historical Museum - Wentworth*

Tom looked up from Elizabeth's journal, his eyes bright with unshed tears. 'She wrote about that night. About how her mother made her promise to carry forward the healing tradition.'

He continued reading from the journal. 'Mother told me about her real father—Samuel O'Byrne, who never knew I existed. She made me promise that if I ever had daughters, I would name one Catherine, so the name would continue. She said O'Byrne women were survivors, that we found ways to turn pain into strength.'

'She did name a daughter Catherine,' Maureen confirmed. 'Catherine O'Byrne Grant, born 1896. Who then named her first daughter Catherine O'Byrne Hinkle in 1922.'

Laura traced her finger along the pressed flowers. 'She kept the name alive through the generations.'

'There's something else,' Tom said, his voice growing quiet. 'Elizabeth writes about finding her mother's letters—the ones Catherine never sent to Samuel.'

He read aloud: '"Hidden in Mother's medical kit, I found three letters addressed to Samuel O'Byrne, Toorak, Melbourne. She'd written them over the years but never posted them. The first, written when I was three, told him about my birth and begged his forgiveness for not contacting him sooner. The second, when I was seven, described our life by the rivers and how she'd named me Elizabeth. The third, written just months before she died, told him she'd never regretted her choice to stay in Wentworth, that she'd found peace by the confluence where the rivers joined".'

Shea wiped her eyes. 'She wanted to reconnect with him but couldn't bring herself to do it.' She looked up at Heath through her tears when he put his arm around her.

'Elizabeth kept the letters,' Tom continued to read aloud. 'Listen. She says, I thought about posting them after Mother died, but Dr Sterling convinced me it would only cause pain. My grandfather, Samuel O'Byrne, was a public figure with a family and reputation to protect. Learning he had an illegitimate granddaughter might have destroyed more than it healed".'

'Wise advice,' Maureen murmured.

Tom turned to the final entries in Elizabeth's journal. '"Today we buried the letters with Mother, as she would have wanted. Her secrets died with her, but her strength lives on in me. I am Catherine O'Byrne's daughter, and I will make that name mean something in this place she chose as home".'

'She buried the letters with Catherine?' Tom asked.

'According to this, yes. Elizabeth felt it was the only way to honour both her mother's wishes and her adoptive family's kindness.'

Maureen stood and walked to a map on the wall. 'The Sterling family plot is in the newer section of the cemetery, but Elizabeth chose to be buried beside Catherine. There's one more thing,' Maureen said, pulling out a final document. 'This is Elizabeth's will, written in 1950. She left money to establish a maternal health fund for women in remote areas. She called it the Catherine Morrison Memorial Fund.'

Tom read the bequest aloud. '"In memory of my mother, Catherine Morrison, who showed me that healing comes from the heart as much as the hands. This fund shall assist women facing difficult pregnancies, ensuring no woman need face such challenges alone".'

'The fund still exists,' Maureen added. 'It's now part of the regional health service. Hundreds of women have received support over the decades, all thanks to Catherine's daughter honouring her mother's memory.'

Shea stood, her expression thoughtful. 'So, Catherine's story didn't end in tragedy. It ended in transformation—her pain became purpose, her exile became belonging, her shame became a foundation for helping others.'

'Exactly what the O'Byrne women seem to do,' Tom observed. 'Turn difficulties into strength, loss into service to others.'

'We've also found burial records,' Maureen said gently. 'Elizabeth Grant is buried in the old section of Wentworth Cemetery. Would you like to visit her grave?'

# Chapter 35

*Wentworth Cemetery*

The old section of the cemetery sat on a gentle hill overlooking the river confluence, shaded by ancient river red gums that had witnessed more than a century of farewells. Tom, Laura, Shea, and Heath walked slowly among the weathered headstones, some so old their inscriptions had been worn smooth by time and weather.

'Here,' Maureen called softly from beneath a large gum tree. 'This is Catherine's grave.'

The headstone was simple but well-maintained, the inscription still clearly legible:

*Catherine O'Byrne Morrison*

*1847 - 1884*

*Beloved Healer, Devoted Mother*

*She Found Her Way Home to the Rivers*

Beside it stood a smaller, newer headstone:
*Elizabeth Catherine O'Byrne-Grant*

*1874 - 1966*

*beloved adopted daughter of James and Flora Sterling*

*cherished mother and grandmother*

*Beloved wife of Henry Grant and mother of John, Robert,*

*Catherine, Florence and Edith.*

*'She carried forward the healing hands'*

Shea knelt beside the graves, her fingers tracing the inscriptions with reverence. 'She lived,' she whispered. 'Catherine lived, and Elizabeth grew up loved and safe.'

'And Elizabeth became a healer too,' Tom observed, reading the second headstone again. 'The tradition continued.'

Laura wiped tears from her eyes. 'Thirty-seven years old when she died. So young, but she'd built something beautiful. She'd saved Elizabeth, given her a good life.'

Heath stood quietly behind Shea, his hand resting gently on her shoulder as she grieved for an ancestor she'd never known but somehow understood completely.

'Look at the dates on Elizabeth's stone,' Maureen said softly. '1874 to 1966. She lived a full life—ninety-two years. She married, had children, and became the town's unofficial midwife just like her mother. The Grant family were pillars of this community for generations. Three daughters and two sons. The Grant family line continued until the 1980s, when the last descendant moved away. But Elizabeth herself lived until I was a young woman—I actually remember her. She was in her nineties, but still sharp as a tack. Used to tell stories about her mother, about the early days of Wentworth.'

Tom was studying both headstones carefully. 'The fact that they buried Elizabeth beside Catherine, even though she was adopted... that suggests the Sterling family honoured Catherine's memory and made sure Elizabeth knew her origins.'

'That's exactly what happened,' Maureen confirmed.

The revelation that Catherine's legacy had continued, that her story had been preserved and honoured by the family who'd adopted Elizabeth, felt like a gift beyond anything they'd hoped to find.

'We found her,' Shea said simply. 'We found Catherine, and she was exactly who we hoped she'd be. Strong, loving, someone who turned her pain into purpose.'

Tom moved away from the headstone, the emotion visible on his face. 'The pattern continues across generations. O'Byrne women find ways to heal—themselves and others.'

'So where does this leave your research?' Laura asked. 'You've solved Catherine's mystery, but there are still gaps in the family tree.'

'Actually, I've been thinking about that. We know Catherine had a younger sister—Róisín O'Byrne, born in 1864. She appears in Samuel's household records until 1882, then vanishes just like Catherine did.'

'Another missing sister?'

'Possibly. Samuel's records show Róisín as intelligent, strong-willed, interested in women's suffrage and social reform. She disappears from Melbourne society at eighteen.'

Maureen looked intrigued. 'Another young woman who may have faced scandal or made choices that conflicted with society's expectations?'

'It's possible. The pattern would fit—O'Byrne women throughout history facing impossible situations and finding ways to survive them with dignity.'

'So, your next research project is finding Róisín?' Maureen asked.

Tom nodded to Maureen. 'I'll have to see how much time our daughter has when she has their baby. She's as interested as I am.' He turned to Shea with a smile. 'But I suspect another of my daughters is getting more interested now that she lives in

Wentworth.'

As they prepared to leave the cemetery, Maureen walked them to the car. 'Catherine would be proud, I'm sure,' she said. 'It seems that she wanted to be someone who helped others. Through Elizabeth's work, the memorial fund, and now through your research bringing her story to light, she achieved exactly what she hoped for.'

Walking back to their car, Shea linked her arm through her father's. 'I'm glad we found her. Glad we know she was happy, that she made a good life for herself and Elizabeth.'

'Me too. And I'm grateful you led us here, even if you didn't know you were following in Catherine's footsteps.'

'The rivers called to both of them,' Laura observed. 'A century and a half apart, but the same pull towards healing and new beginnings.'

Tom nodded, looking towards the confluence visible in the distance. 'The O'Byrne legacy continues. Different times, different challenges, but the same strength passing from mother to daughter, generation after generation.'

As they drove away from the cemetery, Shea's phone buzzed with a text message. She read it quietly, then looked up at the others with a wide smile.

'That was Cat. She's been to see the obstetrician today and everything's good. The baby is healthy and strong.'

Laura reached back from the front seat to squeeze her daughter's hand. 'I'm so excited. Not long to go now, and I'll be a grandmother, and you'll be an aunty.'

Shea smiled and glanced across to Heath, who sat beside her in the back. This was the happiest she'd been for a long time.

# Chapter 36

*Wentworth*

That morning after Tom and Laura's early departure, Shea walked into her room to the sound of her phone buzzing insistently on the bedside table. She glanced across the empty bed, missing Heath's presence—he'd kissed her goodnight at the door but gone back to his own place, not wanting to complicate things with her parents visiting. She was still emotional from discovering Catherine's grave, and the solitary morning felt lonelier than it usually did.

She'd stayed up late with her parents and Heath, poring over Catherine's journals and discussing the remarkable discoveries they'd made at the historical society.

Her head felt thick with sleep and too much wine from their celebratory dinner.

The caller ID made her blood run cold: **David Mason**.

She let it ring out, but within seconds it started again. Shea's hands were shaking as she finally answered.

'What do you want, David?'

'Shea.' His voice was different—strained, almost breathless. 'Thank God. I've been trying to reach you for ages.'

'It's eight in the morning.'

'I know what time it is. I haven't slept. I've been driving all night, and I need to see you. We need to talk.'

The blood drained from Shea's face. 'You've been driving? Where are you?'

'I'm here. I'm in Wentworth. I'm sitting outside your cottage right now.'

Shea crept to her bedroom window and peered through the curtains. A dusty white sedan was parked across the street; David's familiar figure hunched over the steering wheel. Even from this distance, she could see the manic energy in his movements as he gestured while talking on the phone.

'David, I want you to leave. Right now.'

'I can't leave, Shea. Not until we sort this out. Not until you understand what you've done to me.' His voice cracked with emotion. 'Do you have any idea what the last year has been like? Living with what you did? What you took from me?'

'I didn't take anything from you. The miscarriage wasn't my choice—'

'Don't.' The word came out sharp, dangerous. 'Don't lie to me anymore. I know what really happened. I know you got rid of our baby because you were too selfish to see what we could have had together.'

Shea's chest tightened with familiar panic, but underneath it was a growing anger. 'That's not true, and you know it. I lost the baby, David. I grieved for that baby too—'

'You murdered our child!' The words exploded from him, loud enough that she could hear them both through the phone and drifting across the quiet street. 'You took the only good thing in my life and you threw it away like it meant nothing!'

Through the window, Shea watched him get out of the car, pacing back and forth on the footpath while he shouted into the phone. His clothes were wrinkled, his hair unkempt, and even from a distance she could see the wild, unfocused quality of his movements.

'David, listen to me. You're not well. You need help—'

'I need you!' He was walking towards her gate now, his free hand gesturing wildly. 'I need you to stop running away and face what you've done. We could have been a family, Shea. We could have been happy, but you destroyed it all!'

'I'm hanging up now, and I'm calling the police.'

'No, wait—Shea, please. I'm not here to hurt you. I just need you to understand. I need you to see what your choices have done to me.' His voice broke into something that sounded almost like sobbing. 'I can't sleep, I can't eat, I can't think about anything else. Every day I wake up and remember that our baby is dead because of what you did.'

Shea could see him at her front gate now, his shoulders shaking. The sight of his distress stirred unwelcome sympathy alongside her fear. This wasn't the cold, controlling man she remembered from Broken Hill. This was someone who seemed genuinely broken, lost in a delusion that had consumed him.

'David, I'm going to hang up now. I want you to get back in your car and drive to the Wentworth Hospital. Tell them you need help. Tell them you're having thoughts that aren't based in reality.'

'Reality?' His laugh was harsh, bitter. 'Reality is that I loved you more than you deserved, and you repaid that love by killing our child. Reality is that I've spent a year trying to understand how someone could be so heartless, so cruel—'

The line went dead as Shea ended the call, her hands trembling as she immediately dialled Heath's number.

'Shea?' Heath's voice was instantly alert despite the early hour. 'What's wrong?'

'David's here. He's outside my house, and he's... Heath, I think he's having some kind of breakdown. He's talking about things that aren't true, and he seems completely convinced they're real.'

'I'm on my way. Lock your doors and don't go outside. If he tries to get in before I get there, call the police.'

Through the window, Shea watched David pace her front yard, occasionally looking up at the house with an expression of desperate pleading. He'd started talking to himself, gesturing as if having an animated conversation with someone invisible.

When Heath's car pulled up ten minutes later, David spun around with wild hope in his eyes, as if expecting Shea to emerge. Instead, Heath got out, moving with deliberate calm as he approached.

'David?' Heath's voice carried across the quiet street. 'I'm Dr McGregor. Shea asked me to come and check on you.'

David's expression changed rapidly from hope to confusion to rage. 'You're the one, aren't you? The one she's been seeing. The replacement for what she destroyed.'

'I'm a doctor, David. I can see that you're in distress. When did you last sleep? Or eat?'

'I don't need food. I don't need sleep. I need Shea to tell me the truth.' David's voice was rising again, his movements becoming more agitated. 'I need her to admit what she did to our baby.'

Heath moved closer, his hands visible and non-threatening. 'David, I'm going to tell you something important. Shea had a miscarriage. That means the pregnancy ended naturally, through no action of hers. She grieved deeply for that loss.'

'That's a lie!' David's voice cracked. 'She killed our baby because she didn't want to be tied to me. She was ashamed of me; she thought she was too good for someone like me.'

'I can hear how much pain you're in,' Heath said gently. 'Loss like this can make us think things that feel very real but aren't based in fact. When did you last speak to a counsellor or a doctor about these thoughts?'

From her window, Shea watched the exchange with her heart in her throat. Heath was handling it exactly right—calm, professional, non-confrontational—but she could see the dangerous edge in David's posture, the way his hands clenched and unclenched at his sides.

'I don't need a doctor. I need Shea to stop hiding and face me!' David shouted towards the house. 'I know you're in there, Shea! I know you can hear me! Come out and tell me the truth!'

Heath stepped slightly between David and the house. 'David, I need you to listen to me. You've driven through the night, you're exhausted, and your thinking isn't clear right now. Let me help you. Let me drive you to somewhere safe where you can rest and get the support you need.'

'Support?' David laughed bitterly. 'What support did our baby get when Shea decided it was inconvenient? What support did I get when she just disappeared, leaving me to deal with the grief alone?'

'David, you're experiencing something called delusional thinking. It feels completely real to you, but it's a symptom of mental distress, not reality. Shea didn't choose to end her pregnancy. She lost a baby she wanted, and she's been grieving that loss.'

The word "delusional" seemed to trigger something in David. His face contorted with rage, and he took a step towards Heath. 'Don't you dare try to tell me I'm crazy! I know what happened! I lived it!'

Heath held his ground but raised his hands peacefully. 'I'm not saying you're crazy. I'm saying you're in pain, and that pain is making you see things differently than they actually happened. This is treatable, David. You can feel better than this.'

'The only thing that will make me feel better is Shea admitting what she did!' David's voice rose to a shout. 'Shea! Come out here! Face what you've done!'

Inside the house, Shea made a decision. Watching David's escalating distress, seeing the genuine anguish beneath his delusions, she couldn't hide any longer. Whatever risk this posed to her safety, David was clearly in crisis and needed help.

She opened her front door and stepped onto the veranda, staying well back from the gate. 'I'm here, David.'

David's entire body sagged with relief at the sight of her. 'Shea. Oh, thank God. I knew you were there. I knew you wouldn't abandon me completely.'

'David, I need you to listen to me very carefully,' Shea said, her voice steady despite her racing heart. 'I didn't have an abortion. I lost the baby naturally, and it broke my heart. I grieved for weeks, and I'm still grieving.'

'No.' David shook his head violently. 'No, that's not what happened. You were relieved when you lost it. You said it was for the best.'

'I said losing the baby was probably for the best because we weren't ready to be parents together. Because we didn't have a relationship. But I never, ever chose to end that pregnancy.'

'You're lying.' But some of the certainty had gone out of his voice, replaced by a confused desperation. 'You have to be lying. Because if you're not lying, then I've been...' He trailed off, his face crumpling.

Heath moved closer, his voice gentle. 'David, grief can sometimes make us construct explanations for loss that feel less painful than accepting that bad things sometimes just happen.

It's easier to blame someone than to accept that life is sometimes random and cruel.'

David sank onto the kerb, his head in his hands. 'But I've been so angry. For so long. And if she didn't... if it wasn't her fault...'

'The anger was real,' Heath said, crouching beside him. 'The grief was real. The loss was real. But the explanation your mind created to cope with that loss wasn't accurate.'

'I'm so tired,' David whispered. 'I'm so, so tired.'

'I know you are. And I'm going to help you. We're going to get you somewhere safe where you can rest and start to heal.'

Shea watched from her veranda as Heath gently convinced David to let him drive him to the hospital. David didn't resist, seeming almost relieved to finally surrender the burden of his delusion. As Heath helped him to the car, David looked back at Shea with eyes that were suddenly clear and full of shame.

'I'm sorry,' he said quietly. 'I'm so sorry, Shea. I think... I think I've been very sick.'

'I know you have been,' Shea replied, her own eyes filling with tears. 'And I'm sorry too, David. I'm sorry you've been carrying this pain alone.'

As Heath's car disappeared down the street, Shea sank onto her front steps, emotionally drained. The confrontation she'd feared for months was over, but not in any way she could have anticipated. David hadn't been the predatory stalker of her nightmares, but a man whose grief had twisted into something unrecognisable, whose mental health had deteriorated to the point where fantasy and reality had become indistinguishable.

Her phone buzzed with a text from Heath: **Getting him**

**admitted for psychiatric evaluation. He's not dangerous, just very unwell. I'll call you later.**

Shea put her hands over her face and cried again—for their lost baby, and for what that one night had done to David's already fragile mental state.

She wasn't sure how long she sat there, but she heard footsteps on the path and looked up to see Heath walking towards her. He'd returned on foot, having left his car at the hospital.

'How is he?' she asked, wiping her eyes.

'Settled. The psychiatric team thinks he'll respond well to treatment once they get his medication balanced.' Heath sat down beside her on the step. 'How are you?'

'I don't know. Relieved, I think. And sad.' She leaned against his shoulder. 'I keep thinking about how different things might have been if he'd gotten help months ago.'

'You can't carry that,' Heath said gently, his arm coming around her. 'His illness isn't your responsibility.'

They sat quietly in the fading afternoon light. The tension she'd carried for so long finally left her body. The crisis was over. David would get the help he needed, and she could move forward without fear.

'Thank you,' she said quietly. 'For everything today. For handling it so calmly, for making sure he got proper care.'

Heath pressed a kiss to the top of her head. 'You don't need to thank me for caring about you.'

The simple words, spoken with love, filled her heart. Shea turned to look at him, seeing her own feelings reflected in his eyes.

'I love you,' she said softly, the words coming naturally now that the fear was gone.

'I love you too,' he replied, cupping her face gently. 'We're going to be all right, Shea. All of us.'

As they sat looking at the river, Shea believed him completely.

# Chapter 37

Shea's phone rang late afternoon. Laura's name appeared on the screen.

'Hi, Mum.'

'Darling, are you all right? We're home safely, but Dad had this strange feeling we should ring you.'

Shea looked at Heath, who nodded encouragingly. 'Actually, Mum, something did happen this morning. But it's resolved now. The man I mentioned—David—he came to Wentworth. He's been quite unwell mentally, and Heath helped get him to hospital for treatment.'

'Oh, sweetheart. Are you safe? Do you need us to come back?'

'I'm safe. Heath handled everything perfectly. But Mum... I think it's time I told you and Dad the whole story about why I left Broken Hill.'

'We're listening, love.'

Over the next twenty minutes, Shea found herself telling her mother everything—the brief relationship with David, the accidental pregnancy, the miscarriage, David's harassment through months of messages, fleeing to Melbourne, and finally this morning's confrontation.

Laura was quiet for a long moment after Shea finished. 'Oh, my darling girl. You've been carrying this alone for so long.'

'I didn't want to worry you. And I was ashamed.'

'Ashamed of what? Falling pregnant isn't a crime, losing a baby isn't your fault, and that man's illness certainly isn't your responsibility.' Laura's voice grew fierce with maternal protection. 'You handled an impossible situation with incredible strength.'

'Dad's going to be upset that I didn't tell him.'

'Your father will be upset that you felt you couldn't tell him. There's a difference.' She could hear Laura speaking quietly to someone in the background—Tom, clearly. 'We're proud of you, Shea. For surviving this, for rebuilding your life, for getting that poor man the help he needed.'

After the call ended, Heath squeezed her hand. 'How do you feel?'

'Lighter. Like I've been holding my breath for months and can finally exhale.' She leaned against his shoulder. 'Thank you. For this morning, for everything.'

'You don't need to thank me. This is what people do for each other when they care.'

Shea jumped when someone tapped on the front door. As she glanced out the window, she noticed a police car parked outside and opened the door.

'Miss O'Byrne? Is Dr McGregor here?'

'Constable Matthews.' Heath stepped around Shea, extending his hand. 'I was waiting for your call.'

'I wanted to follow up on this morning's incident. The hospital contacted us about Mr Mason's admission.'

'How much do you need to know?' Shea asked, standing beside Heath.

'Just enough to complete our report. Dr McGregor has already provided the medical context. We understand Mr Mason was experiencing psychiatric symptoms and has been admitted for treatment?'

'That's correct,' Heath confirmed. 'No charges are

warranted. This was a mental health crisis, not criminal behaviour.'

'And you're satisfied with the resolution, Ms O'Byrne?'

Shea nodded. 'I just want him to get better.'

'Right then. We'll keep the incident on file, but no further action is required unless you request it.' Matthews looked between them. 'You did the right thing, both of you. Too often these situations escalate because people don't know how to respond to mental illness.'

After the constable left, Heath's phone buzzed with a text message. He checked it and smiled. 'Update from the hospital. David's responding well to initial medication. His thinking is already clearer.'

'That's good news.'

'The psychiatrist wants to speak with you at some point, if you're willing. Not for David's treatment, but to help you process your own experience of being harassed by someone with untreated mental illness.'

'Would you come with me?'

'If you want me to.'

They went inside, and Heath cooked dinner while Shea called her sisters. Each conversation was difficult but ultimately healing—Cat's fierce protectiveness, Róisín's practical advice about dealing with harassment, Erin's empathy as someone who'd faced her own dangerous situation, even young Bridget's indignation on her behalf.

'They all want to drive up here immediately,' Shea told Heath as she ended her call with Bridget.

'Do you want them to?'

'No. I want to keep moving forward, not looking back.' She paused. 'Though I think I'd like to visit home soon. See everyone together, without secrets this time.'

'That sounds healthy.'

Late that afternoon, Dr Patricia Williams from the hospital's psychiatric unit called. She was warm but direct, explaining David's condition and treatment plan.

'Mr Mason is responding very well to medication. His delusional thinking has largely resolved, and he's experiencing significant remorse about his behaviour towards you. He'll need ongoing treatment, but his prognosis is quite good.'

'What caused this to happen?'

'Complicated grief, combined with social isolation and probably some underlying depression. When people don't process traumatic loss properly, sometimes their minds create alternative explanations that feel more manageable than random tragedy. His delusion that you'd chosen to end the pregnancy gave him someone to blame, which felt less painful than accepting that pregnancy loss just happens sometimes.'

'Will he want to contact me again?'

'Unlikely. Part of his recovery involves understanding the harm his illness caused you. He's agreed to a no-contact order as part of his treatment plan. If he does try to reach out, it would indicate his treatment isn't working.'

That evening, Shea and Heath sat on her deck watching the sun set over the river confluence. The same view that had become her sanctuary now felt like a symbol of new beginnings rather than escape from the past.

'What are you thinking about?' Heath asked.

'How different everything feels now. This morning, I woke up afraid, carrying secrets, looking over my shoulder. Tonight...'

'Tonight?'

'Tonight, I'm sitting here with someone I care about, my family knows the truth, and the person who's been haunting my thoughts is getting the help he needs. It's like the whole world has shifted.'

Heath was quiet for a moment. 'Where does that leave us? Now that you don't need protecting anymore?'

'Is that what you think you were doing? Protecting me?'

'Partly, maybe. Though I'd like to think there was more to it than that.'

Shea turned to face him properly. 'Heath, you've seen me at my most vulnerable, helped me through crisis, and never once made me feel weak or broken. If anything, you've helped me remember how strong I actually am.'

'You are strong. Stronger than you know.'

'So where does that leave us?' She echoed his question back to him.

'Wherever we want it to leave us. No pressure, no timeline, no expectations except that we keep being honest with each other.'

'I'd like that very much.'

# Chapter 38

The call came at three in the morning.

Shea's phone buzzed insistently on her bedside table, dragging her from the first peaceful sleep she'd had in weeks. Since David's departure and the involvement of mental health services, she'd finally begun to feel like she could breathe again. Heath had been a steady presence through it all, never pushing, just there when she needed him.

'Shea?' Logan's voice was tight. 'Cat's having contractions. We're heading to the hospital in Broken Hill now.'

Shea sat bolt upright. 'How far apart?'

'Ten minutes. Maybe a bit less.' Shea could hear Cat's laboured breathing in the background, a sound that made her chest constrict. 'The baby's not due for another month. I'm worried. We're almost to Wilcannia, and an ambulance is meeting us at the junction of the highway.'

'How did she go on the dirt road?'

'She's fine, between contractions.'

'Focus on driving safely. Have you called Mum and Dad?'

'Yes. They're on the road about half an hour behind us.' Logan's voice was fading out as service dropped. 'Can you call the girls?'

'I will. I'm leaving now, I'll meet you at the hospital in Broken Hill. We should get there about the same time.'

After hanging up, she called her sisters and shared the news, promising to keep them in the loop as the night progressed, and then dialled Heath's number.

'Shea? Is everything all right?' His voice held concern.

'Cat's gone into labour early. I'm driving to Broken Hill now.' She was already pulling out clothes with her free hand. 'I just thought I'd let you know in case you were worried when you couldn't find me tomorrow.'

'I'll meet you at your cottage in ten minutes. Wait for me.'

'Heath, you don't have to—'

'Yes, I do.' His voice was gentle but certain. 'I'll see you soon.'

##

The drive to Broken Hill felt endless. Shea kept her phone on speaker, staying connected with the unfolding drama. Róisín was driving up from Adelaide with Seth, while Erin and Jack were not far away in Menindee. Only Bridget was out of reach, not answering her phone.

When Shea and Heath arrived at the hospital, Logan was pacing the maternity ward waiting room. His usually neat appearance was dishevelled, his shirt half-untucked, his hands running repeatedly through his hair.

'How is she?' Shea asked, immediately moving to his side.

'They've given her steroids for the baby's lungs and something to try to slow the contractions.' Logan's words came out in a rush. 'But they might not be able to stop it. The baby might come tonight, Shea. Eight months. That's too early. What if the lungs aren't developed enough? What if there are complications? What if—'

'Logan.' Heath stepped forward and placed both hands on Logan's shoulders. 'Take a deep breath.'

He guided him through a breathing exercise. Four counts in, hold for four, out for eight. Repeat.

'That's it,' Shea said as Logan's breathing gradually slowed. 'Now tell me what the doctor actually said.'

Logan managed a shaky smile. 'Dr Peters said that babies born at thirty-six weeks have excellent outcomes these days. The NICU is prepared if needed, but Cat's vitals are good and the baby's heart rate is strong.'

Heath nodded. 'And she's in the best place.'

'I know.' He slumped into a plastic chair. 'Cat needs me to be strong right now, and instead I'm falling apart in the waiting room.'

'A typical expectant father,' Heath smiled. 'I've seen worse.'

Before Logan could respond, a nurse emerged from the birthing suite. 'Mr Wainwright? Your wife is asking for you. And she asked for her sister Shea as well.'

***

Cat looked small against the white hospital sheets, her face flushed with exertion but her eyes bright with determination. The foetal monitor beeped steadily beside her, and an IV drip fed into her arm.

'There you are,' she said to Shea, her voice slightly breathless. 'I was hoping you'd make it before this little one decides to make an appearance.'

Shea moved to Cat's bedside, taking her sister's hand. 'How are you feeling?'

'Like I'm about to meet my baby a month early,' Cat said with a weak smile. 'The contractions slowed down for a while, but they're picking up again. Dr Peters thinks we're probably having a baby tonight.'

Logan had moved to Cat's other side, and Shea watched

as he leaned over and kissed her, his love for his wife overriding his worry.

'Whatever happens, we're ready,' he said, bringing Cat's hand to his lips. 'All three of us.'

'Actually, all five of us,' came a familiar voice from the doorway. Tom and Laura appeared, still in their hastily thrown-on clothes, but their faces full of love and concern.

The next few hours blurred together. Contractions that strengthened and then eased, medical consultations delivered in calm, professional tones.

Shea found herself thinking of Catherine O'Byrne, living and working in a cottage by the river more than a century ago, with no medical support and no family around her. The contrast highlighted how much had changed, and yet how similar this moment was—the anticipation, the fear, and the fierce love that preceded new life.

Just after dawn, Dr Peters made the decision.

'The contractions are too strong and too regular to stop now,' she announced. 'Let's have this baby.'

# Chapter 39

Shea stood by Cat's shoulder, offering ice chips and quiet encouragement. Logan was on the other side, and Cat was holding his hand tightly. Heath, Tom, and Laura were in the waiting room.

'I can see the head,' Dr Peters announced. 'One more push, Cat.'

Logan whispered encouragement, and suddenly the room filled with the demanding cry of a very indignant baby.

'It's a girl!' Dr Peters lifted the tiny, perfect infant. 'Born at 8:47 a.m., and listen to those lungs.'

Through her tears, Shea watched Logan's face transform. All the worry dissolved and turned into pure wonder as he looked at his daughter.

'She's so small,' he whispered, but his voice held awe, not concern.

'She's perfect,' Cat said, exhausted but radiant. 'Look at her, Logan. She's absolutely perfect.'

The baby weighed seven pounds, three ounces—a healthy weight. Her breathing was strong, her colour good. After a quick assessment, Dr Peters placed her on Cat's chest.

'Emma Rose O'Byrne-Wainwright,' Cat announced, looking down at her daughter. 'Welcome to the world.'

The waiting room had filled with O'Byrnes by the time Shea emerged with the news. Tom was reading a farming magazine, while Laura paced near the window. Heath sat chatting to Erin and Jack, who had arrived since Shea went into the birthing suite an hour ago.

'You have a granddaughter, Mum and Dad,' Shea

announced, and the room erupted in joy and relief. 'And she's absolutely perfect.'

Laura burst into tears, and Tom wrapped his arms around his wife. 'Our first grandchild,' he said, his eyes glinting with happy tears.

Heath approached Shea, his eyes questioning. She held out her arms and sighed with happiness as he held her close; it felt so right to have him there.

'Thank you for coming with me,' she said simply.

'Thank you for letting me be here.'

The doors flew open and Róisín appeared in the doorway, one hand pressed against her lower back and the other resting on her rounded belly. The drive from Adelaide had clearly taken its toll—her face was pale with fatigue, but her eyes were bright with excitement.

'How is she?' Róisín asked immediately, accepting Seth's steadying hand as she lowered herself carefully into one of the empty chairs. 'We left as soon as Shea rang.'

'Cat is well, and your new niece is beautiful,' Shea said, watching her sister try to find a comfortable position. 'I've just left Logan and Cat in there meeting Emma Rose.'

'A niece,' Róisín breathed, her hand moving unconsciously over her own bump. 'Our babies are going to be so close.'

Erin stood and came over to sit beside her two sisters. 'I couldn't miss this,' she said, settling into the chair beside Róisín with a small grunt of effort. 'Our turn next, Ro.'

##

Later that morning, they took turns visiting Cat's room in small groups. Emma Rose O'Byrne-Wainwright slept peacefully in her mother's arms while Logan sat beside the bed, grinning like a Cheshire cat.

'She has the O'Byrne chin,' Laura observed during her turn to hold her granddaughter.

'And Logan's nose,' Cat added fondly. 'Poor little thing.'

'My nose is distinguished,' Logan protested.

When it was Shea and Heath's turn to visit, Cat studied them with tired but perceptive eyes.

'You two look good together,' she said.

'Cat.' Shea shook her head.

'I'm just saying. Heath brings out your strength.'

Heath squeezed Shea's hand gently. 'I think your sister's very wise.'

'Don't encourage her,' Shea said, but she was smiling.

##

That evening, as the family finally began to disperse, Shea walked with Heath to the hospital car park. The birth was over, Emma was healthy, and Cat was already talking about going home in the next few days.

The Broken Hill spring evening wrapped around them like a gentle embrace, the air still holding the day's warmth but touched with the promise of a cooler night ahead. Above them, the first stars were beginning to appear in the deepening sky, and somewhere in the distance, the sound of evening traffic on the Barrier Highway had settled into a quiet hum.

'It's been quite a week, hasn't it?' Heath observed, his hand finding hers as they walked slowly between the rows of cars.

Quite a week indeed. David's breakdown and departure, the involvement of mental health services to ensure he got proper care, and now Emma Rose's early but safe arrival. Shea was emotionally wrung out but also happy.

'I keep thinking about how different things could have been,' she said. 'If David hadn't been able to get help. If Emma had come earlier, or with complications.'

'But they didn't,' Heath said gently, stopping to turn towards her. 'David is getting treatment. Emma is healthy. Cat and Logan are happy.' His thumb traced gentle circles across her knuckles. 'And you're safe. That's what matters most to me.'

The tenderness in his voice made her chest tighten with emotion. Over the past weeks, she'd watched Heath guide her through every crisis with steady calm, offering support without overwhelming her, being present without demanding more than she could give.

'I love your positive outlook on life,' she said with a smile.

They'd reached Heath's car, and Shea turned to face him, suddenly aware of how much had changed in such a short time. The car park lights cast a warm glow around them, creating an intimate circle of light. The scent of eucalyptus drifted on the gentle breeze, mixed with the faint aroma of the hospital's garden beds.

'I used to think that caring about someone was a risk,' she said. 'But watching Logan today, seeing his love for Cat and Emma, was an amazing experience. One I will cherish for the rest of my life.'

'Maybe an experience you'll have one day.' Heath put his arms around her, drawing her close, and she closed her eyes, breathing in his familiar scent—clean soap, a hint of aftershave, and something uniquely him that made her feel safe.

'I'm scared,' she admitted, her voice barely above a whisper.

'Of what?'

'Us. Of hoping. Of believing this could last.'

Heath rested his cheek against hers, his breath warm against her ear. 'What if we just take it one day at a time? No promises about forever, no pressure about the future. Just... this. Today. Tomorrow. See what happens.'

It was such a reasonable approach, and there was something deeply appealing about the idea of building something slowly, carefully, with full attention to creating a foundation strong enough to weather whatever storms might come.

'One day at a time,' she agreed, pulling back to look into his eyes.

In the soft light, Shea could see everything Heath felt for her in his expression—the tenderness, the hope, the careful patience that had allowed her to heal at her own pace.

'Shea,' he said quietly, his hands framing her face with infinite gentleness. 'I love you. I know it's complicated, I know we're taking things slowly, but I need you to know that. I love who you are, how strong you've been, how you've let me be part of your journey back to trusting again.'

The words hung in the warm evening air between them, and Shea stood on her toes and pressed her lips against his. 'I love you too,' she murmured against his mouth.

As they kissed under the hospital car park lights, Shea felt something she'd forgotten existed—pure, uncomplicated joy. The night seemed to shimmer around them, the spring air carrying the promise of new life and a new beginning, and for the first time in longer than she could remember, Shea allowed herself to believe that she deserved this happiness.

When they finally broke apart, both breathing unsteadily, Heath smiled down at her with such love that her heart seemed to expand in her chest.

'One day at a time,' he repeated softly.

'One day at a time,' she whispered back.

# Chapter 40

The morning light filtered through the lace curtains of Shea's Wentworth cottage as she packed the last of her belongings into cardboard boxes. After days of soul-searching, she'd finally made the decision that felt absolutely right—following Heath to his rural posting in Broken Hill. They were moving in together, a step that still filled her with quiet amazement at how much her life had changed.

She found herself humming as she wrapped her coffee mugs in newspaper, then caught herself and smiled. When had she started singing again? It had been so long since music had naturally bubbled up from within her that she'd almost forgotten what it felt like to be unconsciously happy.

The phone call from Rod le Cerf two weeks ago had been flattering—an offer to return to veterinary nursing at the practice, especially now that David had moved back to Adelaide and that situation had resolved itself. But declining had been easy.

Her future lay in full-time counselling now, helping other women navigate pregnancy loss and trauma. Heath had already helped her connect with the regional health service in Broken Hill, where there was a genuine need for her skills. She had enrolled in another course and was on her way to gaining more formal qualifications, and was even considering undertaking a degree in clinical psychology. The prospect of deepening her knowledge and ability to help others filled her with purpose.

One of the best things of the past month had been Eliza's visit.

'I knew as soon as I met you that you were the one for my

baby brother,' she'd said to Shea over a glass of wine when Heath was working late one night. They'd been sitting on Shea's small veranda, watching the river flow past in the gathering dusk.

'Really?' Shea had asked, curious about this woman's intuition. 'What gave it away?'

'The way he talked about you after he met you that first night at the pub. He told me about the way you looked at him. Like you were seeing him, really seeing him, not just the charming exterior he shows most people.' Eliza had taken a sip of wine, her expression thoughtful. 'Heath's always been the caretaker, you know. Even as a child. As our parents aged, he felt responsible for everyone. He's spent years looking after others but never really letting anyone look after him, especially since Sarah died.'

'He's told me about Sarah. He loved her very much,' Shea had said quietly.

'He did, but with you...' Eliza had smiled. 'With you, I see him allowing himself to be vulnerable. To need someone. That's huge for Heath.'

They'd sat in comfortable silence for a moment before Eliza had continued. 'And you, Shea—you're finding your way back to trusting, aren't you? Heath told me a little about what you've been through. Not the details, just enough to help me understand why you've both been taking things slowly.'

'It's been worth it,' Shea had admitted. 'Building something real, something solid. I never thought I'd feel this secure with someone again.'

'That's what makes you perfect for each other. You both understand that love isn't just feeling—it's choosing, every day, to show up for each other.' Eliza had reached over and squeezed

Shea's hand. 'And your work with pregnancy loss counselling—Heath says you're exceptional at it. Have you thought about where you want to take that long-term?'

'I'm considering clinical psychology. Maybe specialising in reproductive trauma and grief counselling. There's such a need for it, especially in regional areas where women don't have access to specialised support.'

'You could make a real difference,' Eliza had said with genuine admiration. 'Build something meaningful, help shape how the medical community approaches pregnancy loss. That's a legacy worth building.'

As Eliza stood to leave she pulled Shea into a warm hug.

'I am so pleased that you are moving to Broken Hill with him. He has his joy of life back again. Thank you, Shea.'

'Thank *you*, Eliza,' Shea had replied, understanding that this woman's blessing meant more than sisterly approval—it was recognition that what she and Heath had built together was real, valuable, and worth keeping.

In one way, she felt a pang of sadness about leaving this river town where Catherine had found her happiness and built her healing legacy. But Shea knew her path was to follow Heath, to work together.

Life was wonderful in ways she'd never dared hope for. Each day brought deeper contentment, and she found herself falling more in love with Heath with every passing moment—his steady presence, his gentle humour, the way he encouraged her dreams without trying to direct them. The thought of waking up beside him every morning, of building a life together in their new place, filled her with a joy so profound it sometimes took her breath away.

Little Emma Rose had thrived, growing from a newborn into a robust six-week-old with her mother's determination and her father's steady temper. Cat had adapted to motherhood with typical O'Byrne skill, finding her own pace between caring for Emma, managing the property's accounts, and helping Dad with the family research.

The doorbell rang at ten o'clock. Heath stood in the hallway holding two takeaway coffee cups and wearing the practical clothes he'd adopted for helping her move—old jeans, a faded university T-shirt, and boots that had seen better days.

'Ready for the final assault on your possessions?' he asked, handing her a coffee.

'Just the books left.' Shea gestured towards the towering stacks that dominated her living room. 'I *may* have underestimated how many I'd accumulated in the short time I was here.'

They worked methodically, Heath carrying the heavier boxes while Shea wrapped the fragile items.

'Eliza called yesterday,' Heath mentioned as he hoisted another box. 'The regional health service has signed off on the funding for the new counselling centre.'

'That's good news.' Shea taped up a box of clinical journals. 'Though I still think they're taking a risk on someone without a business degree.'

'You've proved yourself working here. That's better than theoretical knowledge.'

Shea smiled and blew him a kiss. Over the weeks since Emma's birth, their relationship had settled into a natural rhythm. Heath had completed his rural placement and accepted a permanent position at a Broken Hill clinic. They'd bought a small house together on the outskirts of town, close enough to the hospital for his shifts and with enough land for Shea to keep a vegetable garden.

By afternoon, they'd loaded the final boxes into the hire truck. Shea stood in her empty cottage, noting the rectangular patches on the walls where her pictures had hung, the marks on the carpet where her desk had been positioned.

'Second thoughts?' Heath asked.

'No.' She picked up her handbag and keys. 'I think I've been ready to leave for longer than I realised.'

David's treatment had continued to progress well. He'd been transferred to a community mental health program in Adelaide after his initial psychiatric admission and had started working part-time in a city practice while attending regular therapy sessions. Most importantly, he'd stopped trying to contact her. The psychiatric team had helped him understand that his obsession with "fixing" their relationship was part of his illness, not a reflection of genuine love.

The restraining order remained in place, but Shea no longer felt the constant vigilance that had characterised her life for months. She could make plans without looking over her shoulder and could answer her phone without checking the caller ID first.

The drive to Broken Hill took just under three hours, Heath following behind her car in the hire truck.

Their new house sat on five acres of red soil and established gum trees, with a view across irrigation channels towards the Darling. The modest weatherboard cottage had seen better days—built in the 1960s, practical rather than stylish—but Heath had taken one look at the wraparound veranda and declared it had "potential".

'Potential for what?' Shea had laughed, watching him peer optimistically at the peeling paint on the window frames.

'Adventure,' he'd said, which had made her snort with amusement. Heath's idea of adventure typically involved repairing fence posts and planting vegetable gardens.

As they unloaded boxes in the fading afternoon light, their unpacking turned into chaos when Heath discovered Shea had labelled everything with cryptic abbreviations.

'What the hell is "Preg Loss Misc"?' he called from the truck.

'Pregnancy loss miscellaneous,' she called back, wrestling with a box that had split at the bottom. 'Books, pamphlets, probably some tissues that got mixed in. It can go in the spare room.'

'And "K Stuff"?'

'Obvious! Kitchen stuff.'

'This one just says "Crap".'

Shea paused, wiping sweat from her forehead with the back of her hand. 'That would be... crap. Things I couldn't throw away but have no idea what to do with.'

Heath appeared in the doorway, grinning, a box marked "Crap" balanced on his shoulder. 'I love that you have a whole box dedicated to crap.'

'Everyone has a crap box, Heath. We honest people just label it properly.'

As they manoeuvred her desk through the front door—a process that involved much swearing and several near-misses with the door frame—Heath yelped as the desk corner caught his shin. 'Jesus, this thing weighs more than a small car.'

'It's solid wood, you wuss.'

'Wuss? I'll show you wuss.' He made an exaggerated

show of flexing his muscles, which made Shea laugh so hard she nearly dropped her end of the desk.

They set it down in the sunny spare room where Shea planned to see clients. Heath immediately sprawled across it dramatically, arms flung wide.

'Testing the structural integrity,' he announced solemnly.

'Get off my desk, you idiot.'

'Do you think Catherine would approve of your bedside manner?' he asked, not moving.

Shea considered this, looking around the room that would become her sanctuary for helping other women cope with loss. 'I think she'd approve of the honesty. And probably of you lying on my furniture like a teenager.'

When they finished unloading, they sat on the front steps sharing beer and watching the sun set over the water. Heath had found a packet of Tim Tams in one of the kitchen boxes, and they passed it back and forth between them.

'This feels right,' Shea said, gesturing at the property with her beer bottle. 'Not what I ever planned, but right.'

'Plans are overrated,' Heath said, stealing the last Tim Tam. 'Besides, who plans to fall in love with someone who labels boxes "Crap"?'

'Someone with questionable judgement, apparently.'

He bumped her shoulder with his. 'Nope, the best kind.'

# Chapter 41

The call from Erin came on a warm morning while Laura was hanging washing on the line at *Ceann Mara*. The air carried the scent of river gums and the promise of a hot day ahead as she pulled the phone from her pocket. The noise from the cicadas was deafening.

'Mum?' Erin's voice was breathless with excitement and exhaustion. 'You have a grandson!'

Laura dropped the tea towel she'd been pinning up and gripped the phone tighter. 'Oh, darling! How are you? How is he?'

'We're both fine. He was born at six this morning—seven pounds, three ounces. Samuel Jack.' Erin's voice caught with emotion. 'Mum, he's perfect. Absolutely perfect.'

'Samuel,' Laura repeated, testing the name. 'Dad will be pleased.'

'Jack's idea. He said we needed to honour the O'Byrne men who helped shape the women they married.'

Tom appeared from the machinery shed, alerted by Laura's call. She gestured frantically for him to come closer, mouthing, 'It's a boy!'

'Tell us everything,' Laura said, switching to speakerphone so Tom could hear. 'How long were you in labour? Is Jack holding up?'

Erin's laugh was tired but joyful. 'Twelve hours from start to finish. Jack was more nervous than I was—he kept timing my contractions on his phone and double-checking with the midwives about everything. But when Samuel arrived, he just stood there crying and saying, "he's so small, he's so small", over and over.'

'Can we drive up today?' Tom asked immediately. 'Or would you prefer we wait a few days?'

'Come whenever you can. We're staying in the hospital overnight for observation, but we should be home tomorrow.'

After promising to leave within the hour, Laura hung up and stood in the middle of the yard with tears streaming down her face.

'Two grandchildren,' Tom said, wrapping his arms around her. 'Three months apart.'

'Samuel and Emma Rose.' Laura wiped her eyes. 'Now we just have to wait for Róisín.'

They were still getting organised for the drive to Broken Hill when Laura's phone rang again. This time, it was Seth calling from Adelaide.

'Laura? I've got news.' Seth sounded slightly shell-shocked. 'Róisín went into labour this morning. Fast labour— we barely made it to the hospital.'

'The baby?' Laura's heart jumped. Róisín wasn't due for another two weeks.

'She's here. Our daughter. Born an hour ago, six pounds exactly. They're calling her small but healthy.' Seth's voice was full of wonder. 'Róisín's exhausted, but she's incredible. She keeps saying the baby looks like a little bird.'

'What's her name?' Tom asked, leaning close to the phone.

'Mairead Róisín Carter. Mairead is Irish—it means pearl. Róisín chose it months ago, said she wanted something that connected to the family's Irish heritage.'

Laura felt her knees go weak. 'Two babies in one

morning.'

'Sorry?' Seth sounded confused.

'Erin had her baby this morning, too. A boy—Samuel. They're both fine.'

The silence on the phone stretched for a moment as Seth processed this coincidence.

'Two cousins born on the same day,' he said finally. 'That's got to mean something.'

After arranging plans to visit Adelaide later in the week, they hung up, and Laura found herself sitting heavily on the back steps, overwhelmed by the morning's events.

'Three grandchildren,' she said to Tom. 'Can you believe it?'

'The next generation of O'Byrnes,' Tom said, settling beside her. 'Different surnames, but all carrying the family forward.'

They sat in comfortable silence, each processing the fact of becoming grandparents to three babies in such a short time. The family that had felt so fractured during Shea's difficult period was now growing rapidly, bringing new life to *Ceann Mara*.

'We should call Shea,' Laura said eventually. 'She'll want to know about her nephew and niece.'

'And Cat. She'll be delighted that Emma Rose has cousins so close in age.'

'Bridget too, though she might be too busy with university to properly appreciate being an aunt three times over.'

As they made their phone calls, sharing the news and making plans for visits, deep satisfaction settled over Laura. This was what she'd always wanted for her daughters—the chance to build families of their own while remaining connected to *Ceann*

*Mara.*

Later that afternoon, as they drove towards Broken Hill to meet their newest grandson, Tom reached over and took Laura's hand.

'Looks like the O'Byrne family is growing,' he said.

Laura squeezed his fingers. 'We are blessed, Tom.'

# Chapter 42

*Broken Hill - twelve months later*

'Six clients before lunch?' Heath looked up from his coffee as Shea flipped through her appointment book at their small kitchen table. 'That's double what you planned for when you opened.'

'I know.' Shea traced her finger down the page, counting. 'And I've got two more families driving down from Wilcannia this afternoon. Word's getting around.'

'Good word, obviously.' He reached across to squeeze her hand. 'You're making a difference, sweetheart.'

She turned her hand palm up, lacing their fingers together. 'I never imagined it would grow this quickly. Yesterday, Sarah—you remember, my new counsellor? She suggested we start group sessions. For families dealing with recurrent loss.'

'What do you think?'

'I think...' Shea paused, considering. 'I think they need it. God knows I would have given anything for that kind of support when—' She stopped, took a breath. 'When I was going through it.'

Heath stood and moved behind her chair, his hands settling on her shoulders. 'You're giving them what you didn't have. That takes courage.'

She leaned back into his warmth. A year in Broken Hill, and she still sometimes couldn't believe this was her life now. A thriving practice. A partner who understood without her having to explain. Heath's steady presence still caught her off guard sometimes.

'What time's your shift today?' she asked, tilting her head back to look at him.

'Seven till three in ED. Then I've got two med students coming for their rural placement orientation.' He bent to kiss her forehead. 'Should be done by five. Dinner out tonight? That new place on Argent Street?'

'You won't be too tired?'

'Never too tired for you.'

The simple certainty in his voice made her chest tight. 'My last appointment is coming at four,' she said, standing to walk him to the door. 'Remember them? The Wrights? They lost their third baby at twenty weeks.'

'How are they doing?'

'Better. But this month would have been her due date.' Shea watched him check his pockets for his keys. 'I might be late if they need extra time.'

'Take all the time they need.' Heath paused at the door, cupping her face in his hands. 'These families are lucky to have someone who really understands.'

After he left, Shea stood in their small kitchen, listening to his car pulling away. The morning sun slanted through the window, warming the spot where they'd stood together. She thought about the office she'd rented in town, the receptionist she'd hired last month, the second counsellor who'd started this week.

Most of all, she thought about the women who sat across from her each day, their grief so familiar it made her chest ache. They came from all over the region now—some driving three hours just to sit with someone who could say, "I know. I've been there too," and mean it.

Her phone buzzed. A text from her receptionist: 'Mrs Cartwright just called. Wondering if you have any cancellations today. She's had another positive test, and she's scared.'

Shea typed back quickly: 'Tell her to come at lunch. I'll make time.'

She always would.

##

The full moon rose over the Mundi Mundi plains, turning the endless red earth silver-white and making the horizon shimmer where the curve of the earth fell away into darkness. Heath had suggested the drive out to Silverton after dinner, taking the familiar road through the scrub to the lookout where you could see forever.

'You can actually see it tonight,' Shea said, leaning against the wooden rail. 'The curvature. Like the world just drops away.'

Heath stood beside her, his hands restless on the weathered timber. Twenty-five kilometres from Broken Hill, and it might as well have been another planet—nothing but spinifex and saltbush stretching to that impossible horizon.

'You're fidgeting,' she observed. 'Are you alright?'

'I'm fine.' He shifted his weight. 'Actually, no. I'm terrified. I've been waiting for this full moon for ages.'

She turned to look at him properly. In the moonlight, his jaw was tight, his shoulders tense.

'Terrified of what?'

'Of asking you something and having you say no.'

Her heart stuttered, then steadied. She knew what was coming. Had suspected for weeks, maybe longer. The surprise was her complete lack of panic.

'What's the question?'

He turned from the vast plains to face her, taking a breath that lifted his whole chest. 'I know we said we'd take things one day at a time. I know you've got every reason to be cautious—'

'Heath—'

'Let me finish. Please.'

She nodded, the wind picking up loose strands of her hair.

'I don't want just one day at a time anymore. I want all the days. I want to wake up next to you when we're seventy and you're still labelling boxes "crap" and I'm still pretending I know how to fix the washing machine.' His voice caught. 'I want to build something with you that lasts.'

He reached into his pocket and pulled out a small velvet box, holding it between his palms while the endless plains stretched out behind him.

'Shea O'Byrne, will you marry me?'

The wind stilled. Even the distant dingoes were quiet. The whole outback seemed to be holding its breath.

'Yes.' The word came out on a laugh. 'Yes, absolutely yes.'

Heath's whole face changed—relief flooding through him as his hands shook opening the box.

'I should probably give you the ring. It's not much—'

'Heath.' She covered his hands with hers. 'I don't care about the ring.'

'Still.' He opened the box. A simple white gold band, a small, clear diamond that caught the moonlight like a tiny star. 'It was my grandmother's. She would have loved you.'

Her eyes burned as he slipped it onto her finger. Perfect fit.

'It's beautiful.'

'So are you.'

He kissed her then, there at the edge of the world with the moon rising higher and the ancient land spreading out in all directions.

'I love you,' she said when they broke apart. 'Not carefully, just... completely.'

'I love you too. One day at a time, for all our days.'

They stayed at the lookout watching the moon traverse the enormous sky, talking about wedding dates and work schedules, whether they wanted children, and when they would tell their families.

As they walked back to Heath's ute, Shea looked out one more time at that amazing horizon. The ring caught the moonlight as she reached for Heath's hand.

This was it—the beginning of the best part of her story.

# Chapter 43

Tom O'Byrne stared at his phone, reading Bridget's latest text message for the third time. It was nearly midnight on a Thursday in late March, and his youngest daughter was asking to borrow money for "study materials and networking events".

'She's not answering her phone again,' Laura said, emerging from the kitchen with two cups of tea. 'I've tried calling four times this week.'

They settled at the kitchen table, where so many family discussions had taken place over the years. The house felt too quiet with only the two of them—a preview of the empty nest years that lay ahead. Emma Rose's toys were scattered across the living room from her latest visit with Cat, and the sight of them made Tom think about how quickly time passed, how fast children grew away from the people who loved them most.

'When did we last have a proper conversation with her?' Tom asked. 'Not just these random text messages asking for money or telling us she's too busy to come home when the others come home.'

'Christmas. And even then, she spent half the time on her laptop or talking about some AI company.' Laura wrapped her hands around her mug, seeking warmth against the cool autumn evening. 'She barely ate, kept checking her phone every few minutes. I thought it was just exam stress, but...'

The change in Bridget had been gradual but unmistakable. Through her first year of computer science, she'd been focused and enthusiastic, calling home regularly to share stories about her studies and code she was learning. She'd Face Timed them regularly, keeping in touch with family news.

But somewhere during the second year, something changed. The phone calls became shorter and less frequent. Her grades, while still passing, had dropped from distinctions to bare credits. And then they met the cause of it when she'd Facetimed and introduced them to her "friend", Antony Saar.

'I'm worried about her living situation,' Laura continued. 'She moved out of college accommodation halfway through last year, said she'd found a better place. But when I asked for the address, she was vague about it.'

Tom frowned. 'What do you mean, vague?'

'She gave me a suburb, but not a street address. Said she was "between places" and would send details once things were "sorted out." That was six months ago.'

'Maybe we should drive down to Sydney,' Tom suggested. 'Just show up at the university and see what's actually going on.'

The idea had merit, but Tom knew Bridget well enough to understand that an unannounced parental visit would likely drive her further away rather than bring her closer. She'd always been the most independent of their daughters, even as a child, insisting on doing things her own way, in her own time.

'Did you see her Instagram posts from last weekend?' Laura pulled out her phone and scrolled through social media images. 'Look at this.'

The photos showed Bridget at what appeared to be an expensive restaurant in Sydney's CBD, dressed in clothes they definitely hadn't paid for. Her hair had been professionally styled, and she wore makeup that looked expensive and expertly applied. She was surrounded by people significantly older than university students—men and women in their thirties wearing designer clothes and expensive watches.

'Who are these people?' Tom studied the faces in the background. 'They look like they could be her professors, except...'

'Except professors don't usually take students to restaurants that charge two hundred dollars for dinner,' Laura finished. 'And look at her expression. She's smiling, but it doesn't reach her eyes. She looks like she is performing.'

That was exactly the word for it, Tom realised. Bridget looked like someone playing a role rather than enjoying herself. There was something brittle about her posture, something forced about the way she leaned into the group.

The latest concerning development was Bridget's sudden fluency in startup jargon. Her text messages had become peppered with phrases like "disruptive innovation", "paradigm shifts", and "revolutionary applications". She talked about AI and machine learning with the confidence of an expert.

'She asked me yesterday about our financial situation,' Tom said carefully. 'Wanted to know about the property's value, whether we had any investment portfolios, that sort of thing.'

Laura's eyebrows rose. 'Why would she need to know that?'

'She said she was doing a project on agricultural economic software. But the questions were too specific, too focused on liquid assets.' Tom paused, remembering the conversation that had left him unsettled. 'She also asked about our family investments, and whether we knew anyone local with significant capital looking for "ground-floor opportunities".'

'That doesn't sound like any computer science project I've ever heard of.'

They sat in silence for a moment, each processing the

implications. Outside, the night sounds of the river country continued their ancient patterns—water flowing past, night birds calling, the gentle creak of old timber settling. These sounds had provided comfort through four daughters' various crises, but tonight they felt distant, unable to reach whatever was troubling their fifth child in the city.

'I think she's gotten involved with something that's not what it appears to be,' Tom said finally. 'The question is, how do we help her see that without pushing her away completely?'

They'd watched this pattern before with other families in the district—bright young adults who got swept up in schemes that promised easy money or fast success. The perpetrators were always sophisticated, always targeting intelligent, ambitious young people who thought they were too smart to be fooled.

'Should we call Shea?' Laura asked. 'She might have some insight into this kind of thing.'

Tom nodded. Shea's counselling background had given her skills in handling delicate family situations, and she'd always been close to Bridget. More importantly, she understood what it felt like to get involved with someone who didn't have your best interests at heart.

Before he could respond, his phone buzzed with another message from Bridget. This one was longer, more detailed, and somehow more troubling than her usual brief requests.

'What does it say?' Laura asked, noting his expression.

Tom read the message aloud: 'Dad, I know I haven't been great at staying in touch lately, but I've been incredibly busy with an amazing opportunity. I'm working with some brilliant people on something that could change everything—not just for me, but for the entire agricultural industry. I can't say too much yet because we're in stealth mode, but I think you and Mum would be really excited about what we're building. Can we talk soon? I'd love to share some of this with you.'

Laura leaned back in her chair. 'That's the longest message she's sent in months.'

'And the most concerning,' Tom added. 'Listen to the language—"amazing opportunity," "brilliant people," "change everything," "stealth mode". It's like she's reading from a script.'

'What kind of script?'

'The kind that separates young people from their families and their money.' Tom set his phone down carefully. 'I've read about this language before, at those seminars they run in town halls. The ones that promise to teach you the "secrets" of real estate investment or cryptocurrency trading.'

Laura's face paled. 'You think she's involved in some kind of pyramid scheme?'

'I think she's involved with people who are very good at making intelligent young adults feel special and chosen. People who understand exactly how to exploit ambition and idealism.'

They discussed their options late into the night. Confronting Bridget directly would likely trigger her defences and push her deeper into whatever situation she'd found herself in. Ignoring the warning signs felt like abandoning her when she might need them most. The middle path—expressing concern while maintaining connection—required careful navigation.

'I'll text her back tomorrow,' Tom decided. 'Tell her we're looking forward to hearing about her project, but that we'd prefer to discuss anything involving the family or the farm in person. Keep it positive but set some boundaries.'

'And if she doesn't want to come home?'

'Then we'll know we're dealing with something more serious than we thought.'

As they finally headed to bed, both were thinking about their other daughters and how differently their young adult years had unfolded. Cat had made her share of mistakes but had always remained grounded in family and place. Róisín had gone through a rebellious phase but had never lost her fundamental connection to her values. Erin had married young but had chosen a partner who understood and respected the family's bonds. Shea had faced the most serious crisis, but even at her lowest point, she'd never disappeared from their lives entirely.

Bridget's situation felt different. More calculated, more deliberate. As if someone had identified her ambitions and her independence as vulnerabilities to be exploited rather than strengths to be celebrated.

The river flowed past in the darkness, carrying a message about patience and persistence, about waiting for the right moment to act. But Tom found himself wondering if patience was always the right approach, or if sometimes love required more immediate action, even at the risk of pushing away the person you were trying to save.

His last thought before sleep was of Bridget as a child, stubbornly insisting she could fix the broken gate latch herself, refusing all offers of help until finally accepting his guidance only when she realised her own efforts weren't working. He hoped that same stubborn independence would eventually lead her back to the people who loved her most.

# Chapter 44

*Ceann Mara - two months later*

'Everyone, this is Antony Saar,' Bridget announced with forced brightness. She quickly added, 'Antony, this is my family.'

The introductions were performed, and several "nice to finally meet you" were exchanged. Antony handed Tom an obviously expensive bottle of wine with the air of someone who'd Googled "appropriate host gift".

The hug between mother and daughter was stiff, Bridget pulling away quickly.

Shea twisted her engagement ring so the diamond faced inward, hidden against her palm. Through the kitchen window at *Ceann Mara*, she watched Heath help Tom with the barbecue, their easy conversation a stark contrast to the knot of anxiety in her stomach. Not about the engagement announcement—that brought only joy—but about what she could see happening near the verandah.

Antony Saar stood there, gesturing enthusiastically whilst explaining something to Laura. Even from across the garden, Shea could read her mother's body language—polite on the surface, wary beneath. The fixed smile meant Laura was managing a difficult situation whilst trying to keep the peace for everyone else.

'Nobody suspects a thing,' Cat said, appearing at her elbow with Emma Rose on her hip. She immediately reached for Shea's earrings with sticky fingers.

'Good. I want to see Mum's face when we tell them.'

Shea gently redirected Emma's grabbing hands. 'When are Róisín and Seth getting here?'

'Any minute. Róisín texted that Mairead played up in the baby seat, and they've had several stops. Where's Erin?'

'She's putting Samuel down for a sleep. He's teething and cranky.' Cat's expression shifted as she followed Shea's gaze. 'I hope this goes well. With Antony here. A different boyfriend to what I expected from Bridget.'

'Business partner,' Shea corrected automatically, though the distinction seemed increasingly meaningless.

'Please.' Cat's voice dropped as they watched Bridget hover near Antony, her posture deferential in a way that made Shea's counsellor instincts flare. 'Look at how she watches him. Like she's waiting for permission to breathe. And he knows it too—been dropping MIT and Stanford into every second sentence since they arrived.'

Through the window, they watched Antony corner Tom, launching into what appeared to be a technical explanation complete with hand gestures that suggested graphs and trajectories. Tom nodded along, but his eyes found Laura's across the garden—that married couple telepathy that said "we'll discuss this later".

'Predictive modelling for agricultural applications,' Cat mimicked Antony's earnest tone. 'Addressing gaps that established companies are too conservative to tackle.'

'Revolutionary disruption of traditional farming methods,' Shea added. 'Paradigm shifts in agricultural technology.'

'Christ, does he ever just have a normal conversation?' Logan appeared at Cat's side.

Róisín and Seth drove in, and within minutes, the quiet

garden exploded into cheerful chaos.

The adults watched with pleasure and chuckled—except for Antony, Shea noticed, who watched the arriving children with an expression of someone observing something unpleasant.

'Bridget and her friend, Antony, are staying a week, apparently,' Cat said quietly, still watching Antony.

'What?' Róisín had appeared beside them, Mairead squirming to get down and join Emma Rose on the play mat. 'Mum agreed to that?'

'First she's heard of it. Bridget just announced it five minutes ago.'

Shea saw her parents exchange another look—Tom's jaw tightening, Laura's smile becoming even more fixed. The family gathering that should have been about sunshine and shared meals was already taking on an undercurrent of tension.

'What are we gossiping about?' Erin joined them.

'Bridget's new friend,' Cat nodded towards Antony, who was now showing Tom something on his phone. 'The one who found Stanford too constraining for real innovation.'

'Oh God, he actually said that?' Erin laughed, though her eyes remained concerned. 'Dad must be having a field day.'

'He's being polite. So far.' Shea watched her father's carefully blank expression as Antony explained why traditional farming methods were obsolete. 'But if he criticises the vineyard or Dad's cellar...'

The vineyard was Tom's pride—three generations of careful cultivation, vines that had survived drought and flood, wine that had won regional awards. Antony was gesturing towards it now with the casual dismissiveness of someone who saw only inefficiency where Tom saw heritage.

'Lunch is ready!' Laura called, her voice carrying that particular brightness that she used when trying to make sure everyone was happy. The tone that said "everyone will be civilised because I say so".'

They gathered around the long table under the peppercorn tree—all five sisters, their partners, the three babies in high chairs. The seating arrangement told its own story: Bridget positioned herself beside Antony rather than between her sisters as she normally would. The physical distance was small but significant.

The children's laughter and jabbering should have lightened the mood, but somehow it only highlighted the tension at the adult end of the table. Antony dominated the conversation, explaining his vision for agricultural technology whilst barely touching Laura's carefully prepared meal. Bridget hung on his every word, her own plate untouched.

'The integration of AI-driven analytics with real-time satellite imagery will revolutionise crop management,' Antony was saying, apparently unaware that half the table had glazed over. 'We're talking about preventing disease outbreaks before they happen, optimising breeding programmes for maximum genetic diversity, reducing mortality rates by up to thirty per cent.'

'Based on what data?' Seth asked, his data-analyst mind engaging despite himself.

'Proprietary algorithms developed through extensive machine learning protocols,' Antony replied smoothly—an answer that sounded impressive whilst saying nothing at all.

Heath caught Shea's eye from across the table and mouthed, 'Now?'

She shook her head slightly. Not yet. Let Bridget's

boyfriend—business partner, whatever he was—finish his performance.

After the main course, when Emma-Rose was finger-painting with mashed potatoes, Antony stood.

'I'd like to propose something,' he said.

'Oh Christ,' Cat muttered. Róisín kicked her under the table, though her own expression suggested similar sentiments.

'Bridget and I have been working on something revolutionary. With the right investment—'

'Actually,' Heath stood too, smoothly cutting Antony off mid-pitch. 'If we're making announcements...'

He reached for Shea's hand, pulling her gently to her feet. The ring she'd been hiding all morning caught the spring sunlight as she turned it around, the small diamond throwing tiny rainbows across the table.

'We're engaged.'

The table erupted. Laura's hands flew to her mouth, happy tears filling her eyes. Tom's face broke into the biggest grin Shea had ever seen. Cat whooped loud enough to wake the cockatoos in the river gums, while Róisín was crying too. Erin knocked over her water glass in her rush to hug them.

'When?' Laura was around the table in seconds, pulling them both into fierce embraces. 'How? Oh, darling girl!'

'I proposed at Mundi Mundi Lookout.' Heath's arm stayed firm around Shea's waist as everyone converged on them. 'I know I should have asked your permission first, Tom—'

'Nonsense,' Tom said gruffly, pumping Heath's hand before pulling him into a back-slapping embrace that said more than words could. 'You've been family since the day you brought her home. Welcome to the family, son. Officially.'

Seth clapped Heath on the back. 'You're a brave man. Four sisters-in-law.'

'And don't forget a mother-in-law,' Jack added, grinning. 'She's the one who really runs things.'

'Oi!' Laura protested, though she was laughing through her tears.

Bridget hugged them both, though her smile seemed forced. 'Congratulations,' she said, her voice oddly formal. 'When's the wedding?'

'We haven't decided yet,' Shea said, studying her youngest sister's face. 'Something small, probably. Just family.'

'Family's not small,' Róisín pointed out. 'Have you counted us lately?'

In the midst of the celebration, Shea caught sight of Antony still standing by his chair, his investment pitch derailed, his expression calculating as he reassessed the family dynamics. She saw him lean towards Bridget and whisper something that made her sister's genuine smile—the one that had briefly appeared—fade back into that careful, bland expression.

'This calls for champagne!' Laura was already heading inside. 'The good stuff from the cellar! Tom, help me?'

'Is that an antique ring?' Erin peered at Shea's hand, her own wedding ring catching the light as she examined it.

'Yes, Heath's grandmother's actually.'

'It's perfect.' Róisín squeezed her tight. 'You're perfect together. I knew it the minute I met him. Remember? I said he looked at you like Dad looks at Mum.'

'Soppy,' Cat teased, though her eyes were suspiciously bright.

As Tom emerged with bottles and Laura distributed glasses, Shea noticed Antony trying to recapture the spotlight.

'About that investment opportunity—' he began.

'Not today,' Tom said firmly, his tone brooking no argument. 'Today is a family celebration.'

The subtle emphasis on "family" wasn't lost on anyone. Antony's jaw tightened, but he subsided, pulling out his phone to tap at it with barely concealed irritation.

'To Shea and Heath,' Tom raised his glass once everyone was served. 'May you have many happy years ahead, filled with love, laughter, and—' he glanced at the babies covering themselves in juice, '—considerably less mess than this lot generates.'

'Many happy years,' everyone echoed.

The toasts continued, each sister sharing embarrassing stories about Shea that made Heath laugh and Shea threaten violence.

Later, after the champagne and tears and endless questions about wedding plans—'You have to let me do the flowers,' Laura insisted, 'I've been practising on the garden club ladies'—Shea found herself in the kitchen with Heath, washing up while the others sprawled in the garden.

Through the window, she could see the full tableau of her family. Cat sat on the verandah with Emma, teaching her to clap along to a nursery rhyme. Róisín and Seth were attempting to convince Mairead that nap time was overdue. Erin had brought Samuel out from his nap, and Laura was playing with him on her lap.

And there, apart from the rest, sat Bridget and Antony, heads bent over his phone, isolated in their bubble of blue light and hushed conversation about market projections.

'That went well,' Heath said, drying a plate with careful

attention.

'Better than Antony's investment pitch anyway.'

Heath laughed, though his expression grew serious. 'Did you see his face when Tom shut him down?'

'Everyone did. He's not used to being told no.'

'And Bridget?'

Shea sighed, watching her youngest sister through the window. 'She looked relieved for a second. Then scared. Then... nothing. Like she switched herself off.'

'That's concerning.'

'That's learned behaviour,' Shea said quietly. 'I've seen it in my clients. You learn to absent yourself when staying present means conflict with someone who controls you.'

They stood in companionable silence, the kitchen warm with afternoon sun and the lingering smell of Laura's roast for the evening dinner. Outside, Jack had retrieved his guitar and was playing old bush ballads.

'The university position,' Heath said quietly, his voice careful. 'I'm going to take it. Head of rural clinical school. More regular hours, better for...'

'For family planning.' Shea finished, her hand going unconsciously to her stomach.

'If that's something you want to consider.'

She was quiet for a moment, hands still in the soapy water, watching her sisters with their children. The memory of her loss felt less sharp now, though it would never fully fade. 'I've been thinking about it. Not immediately, but maybe in a year or two. With proper support this time. Realistic expectations.'

'I'd like that too.'

A burst of laughter drew their attention outside. 'Your

family looks after each other,' Heath observed.

'Our family,' Shea corrected. 'You're stuck with us now. All five sisters, their partners, and however many grandkids arrive.'

'Could be worse.'

'Could be raining.'

They both laughed at the old joke, but Shea's eyes stayed on Bridget. Her youngest sister stood abruptly, saying something about needing to make a call. As she walked towards the house, she passed Samuel on Laura's knee without looking at him.

As the afternoon wore on, the contrast became more pronounced. The children's giggles seemed to spotlight the awkwardness of Antony's presence, the way Bridget held herself apart from her family as if his look pulled her back whenever she drifted too close to her old self.

When Antony finally announced they needed to leave— 'Important video conference with overseas investors'—no one protested. The goodbyes were stilted, Bridget's hugs perfunctory. She didn't look back as the car pulled away, didn't wave from the window as she always had before.

'I thought they were staying for a few days,' Laura said with a frown.

The silence that followed said more than words could.

'We'll need to watch that situation,' Tom said finally.

'We'll need to watch Bridget,' Laura corrected softly. 'Whatever that situation is, our daughter is drowning in it.'

As the sun began to set, painting the river country in shades of gold and amber, the family gradually dispersed for quiet time with the babies. Shea stood at the kitchen window, Heath's arms around her from behind, his chin resting on her head.

'She'll find her way back,' he said quietly.

'They always do,' Shea agreed, thinking of her own journey, of Catherine O'Byrne's story, of all the women who'd lost themselves in someone else's vision before remembering who they were. 'But sometimes they need help remembering the way home.'

Outside, Jack still played his guitar while Laura sang along softly. The babies were all asleep. It was a perfect family moment—except for the absence that sat like a shadow at the edge of the frame.

Bridget, their brilliant, stubborn, youngest sister, was lost under the control of someone who saw her not as a person but as a resource to be optimised, utilised for maximum return on investment.

But Shea reminded herself today wasn't about that shadow. Today was about Heath's grandmother's ring catching the light, about the promise of building something lasting with Heath, about the family that would stand ready when Bridget finally remembered she could come home.

Cat appeared in the doorway, Emma drowsing on her shoulder. 'We're heading home for an hour or two. Shea?' She paused, her expression serious. 'We're going to need a plan. For Bridget.'

'I know.'

'All of us. Together.'

'I know.'

Cat nodded and left, but her words lingered. Together. That's how the O'Byrne women had always survived—by refusing to let go of each other, even when one of them was trying desperately to disappear.

The story would continue, Shea thought, watching the last light fade across the land that had seen so many generations of women find their way through darkness.

Bridget would find her way back. They'd make sure of it.

# Chapter 45

*March, two years later - Ceann Mara*

'I can't believe she's still with him,' Heath said, watching the dust settle on the dirt road leading to *Ceann Mara*. They'd arrived early to help with Laura's birthday preparations, and the conversation had inevitably turned to Bridget.

Shea shifted in the kitchen chair at *Ceann Mara*, trying to find a position that didn't make her back ache. Almost eight months pregnant, everything was uncomfortable. Alice, as they'd decided to call her after Heath's grandmother, seemed determined to use her mother's ribs as a drum kit. Cat smiled at her; her second pregnancy had been problem-free.

'Happy burfday to you!' Shea and Heath's baby son, James, chanted from the living room, practising for Grandma Laura's party.

'She's not answering her phone again,' Laura said from across the kitchen, setting down her mobile with a worried frown whilst frosting her own birthday cake. 'That's the fourth time this week.'

Through the window, Shea watched the birthday decorations Tom had strung across the verandah flutter in the breeze. Fifty-five today, and Laura had insisted on "just family, nothing fancy". But with five daughters, their partners, and a growing collection of grandchildren, "just family" meant nearly twenty people.

'When did you last actually speak to her?' Shea asked, though she already knew the answer.

'Christmas,' Tom said from his position by the window, watching for cars. 'She spent most of the time on her laptop or talking about some AI company. Barely touched her meal.'

The change in her youngest sister since she'd met Antony had been gradual but unmistakable. Shea remembered Bridget's first year of computer science—the excited phone calls about coding projects, the FaceTime sessions from the computer lab where she'd explain algorithms with infectious enthusiasm.

Through the window, a sleek black car appeared on the red dirt road, navigating the potholes with excessive care.

'They're here,' Tom announced.

Cat was already settling eight-month-old Oliver on a blanket whilst keeping one eye on Emma. 'Quick, light the candles before Antony starts another business presentation!'

'Cat!' Laura admonished, but her lips twitched.

Róisín and Seth arrived with Mairead, who immediately announced, 'It's Grandma's birthday! I brought you a leaf!'

Erin and Jack brought Samuel, who was already organising the other children. 'We need to sing properly. Emma, you stand here. Mairead, you're next to me.'

'I don't want to stand there,' Mairead declared, true to form.

The children's innocent chaos was a distraction from what was coming as Shea watched Bridget and her partner emerge from the car. Her sister had lost weight—her designer dress hanging loose despite obvious tailoring. And behind her...

Antony Saar looked exactly like someone who would drive a car that had never seen honest dirt. But it was his timing that bothered Shea most—who brought business proposals to a birthday party?

'Shall we do cake first?' Laura suggested hopefully as soon as they walked in. 'The children are eager to sing.'

'Actually,' Antony interjected, 'I thought this might be a perfect opportunity to share what Bridget and I have been developing. Family gatherings are ideal for—'

'It's Grandma's birthday!' Emma interrupted with three-year-old indignation. 'We're supposed to sing!'

Tom's face showed relief at his granddaughter's intervention. 'She's right. Business can wait.'

They gathered around the kitchen table, the children vibrating with excitement. James conducted enthusiastically as they murdered the birthday song in three different keys. Laura's eyes were bright with tears—the good kind, Shea noted, the kind that came from having your whole family around you.

'Make a wish, Grandma!' Samuel instructed seriously.

Laura closed her eyes, and Shea saw her lips move slightly. She could guess what her mother wished for.

During lunch, Antony dominated the conversation despite Heath's increasingly obvious attempts to redirect.

'The agricultural sector is ripe for disruption,' Antony was saying whilst the children fidgeted increasingly in their chairs. 'Traditional farming methods are becoming obsolete—'

'Perhaps we could discuss this later?' Heath interjected firmly. 'It's Laura's birthday celebration.'

Antony's eyes flashed with irritation before he caught himself. 'Of course. Though time-sensitive opportunities don't always align with social calendars.'

Oliver started crying. Mairead knocked over her juice. Samuel announced he needed the toilet *right now*. Within minutes, the formal lunch dissolved into cheerful chaos.

'Can we go play?' Emma asked.

'Of course, sweetheart,' Cat said with visible relief.

The children thundered outside, their voices carrying back through the windows. 'I'm the birthday fairy!' Mairead shouted. 'Everyone has to do what I say!'

'There's no such thing as birthday fairies,' Samuel countered.

'There is today!'

Antony pulled out his laptop, apparently unable to resist any longer. 'Let me show you what Bridget and I have been developing.'

Tom's expression was carefully neutral. Laura's smile became fixed. The sisters exchanged glances—Róisín rolling her eyes, Erin's jaw tight, Cat looking ready to "accidentally" spill something on the computer.

The screen filled with charts and data visualisations. 'This is our agricultural monitoring platform...'

As Antony droned on about satellite imagery and proprietary algorithms, Shea watched her family's faces. Tom's polite mask couldn't hide his scepticism. Seth's data-analyst brain was clearly finding holes in every claim. Jack was studying the ceiling with intense concentration. Logan had actually dozed off.

'What's the accuracy rate for your predictive models?' Seth asked, more to break the monotony than from genuine interest.

'Ninety-three per cent for yield prediction, eighty-seven per cent for early disease detection.'

'Based on what sample size?'

'Our initial pilot programmes.'

Through the window, Shea could see that the children had

discovered the garden hose. Water flew everywhere as they shrieked with delight. Even from inside, their joy was infectious.

'Perhaps we should join the children,' Erin suggested. 'It's such a lovely day.'

'Excellent idea,' Laura said quickly.

'But I haven't finished the presentation,' Antony protested.

Heath stood decisively. 'Actually, Antony, could I have a word? Outside?'

They stepped onto the verandah, and though Heath kept his voice low, his posture radiated firm politeness. Shea couldn't hear the words, but she could see Antony's face reddening, his gestures becoming sharp.

'Let's go outside,' Cat suggested. 'Bring your tea, Mum. We'll sit on the grass like we used to.'

They trooped out, Laura carrying her birthday cake, the sisters falling into old patterns. They spread blankets under the peppercorn tree whilst the children immediately swarmed them.

'Grandma, watch this!' Emma demonstrated a cartwheel that was mostly falling over.

'Beautiful, darling!'

'My turn!' Mairead attempted something that might have been interpretive dance.

James toddled over with a handful of dandelions. 'Birthday flowers for Grandma!'

'They're perfect, sweetheart.'

The sisters began singing—old songs from their childhood, the ones Tom used to play on his guitar. Even Róisín, usually too cool for nostalgia, joined in.

'Bridget, come sit with us!' Erin called.

Bridget stood frozen on the verandah, caught between her

sisters' laughter and Antony, who was now arguing with Heath.

'I should...' she gestured vaguely towards Antony.

'It's Mum's birthday,' Cat said pointedly. 'Remember when we used to sit on the grass making her flower crowns?'

'I'm wearing a designer dress,' Bridget said weakly.

'So?' Róisín challenged. 'Since when do you care more about clothes than having fun?'

But Bridget retreated to Antony's side, her hand on his arm as if anchoring herself. Or as if she needed permission to join her own family.

Laura's face fell slightly, but she covered it by tickling James until he giggled helplessly.

'What's disrupting?' Emma asked suddenly, having overheard Antony earlier.

'It means breaking things so you can make them better,' Antony called over, apparently unable to resist educating even a three-year-old.

Emma considered this gravely. 'Mummy says we don't break things on purpose. That's naughty.'

'Out of the mouths of babes,' Laura murmured.

Tom emerged from the house with his guitar. 'Birthday request from the birthday girl?'

'You know what I want to hear,' Laura said softly.

He began playing *The Water Is Wide*, the song he'd sung to her when they were courting. The sisters joined in, their voices harmonising from years of practice. Even the children stopped playing to listen.

Shea watched Bridget's face during the song—saw something flicker there, a memory perhaps of hundreds of afternoons like this, before Antony, before the designer clothes and startup jargon. For a moment, her little sister looked lost, young, uncertain.

Then Antony said something in her ear, and the moment passed. Bridget's face reset to its careful smile.

Later, whilst Antony showed Tom and the other men his sensor prototypes—Tom's expression suggested he'd rather be anywhere else—the women cleaned up in the kitchen.

'He hijacked Mum's entire birthday,' Cat said, attacking dishes with vigour.

'Did you see Bridget's face when we were singing?' Erin asked. 'She wanted to join us.'

'But she didn't,' Róisín added grimly. 'She needs his permission to be herself now.'

'The concerning thing,' Shea said, shifting as Alice kicked, 'is how perfectly he knew today would be ideal for his pitch. Family gathered, everyone relaxed—but he misread the room entirely.'

'Bridget's obviously under his spell,' Laura said quietly. 'She barely wished me a happy birthday. It was as though she'd forgotten why we were here.'

On the verandah, Bridget cornered Tom with her fifty-thousand-dollar investment pitch. Shea could see her father's face—patient but firm, loving but worried.

'Have you invested your own money?' Tom asked.

That telling pause. 'I've invested everything I have—my time, my expertise, my future.'

'That's not the same as money, love.'

The fear that flashed across Bridget's face when Tom gently declined made Shea's chest tight. What consequences would her sister face if she couldn't deliver family money?

As the black car finally departed, the family lingered in

the garden. The children had collapsed in various laps, exhausted from their water fight. James was warm against Shea's side, his pockets bulging with "birthday stones for Grandma" and "special stones for Aunt Bridgie".'

'A lovely birthday,' Laura said with forced cheer.

'The best part was the singing,' Tom said, pulling her close. 'The rest was just noise.'

'She didn't even stay for coffee,' Cat observed. 'He said they had an urgent meeting.'

'Where? Out here? On a Saturday. On Mum's birthday. What a crock of shit.' Erin's disapproval was sharp.

'We stay available,' Tom said firmly. 'Our door stays open. But we don't give them money, and we don't pretend we approve.'

'And when she crashes?' Róisín asked.

'We catch her,' Laura said simply. 'Like we always have. With all of you.'

As evening fell, Shea found herself at the kitchen window where generations of O'Byrne women had stood. Four generations of women who'd faced different battles but the same war—the fight to remain themselves in a world that wanted to reshape them.

'Think happy thoughts, Aunty Shea,' Emma Rose instructed, patting her face. 'Like Mummy said. Happy birthday thoughts for Grandma.'

Outside, Tom played guitar whilst Laura opened her birthday gifts, surrounded by her daughters and grandchildren. Everyone except Bridget, who was probably heading to a Sydney conference room, to perform enthusiastically for Antony's vision.

Her phone buzzed. Bridget: **Sorry we had to leave early. Important investor meeting. Hope Mum understands.**

Shea didn't reply and slipped her phone into her pocket.

The birthday candles flickered in the evening breeze, fifty-five tiny flames that Laura would blow out while wishing for her youngest daughter to find her way home.

The O'Byrne women always found their way back. Eventually.

# Chapter 46

*The confluence - six months later*

The winter sun caught the water where the rivers met, turning the confluence into a sheet of hammered silver. Shea sat on the familiar fallen log, Alice finally sleeping in the pram after a difficult night of teething. She was all Heath's calm temperament during the day and all Shea's stubbornness at three in the morning.

James, now two, was constructing an elaborate fortress from river stones and driftwood. 'For the water dragons,' he explained seriously. 'To keep them safe.'

'Safe from what?' Heath asked, helping him balance a particularly ambitious piece of driftwood.

'From the sad things.'

Even the children sensed it—the shadow that had fallen over the family since Bridget had stopped returning calls three months ago. After Tom's gentle but firm refusal to invest, she'd gradually withdrawn from them. First, the phone calls stopped, then the texts, then she'd blocked them all on social media.

'Your father's thinking about driving to Sydney next week,' Heath mentioned carefully. 'Thought he might try to see Bridget again.'

'She won't answer the door. Mum and Dad have been down twice already.' Shea watched James carefully place a special stone—smooth and white, saved for weeks—in the centre of his fortress. Still saving treasures for Aunt Bridgie, even though he hadn't seen her since Laura's birthday. 'And we're not even sure of the correct address now.'

Her phone buzzed. Sarah from the centre: 'Your sister called again. Asking about "starting over" and "finding yourself after losing everything." I told her you'd call back.'

This was the third time in a month. Bridget hung up each time Shea tried to call her.

'She's reaching out,' Heath said, reading over her shoulder.

'She's testing. Seeing if the door's still open.'

'Is it?'

'Always. That's what family means.'

Alice stirred in the pram, making the small snuffling sounds that preceded full wakefulness. Soon they'd need to get back on the road to home in Broken Hill, back to the routine of bottles and nappies and James's endless questions about everything from clouds to why toast was crunchy.

But for now, Shea wanted to sit and find her calm place where Catherine O'Byrne had once laboured alone, where Elizabeth had planned her midwifery practice, where she herself had chosen to continue after David. Each generation of women finding their way through different betrayals, different losses, different kinds of breaking.

'Do you think Catherine ever imagined this?' she asked Heath. 'Five generations later, her great-great-great-nieces still fighting the same battles in different forms?'

'I think she'd recognise it. The pattern of women having to choose between who they are and who someone else wants them to be.'

James abandoned his fortress to bring Shea a handful of leaves. 'Medicine,' he announced. 'For Aunty Bridgie's sad.'

'That's very thoughtful, sweetheart.'

'Aunty Cat told Emma Rose that Aunty Bridgie got lost.

But lost people can get found, right, Mummy? Like when I got lost in the shop and you found me?'

'Yes, baby. Lost people can get found.'

'Good.' He returned to his building with the satisfaction of a problem solved.

The water flowed past, carrying their worries downstream whilst somewhere in Sydney, Bridget was learning what Shea had learned, what Catherine had learned, what all the O'Byrne women eventually discovered—that you can't build a life on someone else's foundation, no matter how gilded it seems.

'She's strong, and she knows she has family support and love,' Heath said, as if reading her thoughts. 'She'll find her way back.'

'They always do,' Shea agreed, thinking of Catherine choosing survival and transformation over shame, of Elizabeth building her legacy of healing, of herself sitting on this very log, broken but not beaten.

Alice woke properly, demanding attention. As they packed up to leave, James carefully collected four stones—one for each member of their small family—and then, after consideration, a fifth.

'For Aunt Bridgie,' he said firmly. 'For when she comes home.'

His simple faith made Shea's eyes burn. This was what the O'Byrne women did—they held space for each other, even across silence and distance and the kinds of mistakes that felt unforgivable in the moment but became just another part of the story in time.

Standing where the rivers met, Shea thought she could almost see them—all the women who'd stood here before, facing their own confluences, choosing their own directions. Catherine's courage flowing into Elizabeth's compassion, then into generation after generation of women who refused to disappear.

Bridget would find her way back to this place, to this family, to herself. And when she did, there would be river stones waiting, saved with love by a little boy who knew that lost people could always be found.

The story would continue, Shea thought, watching the last light fade across the land that had seen so many generations of women find their way through darkness.

Bridget would find her way back. They'd make sure of it.

# Epilogue

Bridget stared at the lines of code scrolling across her laptop screen, the cursor blinking accusingly at the end of an incomplete function. The Darlinghurst apartment felt suffocating despite its floor-to-ceiling windows and designer furniture. Everything here belonged to Antony—the furniture, the lease, even the laptop she was typing on.

'The predictive algorithm needs to be more sophisticated,' Antony called from the kitchen, his voice carrying that edge it always had when he was stressed about investor meetings. 'We need to show actual agricultural applications, not theoretical frameworks.'

She rubbed her temples, squinting at the screen. The code made no sense. Half the variables weren't defined, and the functions called libraries that didn't exist. When she'd pointed this out to Antony last week, he'd dismissed her concerns with a wave of his hand.

'You're thinking too literally, Bridge. This is conceptual programming. We're showing potential, not building production-ready software.'

But potential for what? She'd been asking herself that question for months now, ever since she'd dropped out of computer science to work full-time on what Antony called "revolutionary agricultural technology". The decision had felt bold at the time—she was going to change the world, disrupt an entire industry. Now, sitting in front of code that wouldn't compile, she wondered if she'd made the biggest mistake of her life.

'Bridge!' Antony appeared in the doorway, already

dressed in his expensive suit for tonight's investor party. 'Have you finished the demo presentation?'

'The code doesn't work,' she said quietly, not looking up from the screen. 'I can't demonstrate something that crashes every time I try to run it.'

His face darkened. 'What do you mean it doesn't work? We've been developing this for eight months.'

'That's what I'm trying to tell you. Look at line forty-seven—this function calls a machine learning library that we haven't installed. And the database connections on line sixty-three reference tables that don't exist.'

Antony strode over and peered at the screen, his jaw tightening. For a moment, Bridget saw something flicker in his eyes—confusion, perhaps even panic. But it was quickly replaced by his usual confident mask.

'This is just a prototype,' he said dismissively. 'The investors understand that. They're investing in the concept, not the current iteration.'

'But what if they ask technical questions? What if they want to see it actually work?'

'They won't. These people don't understand code. They understand market opportunity and return on investment.' He straightened his tie, already moving away from the problem. 'Just make the presentation look impressive. Use plenty of charts and technical terminology.'

Bridget's stomach churned. 'Antony, I think we need to step back and actually build something that works before we—'

'We don't have time to step back.' His voice cut through hers like ice. 'Do you have any idea how much money I've already invested in this? How much I've sacrificed to get us to this point?'

The guilt hit her like a physical blow. He'd given up his Stanford PhD for this project. He'd moved to Sydney, rented this expensive apartment, and bought her clothes so she'd look the part at investor meetings. She owed him everything.

'I'm sorry,' she whispered. 'I'll fix the presentation.'

'Good. And Bridge?' His voice softened, the way it did when he was manipulating her back into compliance. 'Remember what we talked about. You're brilliant, but you need to trust me on the business side. I know what these investors want to hear.'

After he left, Bridget sat staring at the broken code until her eyes burned. She tried calling Shea but hung up before it connected. How could she explain that she was working on a project that didn't actually exist? That the man who she considered her partner might not understand the technology any better than she did?

The worst part was the growing suspicion that Antony had never expected her to actually build anything. He needed her to be the "technical co-founder", the brilliant young programmer who gave credibility to his pitches. But every time she tried to create something real, he deflected, delayed, or found reasons why it wasn't necessary yet.

She closed the laptop and got ready for the party, choosing the black dress Antony had bought her last month. It had cost more than her family spent on groceries in two weeks, and she still felt like she was playing dress-up.

The investor party was held in a Surry Hills warehouse converted into a startup incubator. The exposed brick walls and industrial lighting were supposed to suggest innovation and authenticity, but to Bridget, it felt cold and artificial. She stood beside Antony as he networked, her role reduced to smiling and nodding when he introduced her as his "technical co-founder and machine learning expert".

'Bridget developed our proprietary algorithms,' he told a grey-haired man with an expensive watch. 'She's brilliant—graduated top of her year in computer science.'

The lie rolled off his tongue so easily. She hadn't been at the top of her year. She'd spent too much time on Antony's projects to focus on the third year of her degree. Every time he said it, she felt smaller, more complicit in whatever this was becoming.

'Tell me about the accuracy rates,' the investor asked, turning to her with genuine interest. 'How does your model compare to existing agricultural prediction software?'

Bridget's mouth went dry. 'Well, we're still in the optimisation phase—'

'Ninety-three percent accuracy for yield prediction,' Antony interrupted smoothly. 'Eighty-seven percent for early disease detection. Of course, we're being conservative with those numbers.'

The investor nodded appreciatively, but Bridget caught his questioning look. He knew she hadn't answered his question. She excused herself to get a drink, her hands shaking.

At the bar, she overheard two developers talking about their startup's latest funding round. They spoke casually about version control, deployment pipelines, and user testing—all things that should have been second nature if she was really the technical expert Antony claimed she was.

'Excuse me,' she interrupted, desperate for a connection with someone who understood actual programming. 'I'm working on agricultural prediction software. Have you dealt with integrating satellite imagery APIs?'

One of them looked at her with interest. 'Sure, we did some work with NASA's Earth data. What platform are you building on?'

The question hung in the air. Bridget realised she didn't even know what platform they were supposedly using. Antony always handled the "technical architecture decisions".

'We're still evaluating options,' she said weakly.

The developers exchanged a look—polite but dismissive. They'd recognised her as someone who talked about technology without understanding it. Just like Antony.

She spent the next hour hiding in corners, watching him work the room. He spoke fluently about market disruption and scalable solutions, always deflecting technical questions to "proprietary constraints" or "competitive advantages".'

It was nearly midnight when she went looking for Antony because she was tired and wanted to leave. She found him on the building's rooftop terrace, but he wasn't alone. A blonde woman in her thirties was pressed against him, her hands tangled in his hair as they kissed with obvious familiarity.

Bridget's world tilted. She stood frozen, watching the man she'd sacrificed everything for with his tongue down another woman's throat. The woman pulled back, laughing at something he whispered in her ear.

'Antony?' Bridget's voice came out smaller than she'd intended.

He spun around, his face cycling through surprise, guilt, and finally calculation. 'Bridge. I thought you'd gone home.'

The woman stepped back but didn't look embarrassed. If anything, she seemed amused. 'This is the technical co-founder you mentioned? She's younger than I expected.'

'Miranda, this is Bridget. Bridget, Miranda is one of our potential investors.'

Potential investor. The casual lie made Bridget's stomach lurch. Miranda's dress probably cost more than most people's rent, and she wore it with the confidence of someone who'd never doubted her place in the world.

'How long?' Bridget asked, surprised by the steadiness of her own voice.

'Bridge, it's not what you think—'

'How long have you been sleeping with her?'

The silence stretched between them. In the distance, Sydney Harbour glittered with lights, beautiful and completely indifferent to her humiliation.

'Six months,' Miranda answered when Antony remained silent. 'Maybe seven. Time flies when you're having fun.'

'Miranda—' Antony's voice held a warning.

'What? She was bound to find out eventually. Besides, she seems sweet. Too sweet for this game.' Miranda picked up her purse, kissing Antony's cheek like they were old friends. 'Call me when you sort this out. The offer still stands.'

After she left, Bridget and Antony stood alone on the rooftop. The party continued below them, but it felt like they were suspended in space, orbiting around a truth that changed everything.

'I can explain,' Antony began.

'Can you? Because I'd love to hear how you explain sleeping with an investor while I've been living in your apartment like some kind of kept woman.'

'It's not like that. Miranda and I have history. It doesn't mean anything.'

'History.' Bridget laughed, but it came out broken. 'What about us? What about everything we've been building together?'

'We can still build it. This doesn't change anything between us.'

'Everything between us is a lie!' The words exploded out of her. 'The code doesn't work, Antony. The algorithms don't exist. Half the things you tell investors aren't even theoretically possible.'

His face went carefully blank. 'You're upset. You're not thinking clearly.'

'I'm thinking clearly for the first time in months. You don't understand the technology any better than I do. You're just better at talking about it, and taking the investments.'

'That's not true.'

'Then explain to me how the machine learning model processes satellite imagery. Walk me through the actual code.'

The silence told her everything she needed to know.

'You can't,' she said quietly. 'Because you don't know. You've been using me as window dressing, haven't you? The young, brilliant programmer who legitimises your pitches.'

'Bridge, please. Don't do this. We can work through this.'

'Work through what? The fact that you're sleeping with other women? The fact that our entire business is built on lies? Or the fact that I've wasted two years of my life on something that doesn't exist?'

She turned towards the stairs, but his hand caught her arm. 'Where are you going?'

'Home.'

'This is your home now.'

'No.' She looked around the rooftop, at the glittering city

that had never felt like hers. 'This is *your* life. *Your* apartment, *your* investors, *your* lies. I was just playing a role.'

'If you leave, you'll have nothing. No degree, no job, no future. I gave you everything.'

The manipulation was so transparent now that she almost laughed. 'You gave me expensive clothes and a fake identity. That's not the same thing.'

She pulled her arm free and walked towards the stairs. Behind her, Antony called her name, his voice cycling through anger, pleading, and finally threats about what would happen if she "made this difficult".

But Bridget was already gone, descending the stairs towards street level and the rest of her life. Her phone had seventeen missed calls from her family—they never stopped trying, even when she pushed them away. For the first time in years, the thought of home didn't feel like failure.

It felt like salvation.

Three days later, Bridget was packing her few personal belongings when Antony burst through the apartment door, his usual composure completely shattered. His expensive suit was wrinkled, his hair dishevelled, and there was a wild look in his eyes she'd never seen before.

'Bridge, thank God you're still here. We need to talk.'

She looked up. 'I told you I'm leaving. There's nothing left to discuss.'

'There is. The ASIC investigation—it's not what it looks like. Someone's been feeding them false information about our investor meetings.'

Bridget's blood went cold. 'What ASIC investigation?'

Antony ran his hands through his hair, pacing frantically around the living room. 'They froze our accounts yesterday.

They're claiming we've been running some kind of Ponzi scheme, taking investment money without delivering products. It's complete bullshit, Bridge. You know we've been working on real technology.'

'Have we?' She stood up, her voice steady despite the fear creeping up her spine. 'Because three days ago you couldn't explain how any of our algorithms actually work.'

'That's different. That's just—the investigation is about fraud. They're saying we've been deliberately deceiving investors about our capabilities.'

'Haven't you?'

The question hung in the air between them. Through the floor-to-ceiling windows, Sydney stretched out below them—beautiful, expensive, and suddenly feeling a long way from the red dirt roads of home.

'We've been optimistic about our timeline,' Antony said carefully. 'That's not fraud. That's entrepreneurship.'

'Antony, we don't have any working algorithms. We don't have a platform. We don't even have a coherent business plan beyond taking people's money and promising them "revolutionary technology" that doesn't exist.'

His face went white. 'Don't say that. Not now. If ASIC hears you talking like that—'

'ASIC?' Bridget's voice rose. 'Are you seriously worried about what *I* might tell investigators? What about what you've been telling investors for the past two years?'

'I need you to stand by me on this.' His voice took on that manipulative tone she'd learned to recognise. 'We're partners, Bridge. Partners stick together.'

'Partners don't lie to each other about sleeping with other

women. Partners don't use each other as window dressing for fraudulent investment schemes.'

'It wasn't fraudulent! We believed in what we were building!'

'You never believed in anything except the money.' She picked up her suitcase, checking that everything was packed. 'I'm leaving, Antony. Don't contact me again.'

'If you leave now, you're abandoning me when I need you most.' His voice cracked. 'The lawyers say if we present a united front, if we can show the investigators that we were genuinely trying to develop the technology—'

'Were we? Because I spent two years trying to build something real, and every time I made progress, you told me it wasn't necessary yet. Every time I questioned the technical claims in your presentations, you shut me down.'

Antony's composure finally cracked completely. 'Fine! You want the truth? The truth is that ninety percent of startups are built on bullshit and optimism. The truth is that no one expects the first version to work perfectly. The truth is that Miranda's friends have been pumping money into ventures like this for years, and they don't care about the details as long as the returns look good.'

'Miranda's friends.' Bridget stared at him. 'How many other investors have you been sleeping with, Antony?'

The silence was answer enough.

'Jesus Christ.' She sank into a chair, the full scope of his deception finally hitting her. 'This whole thing—the apartment, the parties, the investor meetings—you've been running a con game. And I was the technical credibility you needed to make it work.'

'It's not a con game. It's venture capital. This is how the

system works.'

'No, it's not. Real startups have real products. Real technical co-founders actually understand the technology they're building.' She stood up, slinging her bag over her shoulder. 'I'm done, Antony. With all of it.'

'ASIC wants to interview you next week,' he called as she headed for the door. 'As a material witness. If you disappear now, it looks like you're running from something.'

She turned back to face him one last time. 'I am running from something. I'm running from the biggest mistake of my life.'

'Bridge, please. I love you.'

'No, you don't. You used me. You only wanted me for what I could do for you. There's a difference.'

The last thing she heard as the door closed behind her was the sound of Antony punching the wall.

*Fifteen hours later…*

The red dirt of the driveway at Ceann Mara looked the same as it had three years ago, before Sydney, before Antony, before Bridget convinced herself that her family's love wasn't enough. She sat in the rental car for a long moment, gathering courage she wasn't sure she possessed.

The front door opened before she could knock. Her father stood there in his work clothes, his face cycling through surprise, relief, and overwhelming love.

'Bridge,' he said quietly, and she fell into his arms like she was five years old again, crying until there were no tears left.

'I made such a mess, Daddy. Such a terrible mess.'

'Nothing that can't be cleaned up,' he said, holding her tight. 'Nothing that matters more than having you home, sweetheart.'

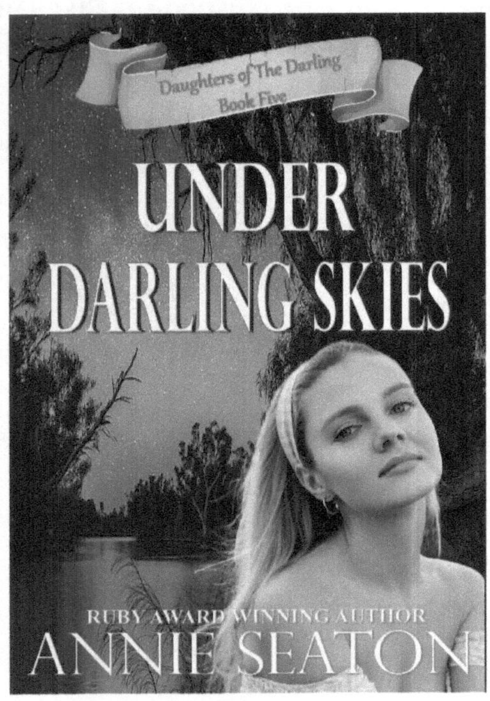

*Book 5*

*Daughters of The Darling*

Bridget O'Byrne thought she was building the future with her brilliant business partner and cutting-edge AI technology. Two years later, she's trapped in Sydney, financially ruined, and under the controlling influence of Antony Saar. When his venture collapses amid fraud investigations, Bridget returns home to *Ceann Mara* with her confidence shattered.

Back on the family property she once couldn't wait to leave, Bridget struggles to rebuild her life. Her path to recovery takes an unexpected turn when she reconnects with Danny Walsh, a quietly competent stockman who was her closest friend in primary school. Danny's contentment with honest work and simple truths challenges everything Bridget thought she wanted.

Meanwhile, Bridget joins Tom and Caitríona to explore the mystery of eleven-year-old Roisin O'Byrne, Catherine's sister, who vanished from Melbourne in 1880. Following Roisin's trail to the goldfields, Bridget begins to understand that sometimes survival requires losing yourself completely before you can find your way home.

A story about manipulation, rebuilding trust, and discovering that the most profound strength often comes from the simplest truths.

Bridget's story, *Under Darling Skies* is the final book in the *Daughters of the Darling* series, will be published in April 2026.

It is now available in print at Annie's store.

**https://annieseatonstore.ecwid.com/Under-Darling-Skies-Pre-order-April-2026-p781513838**

**And for eBook pre-order on all sites.**

eBook: **https://books2read.com/u/meOr99**

# Acknowledgements

The Darling River is one of the most beautiful areas in outback New South Wales. In the spring of 2023, Ian and I travelled the Darling River Run from Brewarrina to Menindee in our caravan, exploring this beautiful landscape.

We stayed at *Trilby Station*, where the inspiration for this story was born. *Ceann Mara* is based on this contemporary station, which has a rich history from the nineteenth century. *Dunleavy* is a fictional version of *Dunlop Station* upriver.

Thank you to *Trilby Station* owners Liz and Gary Murray for allowing me to use information from the historical museum at the campground on *Trilby Station*. We stopped at various sites from Brewarrina to Menindee on the Darling River Run and discovered the beauty of the river. We sat by the water at sunrise and sunset and absorbed the aromas, the beauty of the trees, and the sound of the birds. It is truly a magical place, and if you get the opportunity to travel out there, make sure to do so. There are many beautiful landscapes in Australia, and the Darling River Run is one of the most memorable. In early 2025, we travelled along the Murray River to Wentworth and I was awed by the spirituality of the landscape where the Murray and Darling Rivers join. While we were at the confluence, a funeral envoy of vintage tractors arrived. I have fictionalised that poignant moment in my story while Shea is sitting by the river.

*Beneath Still Waters* is the fourth book in the *Daughters of the Darling* series, and I'm looking forward to Bridget's story, where we will leave the sisters.

Many people supported me in writing this book, and I would like to acknowledge them here.

To the many friends I have made in the writing world over the past fifteen years who constantly support me on my journey, I often say I have found my "tribe", and I value the daily contact with like-minded people all over the world. Again, a special mention and thank you go to my dear friend, critique partner, and editor, author Susanne Bellamy, and to my wonderful proofreader, Roby Aiken.

To my loyal readers, who eagerly await the release of the next book, I invite you to attend my library talks and stay in touch via email and social media to share your enjoyment of my stories. Without readers, there would be no need for stories!

It would be impossible to write without support in your personal life:

To Ian, the love of my life and my research partner, as we travel this magnificent country seeking stories each winter. I could not do this without you. My driver, my chef, my bringer of wine, my fisherman, and my husband of fifty years.

To our children, their partners and our grandchildren: thank you for your love and support.

As always, love and appreciation to my wonderful aunt, Maureen Smith. Sadly, Aunty Maureen passed away in June before this book was published, and I will never forget how she often told me how proud my parents would be of me becoming an author.

To you, the reader: thank you for choosing this book. I hope that you enjoy it and talk about it; word of mouth is the best thing for an author.

Maybe you will want to visit this wonderful part of Australia. I hope you enjoy Shea and Catherine's stories. Bridget's story will be published in April 2026.

Please sign up for my fortnightly newsletter to hear about

my research and my new books. You can find it here:
http://www.annieseaton.net
 I would love to hear from you.

Drop me a line at annie@annieseation.net

Reviews on Goodreads are always welcome and much appreciated!

eBook links:

***https://www.annieseaton.net/books.html***

Print Store:

All books are available in print at Annie's store and on Amazon in paperback.

***https://annieseatonstore.ecwid.com/***

# Awards

2025: Finalist - Romantic Suspense, RUBY award for From Across the Sea.

2023: Winner - Long contemporary novel category, RUBY award for Larapinta.

2023: Finalist - Australian Romance Readers Awards for Kakadu Dawn, the sixth and final book in the Porter Sisters series.

2018 and 2020: Finalist - for the NZ KORU Award.

2017: Winner - Best Established Author of the Year 20'7 AUSROM

2017: Winner - Author of the Year 2014 AUSROM Best Established Author, Ausrom Readers' Choice.

2016, 2017, 2018, 2019: Longlisted - Sisters in Crime Davitt Awards

2016: Finalist - Book of the Year, Long Romance, RWA Ruby Awards for Kakadu Sunset

2015: Winner - Best Established Author of the Year AUSROM